THE EDGE
OF THE
CROWD

T0337229

Previous praise for Ross Gilfillan:

'A novel so rich in its authenticity it can sustain the myriad of twists and turns that keep the reader enthralled and believing to the end.' *The Times*

'This splendid debut novel catches the slurred cadence of Southern speech as neat as shuckin' corn.' *Time Out*

'A charming, atmospheric first novel . . . delightfully conceived.' *Independent*

'Very entertaining first novel. As a debut novel it's impressive stuff and indicates Gilfillan has a big future as a humorous novelist.' *Bristol Evening Post*

'This is an extraordinary book.' *Spectator*

Also by Ross Gilfillan

THE SNAKE-OIL DICKENS MAN

THE EDGE OF THE CROWD

Ross Gilfillan

FOURTH ESTATE • *London*

This paperback edition first published in 2002
First published in Great Britain in 2001 by
Fourth Estate
A Division of HarperCollins*Publishers*
1 London Bridge Street,
London SE1 9GF
www.4thestate.com

A catalogue record for this book is available from
the British Library

ISBN 1–84115–618–3

Typeset in Plantin Light by
Avon DataSet Ltd, Bidford on Avon B50 4JH
www.avondataset.com

Printed and bound by CPI Group (UK) Ltd, Croydon, CR0 4YY

MIX
Paper from
responsible sources
FSC FSC® C007454

For my wife Lisa,
Fae, Tom and Alice
and
Dorothy Gilfillan

1

Wet Collodion

Hyde Park Corner, late in the morning of July 14th, 1851, would try the patience of angels. That, anyway, is the unshake-able opinion of Cornelius Touchfarthing, as he sharply detaches sweat-fastened buttocks from the wagon's dampened leather seat and climbs up on the chest of chemicals that has been stored behind him. Once aloft, he sways dangerously like a mast-top sailor as he searches ahead for the latest impediment to his progress and attracts the disdainful glance of a liveried footman upon a carriage and the interested attention of two sporting gentlemen in a fly. 'What the deuce is it this time?' asks one of them.

Touchfarthing shades his brow and squints into the middle-distance. 'They're letting traffic across the street,' he reports. 'Carriages. Lords and ladies, it looks like. And a squadron of dragoons. Well, it makes a fine picture!'

'Picture be damned!' says one of the passengers in the fly and takes up his newspaper while Touchfarthing, looming above, uses his hands to shape a scene beyond the crush of carriages and broughams, laden wagons and packed omnibuses. Fleshy thumbs crop pavements closely-cobbled with hats and bare heads, making them a variegated living border for a square of scarlet coats, sleekly-groomed horses and glittering carriages.

'A very fine picture indeed!' repeats Touchfarthing to himself.

Shaded by Touchfarthing's corpulence is the slighter figure of John Rankin, who flicks limp reins against his knee as he chats to a lava-haired street-sweeper who has been performing 'cat'un-wheels, ha-penny a tumble!' between the wagon and the stationary carriage alongside. The boy doffs his cap and thanks Rankin for his penny. 'Oh, that an't nothing at all,' Rankin says, jerking his thumb upwards. 'Least, not for a cove what's in the employ of Admiral bloody Nelson!'

'What was that?' Touchfarthing demands and sits down so heavily that the springs bounce and the bottles of chemicals chink loudly in the box.

'Admiral Nelson,' says Rankin. 'I was just saying that Admiral Nelson lived in that there house.'

The bigger man sighs loudly as he swabs his thick neck with a damp and discoloured handkerchief. 'Apsley House is the residence of the Duke of Wellington.'

'That's the fellow,' says Rankin, and turns to wink at the boy who is already ducking under the horse's head and causing Touchfarthing to catch his breath as he slips between the enormous wheels of a great wagon loaded with slate. The driver takes up his whip and for a dreadful moment Touchfarthing fears that the vehicle will move off and that the child will be crushed but the boy reappears among the shuffling crowds on the far pavement, biting his coin before a company of unshod ragamuffins.

Touchfarthing stares in awe at the multitude of street hawkers: the sellers of oranges and thinly cut ham sandwiches, baked potatoes and bottles of ginger beer. Then his attention is drawn towards the long lines of costermongers with their barrows and to the many hawkers of shiny commemorative medals. He considers the fact that this small army is there only to service a much greater force, whose ranks stand four and five deep by the Park rails.

Touchfarthing watches the world go by: young men with beribboned sweethearts; gangs of loudly-singing apprentices;

2

immaculately turned-out recruiting sergeants; a sprinkling of shabby-genteel half-pay officers; two elderly widows in bombazine complaining of the heat; the many-hued faces of foreign visitors; and the walking advertisements whose signboards offer 'cheap beds tonight'. A fascination of individuals now intrudes itself upon his attention: a small portly gentleman with glinting glasses and apoplectic colour prattling with a gaunt cleric whose frock-coat is out at the elbows; a plump and rubescent matron swiping at unruly children with a furled umbrella; and a lean man in black with green-tinted spectacles who stands against a lamp-post unmoving, like a rock in a flowing stream.

'I never saw so many people here in my life,' Touchfarthing mutters to himself. 'Just look at that mob,' he says, louder this time, indicating this swell to his assistant. 'And it's not even a cheap shilling day . . .'

'That mob's our bread and butter,' Rankin says. 'It's their sixpunny portraits what puts meat on our table.'

'For the moment, yes,' Touchfarthing sighs, noting the strange admixture of the crowds, the well-turned-out families lining up with dusty travellers, the quality coalescing in the crush with shopkeepers and tradesmen. 'Perhaps, unlike myself, you don't find it distasteful, all that . . . mingling?' He is overwhelmed, perhaps appalled, by this unnatural colliding of the classes.

Rankin rolls his eyes. 'You know what you've become, Mr Touchfarthing?' he says. 'A stunning snob, that's what.'

Touchfarthing is too hot and too tired to rise to Rankin's bait. They have been stopped outside Apsley House a full half hour but no one has made better headway today: crested carriage has had no more advantage over laden wagon than hansom cab over four-wheeled growler. All have been stilled under the grilling sun as drivers curse and passengers fan away flies drawn by mounting piles of horse dung.

The petrifying spell is broken by a passenger in a hansom. 'Devil take it, I shall walk!' he says and pays off his driver. As if this is the signal that all have awaited, the traffic begins to move again. Rankin shakes the reins and the wagon trundles forward.

Progress is slow. A piece of orange peel crushed on a front wheel takes almost a whole minute to come again to the top. But no matter how slowly they are moving, at last and up ahead vehicles can be seen turning into Hyde Park through the Prince of Wales' Gate, where they are illuminated by sunbeams glancing off the thousands of glass panes housing the Great Exhibition.

II

Rankin does all the work. It is Rankin who unhitches and tethers the horse and Rankin who brings their operation to such a state of readiness that a crowd has already gathered and has begun to hinder preparations with numerous enquiries about the pricing of premium-quality souvenir photographs. A handful of mismatched dining chairs are taken from the wagon and arranged upon the grass where the subjects will sit. The camera nestles upon its tripod sufficiently distant from the Exhibition that a portion of the building may serve as a recognisable background and the angle of view has been adjusted so that the lines of abandoned carriages and other conveyances will be excluded. Even so, Rankin frowns as he emerges from under the black cloth, dissatisfied with the picture on the ground-glass screen.

For once, backgrounding is important. His customers will pay today's high rate only if the photograph associates them with the fabulous edifice. But between the lens and the all-important background are desultory strollers, boys with hoops and vendors of various comestibles. He wishes them vanished. Rankin would also prefer that the visitors examining the exhibits outside the building – a monolithic slab of coal, an assortment of heaped raw materials for use in industry and the biggest ship's anchor Rankin has seen – would take themselves inside. But humankind is not to be avoided today: all about are people of every station and exotic tint. It is hard to remember, and at this moment even more difficult to believe, that a two-minute exposure will entirely eliminate from the scene everything that is in motion.

4

Rankin pitches the dark-tent under an elm tree and into this he installs a brass-cornered and felt-lined box of lenses. Beside the box he places his dishes, scales, weights, funnels, glass measures and a large supply of glass plates. He sends a boy to fill a pail from the Serpentine and now needs only the heavy chest, in which are contained bottles of chemicals for coating, sensitising, developing and fixing of the glass negatives. He exits the tent and begins to drag the trunk towards the tailboard of the wagon. 'I ain't shifting the chemicals by myself,' he calls to Touchfarthing, who stands shaded by the great elm. 'I shan't answer if the box gets dropped.'

Touchfarthing, sipping from a bottle of ginger beer and watching riders upon Rotten Row, makes no reply.

'What you'll have is a box of broken glass and spilt chemicals,' says Rankin, louder. 'And it won't be my fault.'

But Touchfarthing only indicates a pair of riders who have broken into a dangerous canter, sending a small boy and girl fleeing from their path. 'Look there,' he says. 'That's Lord Montague mounted on the roan. With Arthur Vavasour. Well, well! Do you know that when last I saw them they were hardly speaking?'

'No, I didn't know that,' says Rankin, shortly. He purses his lips and drums his fingers on the chest containing chemicals.

'I had their acquaintance at Sibthorpe, you know,' Touchfarthing says, complacently.

Rankin whistles through his teeth and rolls his blue eyes. 'When you're ready, guv'nor,' he says, managing with some difficulty to move the box unaided by the other man.

Touchfarthing approaches the camera as a maestro his piano forte. By separating himself from Rankin and the labours of preparation, it has been made clear to onlookers that it is Touchfarthing who is the artist; and Rankin who is very much 'school of'.

Touchfarthing signals with a ringed finger and Rankin invites the first subject, a well-fed gentleman with a single bushy eyebrow and luxuriant red whiskers, to sit upon a chair. As

5

discreetly as possible, he quietly points out the advantages of a larger photograph frame, of additional prints or of a special patent backing which is guaranteed to prevent fading, before he solicits a shilling and retires to the rope, beyond which interested onlookers have now formed themselves into an orderly queue. Touchfarthing, shrouded by the great black cloth, removes the lens cover and raises his right arm. Eyebrow and whiskers are still as death and eternity seems to pass before the photographer drops his hand and re-covers the lens. The business of the day has commenced.

Rankin must now confine himself to the dark-tent, the conjuror's cloak under which some magic must be performed before the sorcerer's apprentice can re-emerge with his subjects' captured and framed likenesses on the day they visited the Great Exhibition. And it might as well be alchemy to Touchfarthing too. This collodion process is so new that Rankin alone has attempted its mastery and even he has doubts concerning its use on such an important occasion. But Touchfarthing has proved intransigent, insisting that only the very latest method is appropriate for use at the Great Exhibition of All Nations.

With Rankin engaged, Touchfarthing is obliged to attend to the subjects. Before he carefully constrains them in their chairs he will compliment and flatter them or bamboozle them with the science of photography. This, he hopes, will divert attention from the transaction itself, the part of the business Touchfarthing loathes. It is, after all, the transfer of cash that distinguishes the grubbing tradesman from the pioneering amateur.

The ordeal over, he again addresses the camera into which Rankin has inserted a new wet plate and under whose black cloth he buries his head from view. Flattened into two dimensions is how Touchfarthing prefers to view his run-of-the-mill clients. On the ground-glass screen their hats and their 'physogs', their arms and their torsos become mere compositional elements to be arranged in the most pleasing and aesthetic manner. By correcting poor posture, rearranging slack attire and encouraging a sober

6

expression, Touchfarthing considers that he improves on life.

The afternoon passes away. Never has either man worked so hard at the business of photography nor encompassed such a bewildering variety of subjects from every place and of every station: couples from Clapham; families up from Kent; Midlands industrialists; richly-attired visitors from the sub-continent; a fidgeting band of Neapolitan musicians; mechanics and farmers; curates and choristers; sailors on shore leave; the recruiting sergeants, now merrily drunk; Etonians and Harrovians and a class of National school children, the eyes of whose teacher pierce the lens so fiercely that Touchfarthing almost trembles.

The photographer finds this multiplicity repellent: skilled physician follows lowly apothecary as if there were no order in the world. And perhaps this is a singular occasion but no one seems to take offence at such an unnatural commingling of society. Touchfarthing whispers to the busy Rankin, 'Dear me, where is the quality here?'

Touchfarthing would rather maintain distance from the common man and upstart alike. This last taxonomy he most detests. Rankin has tired long ago of Touchfarthing's declamations on these 'self-made counter-jumpers' who 'dress like kings and talk like coal-heavers', but the process is slow and while Rankin is in and out of the dark-tent changing and processing plates, there is little that Touchfarthing can do to avoid unwanted intimacy with hoi polloi and he is further dismayed to discover among his sitters a tendency towards self-publicity.

Mr Hector Trundle, as he tolerates Touchfarthing fussing about his disarrayed neck-wear, announces that he might buy up any of the exotic exhibits he has seen displayed within 'they great glass walls'. He might load up a caravan with power looms and steam hammers and such practical improvements; he might choose the finest satins and silks for his wife (for whom he had a handkerchief passed through the fountain of Eau de Cologne); and should he so desire, it would be within his power to buy up a whole array of novelties: the eighty-bladed pen-knife, the stiletto umbrella, the tableaux of small and expertly stuffed

7

animals. With the possible exception of that Koh-i-Noor diamond, he might slap cash on the table and haul the whole lot back to Salford, Lancashire. In fact, he might do anything he likes except that which this minute he desires most in all the world and that is to scratch his nose.

Jasper Munro considers the Great Exhibition 'a damnable mess'. He sits erect, his hands folded over a silver-topped cane that he has pegged into the earth while Touchfarthing fastens a collar stud and brushes dust from his shoulders. 'Poor classifying, that's what it is,' he is saying. 'No idea of proper categorisation. I saw how it would be from the start, when the Prince announced his intentions. How can you "wed high art with mechanical skill" and avoid an unholy mess? Crystal and fine porcelain here, greasy, thumping steam engines there. It's a fiasco.'

But by no means all those who share their views with Touchfarthing are dissenters. Most, in fact, are evidently impressed by the varied marvels of the Exhibition or simply by the novel experience of entering a structure so vast that it can and does contain fully grown trees. The glass and steel edifice itself is the source of infinite wonder to many more. Mr Colin Caldicott, an engineer 'from Brummagem', informs Touchfarthing that the Crystal Palace is 'a modern marvel'. Touchfarthing nods and prepares to duck under his cloth, but Caldicott holds his arm. 'It's one thousand, eight hundred and forty-eight feet in length. Four hundred and eight feet in height. An area six times that of St Paul's Cathedral!'

'I can well believe it,' says Touchfarthing.

Caldicott shakes his head as he reads in a flat tone from a catalogue on his lap. 'Five hundred and fifty tons of wrought iron. Three thousand, five hundred tons of cast iron. Nine hundred thousand feet of glass. Six hundred thousand feet of wooden planking. Two hundred and two miles of sash bars. Thirty miles of guttering.'

Touchfarthing makes a show of producing and checking the face of his silver pocket-watch but another long minute passes before the sitter folds his catalogue and allows Touchfarthing to execute his shilling commission. For the next three hours the performance is the same – a cast of changing faces, a succession of to-ings and fro-ings between the front-of-house chairs and the backstage dark-tent – and it is late afternoon before the last customer, an impatient young hussar, pockets a dried, framed and wrapped photograph and strides quickly across the Park in the direction of Gore House.

The sun has begun to dip towards the western roofscapes; visitors on foot and on wheels are leaving the Park by every exit. Rankin is squatting by his box, funnelling chemicals into bottles. Touchfarthing is uncomfortably close. 'I feel filthy,' he says. 'Like a wretched tradesman.'

'That was good business we done there,' says Rankin, jingling the purse. 'And I've the one plate left, if you can find a customer.'

'No, that's enough of the mob for one day,' says Touchfarthing. 'That plate is saved for Art. The Exhibition by itself will make a very fine picture, I think.'

'And sell like hot plum-dough,' Rankin agrees. 'But I suppose we'll have to shift everything back to the Gate.'

'You'll do that, will you?' says Touchfarthing. 'While I calculate the longer exposure. Just take the essentials – it's only one picture.'

'And have some vagabond lift everything else? You'd best help out, that's my belief, guv'nor,' says Rankin and prepares to lift the camera from its tripod. He hesitates and nudges the other man. 'Do you suppose that cove got up like an undertaker is waiting his turn?' To Touchfarthing's questioning glance, Rankin indicates a lean, pale-faced man dressed wholly in black. The dark and curling locks which depend from the brim of his hat are longer than fashion allows and he wears a pair of green-tinted spectacles. 'I've caught him watching our goings on earlier,' says Rankin. 'What's 'is lay, do you think?'

'I'm sure he only wants his photograph taken, as do the world and his wife today.'

Touchfarthing's eyebrows interrogate the man, but he makes

no move towards the chairs, only looks a little longer upon the scene before straightening a louche pose and strolling towards the trees, where he becomes a part of a crowd that surrounds the fire-eater whose loud patter and sooty explosions have drawn away the last of Touchfarthing's trade. 'Rum fellow,' Touchfarthing says, frowning as he takes hold of a rope handle. There is a tinkling of glass as the two men swing the great box aboard the wagon.

III

By the Park gates, Rankin fits a new lens upon the camera, into which is inserted the last of the wet collodion plates. They have been ready for the past quarter hour and Rankin is impatient to quit the Park and fill his belly at Simpson's chop-house. He observes that 'Simpson's is very good for their cutlets' and that 'their pies is full of meat with no rubbish', hoping that Touchfarthing will perceive the wisdom of patronising a place of 'unbeatable value' and not squander the day's takings at Alexis Soyer's grand new establishment at Gore House, the wonders of which the hussar has left ringing in their ears. 'Now that's the sort of place we might make useful connections,' Touchfarthing had said. 'It's the sort of place we might waste a lot of money,' Rankin had replied.

A vendor is crying his wares by the Park gates: 'Potatoes, all 'ot!!' and Rankin is debating with himself whether a further economy might be made by expending a couple of pennies there rather than at Simpson's, when Touchfarthing claps his hands and exclaims, 'There, we have it now!' and points towards his magnificent subject. Even Rankin is forced to admit the beauty of the scene before them. Oblique sunlight lends fleeting solidity and sharply defines a thousand sash bars and gracefully curving flights of iron. The roof-lined flags of all nations which fluttered gaily in the morning breeze now hang heavy in the still evening air and nothing distracts from the audacious simplicity of Paxton's ingenious design.

10

'A pity about all those folk cluttering the middle ground,' Rankin says. 'Ain't they got no homes?'

'They won't register on the photograph,' says Touchfarthing. 'Not so long as they keep moving. Now then, I shall have to lengthen the exposure in this light.'

Touchfarthing removes the lens cover and hold up his pocket-watch, timing the exposure while impressively signalling to all about that here is a photographist going about his work. And indeed, in the ground between lens and Exhibition are many careless strollers who appear to take notice and who, perhaps in their ignorance, believe that their presence at the Great Exhibition is being recorded on a photograph.

'I think that will suffice,' Touchfarthing says as he re-covers the lens. 'Take care with your process, Rankin. I think I shall be pleased with this picture.'

'Well, let's 'ave that plate quickly, then,' says Rankin, 'while there's still enough light to make a print.' Rankin disappears inside his dark-tent while Touchfarthing, succumbing to the fatigue of a long and busy day, climbs upon the wagon and settles himself in the largest of the assortment of chairs. He begins to doze, his heavy jowl supported by a hefty hand, and would at any moment have given himself up to a deep and languorous sleep, had not Rankin shaken his knee. 'Guv'nor, you an't going to like this!' he says, pulling the torpid Touchfarthing from his seat. He follows Rankin to his bottles and dishes and from one of these Rankin extracts a square of paper which drips a new pattern of stains upon his already parti-coloured unmentionables.

'Well, what is it?' asks Touchfarthing irritably. His sleep-bleared eyes descry the unmistakeable shape of the great glasshouse before them. 'It looks all right?'

'It ain't quite there yet. But watch here, by the tree.' Rankin holds the developing photograph towards the sunlight and before their eyes the gauzy facsimile darkens and sharpens and detail begins to show: the crazing of the bark on an elm bough, individual panes of glinting glass, the folds of a Union flag.

11

'What's that?' Touchfarthing explodes. He takes himself and the photograph from the dark-tent, the better to examine it by the last rays of the sun. 'Ruined!' he says, his focus fixed upon an unexpected element in his composition. In the bottom corner, separating and becoming distinct from the trunk of a great tree, stands the man in the green-tinted spectacles and funereal clothing. Long exposure has, as the photographer predicted, erased every other idler and stroller from the scene. But this one remains. The subject of the photograph now seems not to be the Great Exhibition but rather a wealthy country gentleman showing off his estate.

It is only a photograph. The Great Exhibition is not disappearing tomorrow, when Touchfarthing might, with some inconvenience to himself, return and take another picture. But there is that about the man's expression, an ironical smile, which seems directed at Touchfarthing himself, that enrages and impels him towards the tree where the man had stood.

'Watch yourself, guv'nor. It an't worth getting the apoplexy for,' Rankin says, as Touchfarthing circumnavigates the tree trunk and scans the vistas beyond for any signs of his uninvited subject. Hot and bothered, he fans himself with the photograph as they walk back to the wagon. 'What kind of fellow is it, do you think, that stands absolutely stock still in the middle of a park for three minutes? Answer me that, John.'

'A very peculiar one,' says Rankin, and looks again at the paper, whose unfixed and evanescent image is disappearing before their eyes, fading away until nothing remains of man, tree or the Great Exhibition itself.

2

Over-exposure

Ten and sometimes twenty yards ahead, a small knife-thin figure in threadbare fustian led Henry Hilditch past the fish merchants and marine insurance offices of Lower Thames Street. They had walked, one before the other, from the West End and the guide showed no sign of slackening his brisk pace nor of indicating proximity to their destination.

Hilditch's footsteps clacked loudly on flint-dry cobblestones. A flaring street lamp briefly distinguished a pale face and hands from uniformly black apparel and showed him to be young. His voice, however, choked with the irritation of dissatisfied middle age. 'A guinea for a bit of mutton and some dressed crab!' he snorted. 'A guinea!' and shook his head as he increased his pace to match that of the small creature scuttling ahead. The decision had been his own and so the folly keener felt.

A temptation to brush buttons with society had lured him from the free and fresh air of Hyde Park to the over-priced and over-decorated restaurant rooms in which he had found himself among a crush of excursionists, the disengorgings of special trains from the Midlands and the North. Gore House, despite its finery and the presence in the kitchens of the remarkable Alexis Soyer, was clearly only another conduit for Exhibition cash.

Conceivably, he could have rescued something from the occasion. He knew that he might have furthered his observations of the London poor by talking to the pot boys, the cellar men, the grooms and the footmen, the under-cooks and scullery maids, to the mob of hungry men and women assembled in hope by the kitchen doors.

The singular occasion of the Great Exhibition was already furnishing unique and significant information. Henry Mayhew, whose startling publications on London's poor were opening wide the eyes of their more affluent neighbours, had himself acknowledged this much. And now, Henry Hilditch, engaged by a rival newspaper to exploit Mayhew's success, had also found much to interest him and much more to provide sensational copy for the readers of the *Morning Messenger*. Mayhew's reporting of the Exhibition would be sensible, worthy and full of facts but it would lack the drama that Henry's editor always insisted upon and which Henry always provided.

As an entrée to the evening's investigations, Hilditch had found himself exchanging banalities with his countryfolk: among the outpourings of Lancashire, the Potteries and the Black Country he encountered a house-builder from York, a confectioner from Pontefract and a landowner he knew by sight from Whitby, men he might have met at any time, in a past life. There was no profit in this nor in the substance of the intercourse itself. Half a mile from the Exhibition, Paxton's glasshouse and its cornucopia of invention was the main course of all conversations.

Enfin, Hilditch admitted, the most valuable contact he had made the whole evening had been with a waiter, whose own personal history Hilditch had quickly dismissed as trite but who had hired out the kitchen boy as his guide for preliminary explorations of London's East End. He had intended to go from Hyde Park directly to an address at which he had been advised he would find the poor at play and material sufficiently interesting for inclusion in his own survey of London's lower classes. Not only would this satisfy the curiosity of his readers

14

but it would go some way towards answering a need of another sort that was lodged deep in the heart of the young man himself.

The waiter had confidently asserted that boy Daniel knew just the place to interest the gentleman and so it proved, but only after the waiter had consented to take a shilling and Daniel himself had pocketed a shiny sixpence.

Now, digested by black anonymous streets and cuts in which one soot-blackened tenement back was the same as the next, Hilditch found himself unwilling host to an insidious and unreasonable dread that had been welling slowly since they had left the West End. The last rays of the sun that had scorched Hilditch's neck all afternoon in Hyde Park had glanced off the dome of Wylde's Monster Globe as they crossed Leicester Square and now it was only when moonlight found access and lit up the name of a street or the sign above a shop or lodging house that he dispelled the fantastical notion that he had wandered down some abysmal path to blackest Hell, and was still in the overworld. In these slums and rookeries were the very subjects of his investigations; he had realised that meeting London's poor on his West End ground was insufficient; that he must eventually follow them to their homes. But now, on his first visit to the deeper reaches of the East End at night, he found himself breathing hard and stumbling to keep up with the boy in a labyrinth of nameless passages. Then, when the inclination to run hell-for-leather until he found a main thoroughfare and a passing cab was strongest upon him, just up ahead he saw light and heard a commotion.

'Whitechapel!' the boy exclaimed, and Hilditch berated himself for his foolishness as he hurried out of the empty by-way into streams of pedestrians. But no sooner had he stepped upon a wide and well-lit street than Hilditch again lost sight of his companion among crowds gathered about line upon line of costermongers' barrows and fish-fryers' stoves. Hilditch held fast his purse and called out, but his 'Halloa, boy!' was lost among a dissonant chorus of street-cries, the braying of donkeys, the sizzling of frying fish and the hubbub of Londoners out on a Saturday spree. He pushed past faces made hellish by burning braziers or jaundiced by grease lamps and candles; knocked down a uniformed beggar outside the Three Tuns; had his coat seared by a fire-eater outside the Alhambra's noisy dancing rooms and roughly apprehended the wrong boy among a crowd of young people leaving the shabby premises of a penny gaff theatre.

'What's your game, guv'nor?' the boy demanded, shaking free of Hilditch's grasp and showing a face pock-marked with disease.

'A mistake only,' said Hilditch. 'See here, I am looking for a boy.'

'I might be that boy. A lot of toffs wants boys here. Depends on your price and what you wants.'

'No, that boy – there!' said Hilditch as he remarked his guide, stroking a small dog clasped by a boy of about his own age. 'Over here, boy, over here!' Hilditch gestured while the pock-marked boy bowed ostentatiously to the other.

'Your 'umble pardon, Dan'll! I didn't know this gent was engaged with you.'

'None o' that, Pineapple Joe,' said Hilditch's boy. 'I'm a respectable fellow in regular employ.'

'Wiv no time for your old pals, is that it?'

'I ha'n't got time for no one tonight,' said the other. 'My old un'll skin me if I ain't home at the soonest.'

'You'll be back, Dan'l Saggers, when he turns on you agin. And then you can 'ave your old spot by the Three Tuns.'

The boy frowned and rejoined Hilditch. Cutting between the premises of a tallow chandler and a sponge merchant they plunged once more into backstreets and alleys. 'That's put us behind and I'm sorry for it,' the boy said. 'But I was 'opin to get the loan of a good dog. A nice little dog might have put my old man in a 'menable mood. But no money no dog, says he. Well, such is life. And now we'll have to be double quick.'

'It must be after eleven now,' Hilditch said. 'Are we not too late already?'

'Wiv luck we ain't, sir. They don't like to start until arter the drinkin when the folks is more free with their money.'

The boy now fairly clipped along, leaping foul gutters and pulling Hilditch through murky alleys which seemed to him a succession of convergences, where buildings staggered ever closer together and each street was narrower and meaner and darker than the last. Black shapes glanced by with rustles of petticoats or rough imprecations. Unbidden, the mind of Hilditch flashed with the memory of a reported murder of a young girl in just such a place and of what perils might beset not only himself but another who might be lost upon these very streets. 'Daniel!' he called out, failing to master a tremor in his voice. 'Where am I?'

Small fingers squeezed his own. 'You're all right, sir. Not far now.' Hilditch took a deep breath and kept the boy's hand as they crossed the entrance to a malodorous court and splashed through water or nightsoil before coming upon a broader and less gloomy street and then a gap in a crumbling brick wall. 'Here we are, safe and sarn!' said the boy and then snatched at Hilditch's sleeve. 'Stop, sir, stop! Mind the steps or you'll break your neck!'

Hilditch took a careful step forwards and discovered that beyond the gap and lit faintly by lights he could not see was a long and precipitous flight of wooden stairs, connecting the road above with a deep railway cutting below. He caught his breath and let the boy go down first. When Hilditch had descended with measured tread to the first of two small landings, he found himself a little above the first-floor windows of a ramshackle and venerable building which was supported on two sides by stout oak buttresses, like a collapsing drunk held up by constables. Below the first-storey windows, from which gaslight glared and illuminated men busy at some work, depended a heavy wooden sign on which might faintly be discerned the image of a grey swan. Under this, two lean men stood behind stacked barrels. These men were engaged in earnest argument with a fatter, much larger third, who was shaking his head vigorously. The exchange was heated and voices raised sufficiently for Hilditch to comprehend.

'There it is. It's a fair offer. You won't do better tonight,' the fat man was saying.

'The agreed price was two guinea. I can't take less'n that, Villum!'

The fat man spat and yanked a string from the other's hand, winding in a large, stocky dog.

'Ten bob's your lot, you thieving gypsy. And you'll still be turning a handsome profit, I've no doubt.'

The man cursed but was dissuaded from further remonstration by the whispered advice of his friend. He pocketed a handful of coins and started up the stairs, querying Hilditch with a glance before disappearing into the gloom. Below, the fat man was stooping to inspect his purchase when he saw the boy, immobile in a pool of sickly window-light.

'Just in time, Dan'l,' he said. 'Now let's be having the money. I'm lucky tonight, I know it!'

The boy made some reply too faint for Hilditch's ears.

'What? You done what?' the fat man roared. 'My ears is bad, Dan'l, you'll have to repeat that 'un for me!'

But without awaiting the reply, he seized at ragged clothing and severely shook the boy's flimsy frame. The fat man looked about him, as if seeking some place to dispose of unwanted rubbish. 'Wait, wait!' the boy cried, but the man was already hurling him off his feet, smashing him against the door post of the inn and causing a big man in an apron to look out from the doorway. 'There'll be time to knock some respect into the villain later, Bill,' he said. 'They're wanting you up my two pair of stairs now.'

But the fat man picked up the boy and struck the side of his head with sufficient force to send him reeling backwards where he lost his balance and tumbled noisily over an empty barrel. Now Hilditch could hear the boy as he protested to his antagonist. 'It weren't my fault, guv'nor! I tole you them rich folk wan't to be trusted!'

The man snatched up the boy and pressed his own fist against a hollow cheek. Hilditch heard a low and menacing rumble like the approach of a distant train.

'Trusted?' the fat man snarled. 'You gets a place hard by the Shibition itself and can't make no money? Don't give me that barrikin. And where's the silver I told you to bone? Don't tell me nothing stuck to you? You're either the laziest boy in London or a stunning imbecile. Look at this – I've got Carver's dog at last and nothing to bet. Curse you, the only money I'll make on it tonight is when I sell it!' He seized a stave of wood and hoisted it above his head.

The boy looked about wildly for some defence and at the same moment footsteps on creaking stairs alerted his assailant to Hilditch's approach. 'Who's that?' the fat man hissed and laid down the wood. He lifted the boy to his feet. 'Is 'e with you, Dan'l?'

The boy nodded and passed a sixpence to the man. 'And he give me this jest fer walking him across town.'

The man looked more carefully at the stranger. 'Did 'e truly? Well, well, that was handsome.' He appraised Hilditch with a top to toe glance, threw him a quick smile and ducked inside the public house.

Hilditch descended the last few steps and regarded the boy. 'I suppose you are hurt?'

The boy dusted off his thin clothes and shrugged. 'That wasn't hardly nothing. I've had wuss'n that. It's all over anywise. I won't remember this once it starts upstairs.'

They pushed past the men at the doorway and others who lined a cramped corridor and entered a packed bar room in which was a crush of bodies and a fug of tobacco smoke, stale beer and unwashed linen. Glasses toppled from slops-laden tables as Henry Hilditch was drawn through a mangle of sandy corduroy, scarlet uniform and spittle conversations.

'Is this the singular spectacle we have come far to see? These people, this pandemonium?' Hilditch shouted, for the bar room was loud with cursing and laughter, soldiers' songs and the insistent barking of dogs.

'Just you foller me and you'll see,' the boy called back as he held open a door.

They mounted a narrow staircase and entered an upper chamber whose area had been greatly enlarged by the removal of a central wall, which arrangement obliged those passing the length of the room to step nimbly through the surviving uprights of a timber frame. Old doors and timbers mounted upon barrels served as tables, and on rough-hewn chairs and makeshift settles were already installed some thirty-five or forty patrons all contributing to a bedlam of chatter and contention. Beyond the timber wall-frame was a room in which more men were grouped about a cleared area of better illumination.

The boy showed Hilditch to a table where an army officer in an unbuttoned tunic sat already and on which there seemed little room for anything more than the Staffordshire bull terrier which stood upon it. The soldier, prising open its jaws so that its saliva pooled on the table, acknowledged Hilditch's arrival with a curt nod as he conversed with a smock-coated man who held his hat doffed beneath his arm.

'Strong teeth, you'll agree, Cap'n?' He parted the dog's legs and cupped pendulous testicles in his hands. 'Two onions in a string bag, eh? He's all dog, Cap'n, just what you want for the fancy!'

The soldier, applying a flaring Lucifer to his pipe of tobacco, kicked the dog from the table and rested polished boots in its place. He removed the pipe and spat out a shred of tobacco. 'Teeth and testicles are very well, but many's the good-looking cur that hasn't earned his meat when set to it.' He turned to Hilditch. 'What say you, sir?'

Henry Hilditch struggled to sort and arrange the loud tumult of strange sights and sounds: the shifting curtain of corduroy, fustian and bombazine; the children appearing with tankards of ale and disappearing with pots and coins; the abnormal number of dogs straining on strings or held in their owners' arms, or peering out from under coats, whose apparent ancestors – petrified in a full range of aggressive poses – were

20

preserved and displayed in glass cases on shelves above.

The soldier nudged Hilditch. 'Well, sir, what say you? Which is the top dog tonight?'

'I couldn't say, I'm sure,' said Hilditch, as if he would much rather avoid conversation and be left to himself.

The boy, who had been awaiting a convenient moment to speak, now held out a hand to Hilditch. 'You'll feel more yourself with a drink inside you. A gent like you would take some port, I 'spect? Or maybe some French brandy? Give me a bob or two and I'll see to it.'

The soldier's moustache brushed Hilditch's ear. 'You keep close, is that it? Well, that might be the wisest course.'

The boy was tugging upon Hilditch's sleeve like a restless puppy. 'Drink, sir? There's champagne, I believe.'

'Champagne, that's the ticket, eh!' said the officer. 'No beer and porter for us, eh, sir?'

'What will it be, sir, brandy or champagne?' said the boy, extending again his small hand.

'No drink,' said Hilditch. 'Not while I am about my business.'

'What's that? You'll not take a drink with Jack Ratcliffe of the Life Guards?'

'No drink, thank you,' said Hilditch, and in retreating behind his coloured spectacles provoked the soldier to swear and then to rise unsteadily.

'Rum sort of fellow you are, sir,' he said and stepped through the frame and into the area beyond, in which someone was ringing a bell. The boy remained at Hilditch's side and sighed theatrically. 'It is conventional to take a drink first,' he declared. 'You must have the drink, you know.'

'This has been a mistake,' Hilditch was saying as the noisy crowds about him pressed into the adjoining chamber. Some peered at him closely as they passed and others laughed at remarks made by the captain which evidently had concerned the newcomer. Even when abroad, Henry Hilditch had never felt such a stranger. He realised that he had been unprepared for such an odyssey and wished for nothing more than to be safely returned to the West End. When he had first taken in this room, he had been delighted at the abundance of exotic subjects, any one of whom would most likely make a memorable portrait for the *Messenger*. Thoughts of over-leaping Henry Mayhew had raced through his mind. He saw *An Entomology of the Working Classes*, by Henry Hilditch. And if just one of these denizens of the streets and alleys of the East End had noticed a strange girl newly come among them . . . But as quickly as these thoughts fled had come the unsettling fear that he had crossed some invisible line and that his presence here was suspected and unwelcomed by all about.

'If you will just see me back upon the high road . . .' he said to Daniel, but immediately he was swept up by the tide of men and women who were crowding through one room and into the other, where, guided by the boy, he now found himself pushed and pulled until he was pressed hard up against the wooden siding of a circular pit about twelve feet in diameter. The pit was empty, though about its walls men were wedged tightly and behind them were others, pushing, shuffling and arranging themselves into positions of better vantage. The larger part of the audience stood upon furniture, sat upon a billiard table or swung their legs from the sills of high windows. Hilditch, hot about the collar, feeling not only the discomfort of his own strangeness, was nauseous too as he breathed the cloying atmosphere of decaying teeth, poor ale and dogs. As he became more accustomed to the scene he perceived that the only object of any interest at that moment to those other spectators whose pipes and elbows hung over the siding was himself.

''E won't see much with 'is blinkers on!' commented a stout woman as someone at Hilditch's back ran a hand over the pile of his coat and observed that it must have cost a bob or two. It was unbearable to be the focus of such attention and to feel like a bug under glass and yet, Hilditch mused, perhaps, in their own way, these people were admiring him. They had already marked him as different. Conceivably, they might think him a princely stranger come among them for a mysterious purpose.

Preoccupied in this way, a sudden blow to his shoulder took him unawares.

'Mind yer back!'

Unnoticed by Hilditch, a man carrying another, larger dog had made his way through the crowd behind and now knocked him roughly as he passed. The dog was offered over the barrier and dropped into the pit.

'Here's a capital dog for someone,' said William Saggers as he stood in the centre of the ring, which was lit from above. He uncoiled a length of rope and threw it over an oak beam, from which depended a great iron fitting with six flaring flames. No sooner was the rope tied off than the animal broke free, leapt into the pit and seized the rope's end, locking its teeth upon a great knot.

'That's the style, Nipper!'

The rope was pulled hard and the dog launched into the air. Flexing the muscles of its neck, it swung from side to side, frantically arranging a better hold for its teeth. These struggles and contortions were observed with keen interest by all about the pit. Saggers stood back and waved a hand at the gyrating animal. 'Did you ever see a stronger dog? Here's more muscles than Billingsgate! Who'll have him? Who'll make me a decent offer?'

The dog gave out joyous, slobbering growls as it arced wildly, but then, unable to unfix its teeth from thick hemp, it started to choke on its own saliva.

'He's had his fill already, Willum,' observed a man. 'What's wanted is a dog with tenacity!'

'I'll show you that!' said the other and before the animal could extricate itself and drop to the floor, William Saggers had taken a guttering candle from a table and slipped it directly beneath the beam. Now whenever the dog passed over the source of heat, it convulsed and thrashed wildly as it tried to remove itself from the source of pain. It swung high but, inevitably, its pendulum course returned it to the flame where it shuddered and flailed with increased violence. The mob cheered with one voice as the squealing dog was scorched again and roundly condemned the soldier Ratcliffe when he stepped into the pit and kicked away the candle. 'Enough, you half-wit, Saggers, I want some dog left, don't I?'

'You'll 'ave 'im, then, Captain? A reg'lar bargain he is, at five guineas.'

'You'll get your money afterwards,' said Ratcliffe. 'Anyone can hang on a rope and no doubt some of us will. I'll see the dog going about his business first.'

The soldier quietened the quaking dog and quit the ring as William Saggers said, 'Bet now, gentlemen, and remember that this fine dog is for sale arterwards to the highest bidder. Never mind that the captain's set 'is expert eye on him.'

Saggers climbed from the pit and stepped up to his chair, an old Windsor carver which was elevated upon some unseen dais and situated at one side of Hilditch. Thus enthroned, he began taking money, giving change and marking slips of paper presented by those about. A shadowy figure without the inn, the ring of gas flames above showed Saggers to be a figure worthy of more particular notice. His face was jowly, his eyes squinty and the line of his mouth thin. Beneath his eyes, below his forehead and lip, shadows had formed that exaggerated the lines of his middle age and his foreshortened visage looked as if it had been sat upon and crumpled, like a mislaid hat. His head weighed upon his shoulders like a cannon ball on a soft cushion, folding into his flabby blue-chinned neck which was squeezed so tightly into its collar that folds of flesh spilled over the top. Neither his waistcoat nor his overcoat were buttoned and nor did it seem possible that the two sides of his apparel could ever be caused to meet.

With the attentions of all fastened upon this individual, Hilditch allowed his terror to subside and to become interested himself. This singularly repulsive specimen was worthy of further study. He would relish introducing him into the well-upholstered homes of the *Morning Messenger*'s readers. The subject of Hilditch's meditations spat and called out, impatiently,

24

'All finished, jintlemin? Then let's have 'em in, Jack!'

Heavy boots clomped upon the stairs and the crowd parted to allow the passage of a sharp-nosed, wiry man who carried some heavy burden. As he came closer, Hilditch saw that it was a cage and within the mesh a dark mass appeared to move. For an instant Hilditch thought that here was some small caged bear but then flaring gas sparked in a hundred tiny eyes and as the cage was jolted against the pit wall, the amorphous shape split apart and rearranged itself at either end and upon the roof of the cage. Tails flicked from the grill like the tongues of lizards; Hilditch heard now the squealing and saw that in the cage was a great mass of brown rats. The man deposited the cage on the floor of the pit. He bent to tie two pieces of string about the bottoms of his trousers, observing that he 'could do wivart rats up there!' and untwisted the loop of wire that fastened the cage.

II

The cage door being let open, the rats – so quick do they move that Hilditch can only roughly estimate that their number is around fifty – pour out on the boards and scatter this way and that, around and about the pit, nosing in crevices and searching for an egress, of which there is none. By Hilditch's side, Captain Ratcliffe struggles to hold back the salivating and growling terrier as it strains and fights to be let go. The rats, sensing extreme danger, pile themselves at the opposing side of the pit, scrambling one upon the other in pyramids of fur and whiskers, screeching and tearing at each other, the topmost jumping hopelessly for the rim of the pit, where a man flashes an amber-toothed grin as he swipes at them with a club.

'All ready, sirs?' calls the wiry man as he shakes free a rat that has fixed itself upon the cloth of his trousers. He climbs from the pit and winks at Ratcliffe. 'Then we'll let the fancy commence!'

The soldier leans forward and drops the dog into the pit. It pauses a moment to size up the situation and then plunges into the largest pile of rodents, snuffling deep among the shrieking, squirming pile until it extracts a fat brown rat on which it fixes its teeth so hard that dark specks of blood appear on the rat's neck. The dog shakes its prey as violently as it was itself shaken upon the rope. It bites harder, forcing more blood from the throat of its victim and then throws the rat upon the floor, where it lies convulsing in its death throes.

The dog darts again at the pile and pulls out another, smaller rat and, making an excited misjudgement, crushes the head in its jaws. It spits out the mutilated animal and despatches three more rats with greater efficiency. Now it has the measure of the job in hand it wags its tail and takes its time, plucking a rat from here, a rat from there; it is content to allow others to race between its legs as it breaks another small neck. So complacent is the dog that an unexpected reversal is all the more alarming.

Once more rushing a number of rats, the dog suddenly withdraws its snout, throws back its head and yelps. A rat hangs heavily from the dog's jowls, its teeth firmly fixed in the soft skin. The dog attempts to shake free the rat and in so doing tears its own flesh. It squeals and backs away from the pain. Injured and confused, the dog turns on the remaining rats with renewed vigour and, loudly encouraged by the spectators who hang over the pit sides and sometimes beat the rats from the walls with sticks, kills one after another in quick succession. The number of dead steadily grows until more are laid stopped upon the floor than are still scattering about the ring.

A man close to Hilditch points to his pocket-watch. 'I count thirty-eight dead or dying. Another twelve in three minutes, my beauty, another twelve!'

'Don't reckon your pot yet,' Captain Ratcliffe says. 'That dog is tiring of the game.'

No sooner has the other replied, 'Says the expert?' than he too sees that the dog's attention is wavering. The gash in its cheek still bleeds and though the number of scuttling rats continues to drop, the dog is dealing out death in a most desultory fashion. The rats themselves appear to sense the

26

change and are becoming bolder. One sits on its hind legs, rubbing its whiskers with tiny paws. Small black eyes glint in the gaslight and Hilditch is seduced by the absurd idea that the thing is praying to him, as some omnipotence holding the gift of life or death, when the dog flies at it, pinning its torso to the floor with sharp claws as it tears off the head with its teeth.

This final violence has thoroughly sated the dog and, pausing to cock its leg and piss against the pile of matted fur near the centre, it sees its present owner and jumps its paws on to the rim of the pit, where its ears are scratched. Unmolested, the last few rats traverse the floor without purpose.

The match over, money changes hands. 'Well, Captain,' William Saggers says when the bets are settled. 'I'll accept your money and then I'll have a little bet myself. We agreed 'pon five guinea, I think?'

Captain Ratcliffe laughs dismissively. 'A farmer might give you a few shillings. That's no sporting dog.'

Saggers' voice falls to a low whisper. 'Don't make a fool of me, Ratcliffe. I must get staked. There's money here tonight, I can smell it!'

'Then sniff it out, by all means,' says Ratcliffe, turning away. 'Just keep your nose out of my pockets.'

Saggers forces a smile but his brow appears to record the passing of darker thoughts. His eyes roam about the room but his gaze is unmet. A man whose attention is engaged before he can avert his eyes, listens to whispers and shakes his head. Saggers raises his voice. 'What? Only five shillings, Bob? And my firm promise that you'll have six on Saturday next? This ain't worthy of you, Bob!'

'Mr Willum, you know I'd never refuse you. But my last tanner went on that dog and I'll go wivart my lunch tomorrow.' Saggers grunts and watches blankly as a new dog sets about his rats. The small carcases are being dropped into a sack when Saggers seizes the boy Daniel and grips him by the neck. 'This is your fault, Dan'l, you've brought me to this! What's a betting man without his capital?'

Hilditch follows the altercation between father and son with interest. He is fascinated by this Saggers, who is clearly a pivotal figure in this alien world and may even, Hilditch thinks, provide him with some vital intelligence. It does not seem unlikely. Just as Hilditch himself has been identified instantly as a stranger, so too would a well-spoken and striking woman appearing suddenly in these parts. It is this woman whose memory has drawn him after her, into the East End of London, and she who impels him into such strange places as this. Engrossed in such thoughts, Hilditch fails to notice that Saggers' eyes are fixed upon him.

'Well, stranger! Dan'l says you've come a long way to see the fancy tonight. But you've yet to make a wager?'

Hilditch is non-committal and only shrugs, in the French fashion.

Saggers says, 'Well, if you're new to the fancy you're wise to watch how it goes first. A man needs to know what he's doing. And know something about dogs, too, eh?'

He leans over his chair and lowers his voice. 'Lucky for you, I'm the 'knowledged expert on matters of a canine nature. Ain't that so, Ned?'

''E's that, all right,' says a man in a garish waistcoat.

'What I propose,' Saggers confides, 'is that I larns you something about the fancy, in return for a small consideration. Through the fault of others, I find myself short. But a gent like you would hardly come out without his tin, eh? Now, to begin, shall we stake five shilling?'

'No, I think not,' Hilditch replies.

'Three, then? Or a round half crown?' Hilditch shakes his head and Saggers frowns. 'I knows my dogs, I tell you. And if we don't win I don't take my consideration. How much fairer can a man be? Give me a shilling and I'll lay it down.'

'No, I really think not,' Hilditch says and turns away. He affects to observe the spectators about the pit, who have resumed their drinking and chatter and are, Hilditch thinks, at least as interesting as the spectacle in the pit. Now that the arena is being cleared once more of dead rats, those gathered about it are talking loudly. Nattily dressed salesmen puff cigars at the side of costermongers who pull on yellow-stemmed pipes and expectorate into the pit. Other fanciers point at dogs in the glass cases, shaking their heads with the gravitas of Oxford dons. One or two nearby have been paying heed to the exchange between the stranger and Saggers, whose brow now furrows as his head inclines quizzically.

'Am I mistaken?' he says, loudly enough for all about to hear should they so wish. Saggers addresses himself to the ceiling. 'Am I under a mishapprehension?' He peers directly into the dark glass of Hilditch's spectacles. 'You is here to enjoy our 'umble entertainment, isn't you?'

Saggers snatches at Daniel who has remained at his side and pulls him closer. 'Dan'l! The gent is here to bet, ain't he?'

Daniel looks about himself, to the door, but interested crowds have stopped up the way of escape. 'No, he an't here to bet.'

'Not here to bet?' announces Saggers, astounded. And then claps his hand to his forehead. 'Hang me for a fool! O'course, that's it, he's here to buy, then!'

'No, he don't want a dog neither.'

'What, then, Dan'l?' says Saggers.

'He said he just wanted to watch.'

Saggers makes his eyes bulge in mock-astonishment but real annoyance prevents further mummery and he booms out, 'To hob-serve? What's the good of that? Who is he, Dan'l? Is he a spy, a Customs sneak maybe?'

Eyes swivel to Hilditch like so many great guns. 'We don't turn away strangers here, sir,' Saggers says. 'We welcomes 'em, takes 'em into our fold. We treats a stranger like our own, so long as they loves the entertainment we provides. And you don't give the appearance of doing that, sir! P'raps you'll explain yourself?'

To those across the pit the stranger appears composed but some who stand closer may observe the sheen upon his lip.

'I'm not a sporting man. I only want to see what goes on here.'

Saggers pauses, weighs up the answer like an Assize judge after a heavy lunch.

'What kind of cove are you, sir? What doesn't get involved?'

'I only want to be a spectator,' says Hilditch. 'I get no pleasure from gambling. I wish only to stand here quietly and watch. But, if that is not permissible, then I will go.'

'No, no, you interest me, sir, and you shall stay,' Saggers says. 'I would like to know what kind of a man is it that can keep isself separate from all others though he stands beside 'em and accepts their 'ospitality.'

'I have no wish to insult you,' says Hilditch. 'You will forgive me if I seem impolite.'

'You're like the missionaries and the meddlers that come about us, all wanting something for nothing.' He shakes his head as he scrutinises the novelty before him. 'What a pale and lifeless thing you are! Do you have no blood in you? Can't you afford no meat? I can hear you've an education. A man can go far with one o' them, they say. But it seems he can't get fat!'

William Saggers slaps his own ample haunches, and looks about for the endorsement of the crowd.

'If you will excuse me, now,' Hilditch begins, but Saggers holds him back.

'I think you care for nothing, sir. I think you are a cold creetur that can worm its way in anywhere, observe and go away again.' He turns again to the silent crowd and receives nods and murmurs of assent before he starts to address Hilditch again. 'Maybe I've seen you at a hanging? We've all observed at hangings, ain't we, mates? But we ain't like fish watching wi'out blinking as some cove dies. We cheers if he's a bad 'un or we cries if he's a pal. But we gets involved, that's for sartain.'

Hilditch, pale as candlewax, fights to keep control of his trembling voice. 'I don't have a lot of money, but I can loan you a shilling, to make your bet,' he says. 'If you will only allow me to watch without further molestation.'

'I shouldn't like to involve you when you didn't want to be

involved,' says Saggers, 'when arter all you had only come here to observe.'

Saggers pushes Daniel before Hilditch, blocking his path. 'You know my boy Dan'l?'

Hilditch meets the wide eyes of the child and nods. Saggers holds the boy's arm with one hand and with his other hand he strokes his face.

'He's a good boy, ain't he?'

'That depends on the purpose for which he guided me here. But I'm persuaded he is.'

'You got here safe, didn't you?'

Saggers speaks loudly, so his voice can be heard above the preparations for the next match. Rats scratch against the boards by which Hilditch stands, confronted by Saggers, while in the periphery of his vision they run pell mell about the pit. A small, sharp-eared terrier yaps excitely in its owner's arms.

'Drop the little feller in,' somebody calls. 'He looks ready for 'en!'

'Wait!' The voice of William Saggers is loud enough to brook further chatter. 'Hold your dog, Isaac. He can have his turn after the diversion.'

News of this diversion daisy-chains about the pit and Hilditch has every man's attention as he turns Daniel about and, with a dog's rope, pinions his arms behind his back. 'Jes' so you isn't tempted to cheat,' he says.

The boy, with a face that is a mixing of shock and rage, protests loudly. 'You promised I shouldn't do this again!'

'And you promised to bring home your money,' his father replies, as he helps the boy up upon a pit-side table. 'Now go on, give the gentlemen their entertainment and there might be something in it for you.'

Daniel stands above the crowd. At first Hilditch thinks the boy's trembling is caused by his precarious perch – the table rocks upon a shortened leg – but then he sees the dark streak upon the boy's trousers and the new puddling upon the tabletop. The boy whimpers softly.

'No good looking at that particular jintleman,' Saggers says. 'He's only a observer! Now, into the pit, Dan'l, or it'll go the worse for you.'

The boy hesitates. He looks again at Hilditch, as if he might penetrate the opaqueness of his disguise. Saggers moves towards him and raises his stick. "E jest needs a little poke,' he tells the crowd, but before Saggers can follow through, the boy jumps to the floor of the pit. He lands hard upon the boards but loses his balance and crashes to the floor. His tied hands are trapped beneath him and for some moments he is unable to rise or to prevent the rats swarming over his legs and chest. Daniel struggles but is at last upon his feet, crying petulantly, 'I ain't doing this again!'

'A half dozen rats in five minutes, Daniel – that ain't asking much, I think, of a dutiful son.'

'I only done two last time,' the boy complains.

Saggers' stick prods the boy towards the largest piling of rats. 'Every one on 'em, Dan'l, or you'll bed in the gutter tonight. I've had my fill of you.'

Tears of anger and frustration flash in the boy's eyes as he crosses the pit and swings a ferocious kick at the writhing mound. As the rats disperse, he stamps hard and crushes the head of one and immediately receives a crack across his own skull from his father's stick. 'None of that, none of that! You bite 'em, same as the dogs!'

Around the ring, bets are being made by the sanguinary men who cheer noisily as the stick flails and Daniel ducks to avoid another knock on the head. The boy resigns himself to his circumstances and falls to his knees before the rats. Screwing tight his eyes, he darts his head among them in the manner of the dogs before him. The topmost creatures escape his incursion by scrabbling over the boy's head, matting his hair and scratching his scalp before they run off down his back. Others dart out from between his legs and around his sides. The boy shuffles about, his head bobs up and down and then he straightens his back and turns about. Blood streams from lacerations to his cheeks, nose and forehead. He has a rat between his teeth, which he quickly traps against the wall while he bites its neck. The rat scratches, fights and squeals as the boy traps it against the wood while he finds a place to make a fatal nip.

'That's the style, boy, that's the style!' Saggers calls.

The boy drops the rat and spits out a piece of its fur. 'Let me go, I'll get you money if you'll let me go,' he implores, but Saggers will hear none of this and shouts, 'Another varmint, lad, go to it!'

Reluctantly, the boy again addresses the quivering rats. This time his small mouth can find no purchase and each time he delves among the animals he receives additional wounding. Not all who cheered before are cheering now. A pop-eyed, florid-faced man urges on the sobbing boy, waving his stick and shouting, 'Kill 'en, Dan'l! Kill 'en, boy!' but Daniel withdraws himself from his quarry and sits back upon his heels with glazed countenance.

Saggers, for all that he seems intent upon the boy, has Hilditch in his gaze. His thin smile is enquiring. 'How do you like our sport now, sir?'

Blood wells in the boy's eyes, drops heavily from a split lip and dapples his shirt front. Wherever bare skin shows, it is crazed with the scratches of sharp claws.

'This is the most damnable thing I ever saw,' Hilditch says.

Saggers prods the boy with his stick. 'Don't stop now! Another rat, damn you!' He begins to push Daniel towards the seething, blood-speckled heap of animation.

Hilditch, who is so close to Saggers that he seems complicit in his every action, clears his throat.

'What's that?' Saggers says.

'That's enough!' says Hilditch.

Saggers affects surprise and cups his ear as he speaks to the assembly at large. 'You ain't about to interfere? Ho, no, I couldn't have heard that!' He leans forward and pokes his stick in the back of the boy's neck. 'Get along, boy, you ain't finished yet!'

Hilditch lays his hand upon the arm that is raising the stick.

'You must stop this. You must have his wounds seen to now!'

'Must I, indeed? This is your opinion?'

'It's the opinion of anyone with an ounce of sanity,' says Hilditch.

'You keep out of this. Can't you do like you said? He'll be taken care of, jest as soon as he's finished.'

'He's finished now, man. Look at him!'

Saggers spits at Hilditch, 'If he leaves that pit now, he leaves this house for ever and ever, Amen. A boy what can't make money is no good to me. Well? Will he leave with you, sir? Will you take him?'

Hilditch hesitates. 'I can't do that.'

'I thought as much,' he says, and turns away. 'Finish them rats, Dan'l. It's like you said. The gent's only here to watch.'

Daniel shuffles towards the rats once more. Saggers throws a halfpenny into the pit and someone else throws a second. Daniel is encouraged by the men about the pit, whose calls are now sympathetic, some even kindly. 'Go on, son,' someone says. 'You're doing stunning.' Over his shoulder, Saggers says, 'You'll recall the way out, sir.'

The crowd makes way before him, and before he knows it, Henry Hilditch is once more outside in the cool night air of the London streets.

3

'Sixpunny Portraits'

At the wrong end of a small tributary off Oxford Street, in an area where strugglers of some ambition might claim a West End address, but others might feel keenly their proximity to the rookeries of St Giles; where spider and web fought dustpan and brush, and the occasional tottering pile of crumbling masonry and broken windows was like an ebony piano key on an otherwise ivory board; and where the owners of flower boxes and neat little shops hoped to raise their neighbours by example alone, a smart black equipage was pulled by four beautifully turned-out horses the full length of the street before it was brought to a halt outside a place of business situated on a corner.

The upper two storeys of this house were much like its neighbours – soot-stained bricks punctured by a double row of three sash windows, all nearly opaque with grime. Below these upper windows appeared the still-white lettering, Touchfarthing. Photographer. The ground-floor sashes had been removed and replaced with a large plate-glass window, behind which were displayed line upon line of assorted photographs framed in tin and silver and representing generations of people of all stations, although those of more obvious standing were allowed their right of precedence and stood to the front of the window, while anonymous fishwives and porters, costermongers and men with dogs lurked in obscurity at the rear.

Dwarfing these were larger portraits framed in wood and gilt depicting whiskery men of business in shiny hats; young, newly-commissioned officers; robust matrons restraining fidgeting infants and there were also the records of young ladies and gentlemen at various stages of their development. Two remov-able glazed panels of sample pictures and frames stood propped in opposite corners. Beneath the window, for anyone sufficiently interested to stoop, was the information:

> *Cornelius Touchfarthing, Photographer. Exact Likenesses taken for as little as 6d, frame included. Miniature and Large sized Photographs taken at Three-quarters or Full length. Reduced Prices for Whole Families and Groups. Personal Visits undertaken to the Homes of Ladies and Gentlemen. Enquire within about our Morocco cases, brooches and lockets.*

The window display was rarely without its cluster of admirers and was treated by much pavement traffic as a free gallery and by the proprietor with mixed feelings. If one half of those who gathered about his window would enter the shop and have their likenesses taken he might be well-pleased, and he was buoyed only by the hope that some who peered into his window told others and these might some day be his customers. In the meantime, he admitted with some reluctance, he would have to resort to more go-ahead methods if he were to keep his head above water.

On this morning a smartly-dressed family stood before his window admiring another family, whose perfect likeness made the attractive centre-piece of the window display. A great gilt frame, such as might have been employed almost without shame at the Royal Academy, encompassed a scene of domestic perfec-tion. The tall, mustachioed patriarch of the group stood sternly to one side with a hand resting heavily on the shoulder of his seated wife, a model of simple chastity. Sitting on a chaise-longue beside her were three children, groomed, scrubbed and stiffly resplendent in their Sunday best. The bases of posing stands, showing between the polished shoes of the boy and the laced-up boots of the elder girl, suggested that this perfect poise had not been achieved without a little ingenuity.

The admirers of this picture turned as one when the sounds of hooves and harnesses alerted them to the arrival of horses and carriage. The conveyance was not a grand affair, but smart and compact and in the best order. Soon the bright crest upon the door was holding the interest of the window-gazers and was very quickly attracting the attention of more pavement traffic, a handful of shopkeepers and one or two street sellers. They gathered about to decipher the emblem and the motto below, waiting for a glimpse of the august occupant, whose identity was protected by a lowered blind. The driver, the collar of his great-coat raised, the brim of his hat pulled low so that he was altogether muffled too well against the clement weather, took all the time in the world descending from his perch and in giving the reins to a crossing sweeper. 'His lordship will not detain you long,' he said loudly, and gave the boy a shiny sixpence. Anticipation rippled through the crowd as the driver tapped upon the carriage door. The blind was let up and from within sounded a stentorian voice. 'We're arrived are we?'

The crowd clustered about the vehicle as the driver opened the door and let down the steps. 'This is the establishment as was recommended, sir,' he said.

'This person is good, is he?' demanded the resounding voice.

'The very best in London, I'm assured,' said the driver.

'And you are certain that he is properly patronised?'

'I'm told the Duke himself calls for Mr Touchfarthing.'

'Well, I hope he's quick. I'm a busy man.'

'I understand told that the whole process is accomplished in five minutes,' said the driver. 'He's also uncommonly cheap.'

'Pshaw!' said the voice within. 'If it's quality I want, I think I can pay for it! Help me out!'

The crowd gathered close about the carriage as the driver extricated from the small cabin a large man in beautiful yet curiously ill-fitting garments. One or two of the shopkeepers touched their forelocks as the driver, crying out 'Make way for his lordship, there!', hurriedly assisted his passenger across the pavement and into the shop doorway. The door opened and closed and its bolt was shot. The crowd pressed against the window, where, above the brass rail of a half-curtain, the party just entered might be seen making its way to the rear of the premises.

'Gorn to have 'is photograph made!' hissed a bent and toothless cress-seller. The two young crossing sweepers who had wormed their way to the front of the crowd now extricated themselves with the same ease. 'You'n see't all at the back!' said one and those with sufficient curiosity shuffled after the sweepers, who had scampered around the corner where a rickety fence enclosed an unusual addition to the photographer's premises. This great glasshouse, the oasis of some forgotten city horticulturist, was now in poor repair, the branches of an apple tree having broken through one corner, and with many of the panes now whitewashed or stuffed with waxed paper and cloth, the annexe was a poor adjunct to the property for anyone but a photographer of limited means, for whom its abundance of northern light made it a perfectly serviceable and capacious studio. Through knots and gaps in the surrounding fence, the boys were commenting on the proceedings within.

''Is lordship's stood agin a great pile of books an' a bit of a pillar, it looks like. There's a door behind 'im and trees and the sea.'

'Sea? In the middle o' London? Shift over an' let me look!'

'It's a pitcher, I mean – what looks like the sea.'

'And don' 'e look savage?' The boy rapped on the glass. 'Like a reg'lar statchoo, aintcha, old feller?' He knocked again and contorted his features so that his eyes bulged and his nose was flattened against the glass. The sitter, sensible of his audience, struggled to maintain his composure. He adjusted his pose, lifting his chin and stroking his luxuriant moustache before fixing his gaze in the far distance.

Shortly afterwards, the muffled driver opened the door of the shop and escorted the noble personage back into his carriage. As soon as the door was closed, he mounted his seat and flicked his whip. The carriage drew away. It turned a corner and then another and then it stopped. The door opened and its passenger alighted and hurried into a tradesmen's entrance behind the glasshouse. The carriage itself turned into the yards of a livery stable where the driver jumped down.

After the great stable doors had been opened and the coach had been wheeled inside and the doors once more closed and locked, a sum of money passed from the hands of the driver into those of a cheerful man in a checked waistcoat and top boots.

The passenger meanwhile had hurried across a yard, through the glasshouse and into the kitchen door of the photographer's premises. Throwing off his jacket in the partitioned kitchen that served also as dark-room, he prised off his shoes and pulled on his familiar stained jacket and trousers. Once reattired and having paused just long enough to catch his breath, he strode over to the front door. Here he stopped suddenly as if struck by an idea. Carefully, he stripped the moustache from under his nose and slipped it into a pocket of his trousers before opening wide the street door.

'A good afternoon to you,' he said to the still curious and bemused throng without. 'I hope I haven't kept anyone waiting. I was obliged to prepare a photograph for a most important client. But I am free now – I can see the first sitter in just a moment. Photographs can be made by my assistant Mr Rankin for sixpence or for only twopence more you can elect to be photographed by myself in person. Now, who will be first today? This little fellow' – he addressed a woman with a baby wrapped in her shawl – 'will make a charming picture. If his fortunate mother would like to take him through to the studio at the rear?'

Cornelius Touchfarthing, recumbent in the chair that had been warmed by a succession of sitters that afternoon, accepted the cup of tea that had been placed in his hand by John Rankin, without any sign of acknowledgement. 'What a shabby business, John,' he sighed. 'I am defiled.'

Rankin drew up a stool and placed a plate of buttered toast on the box of chemicals that was between them. 'Well, it ain't as straight as I could want but it's taken care of the rent.'

'But the indignity of it all, John. I felt like a player in a pantomime.'

'There ain't no reason we have to do it regular. It won't work for us if we *do*. But something like that will get us known. It's you what said we needed the patronage of the nobs.'

'Upon my word, we do, John.'

When the cups had been emptied, Rankin refilled them, fussing about a little spilt milk upon the tray and pouring the tea from the leaky pot with all the daintiness of a lady's maid. 'That's all well and good if we gets enough of 'em to make a go of it. But as it is we've got a roaring trade in sixpunny portraits. We might get set up in that line alone.'

'But do you look at our subjects, John. Shopkeepers. School-teachers. A chimney sweep and his family, for goodness' sake! If we keep on in this way we'll drive off the better customers. There will be no more well-to-do families, army officers and distinguished businessmen then.'

'There ain't any now. Or 'ave you forgot how you bought them pictures in the window?'

'Only to encourage respectable business of our own, John. I didn't set up here to produce penny keepsakes. We must establish ourselves in the right circles as quickly as we can. There are not more than a dozen commercial photographers in London today but in only a few months it will all have changed, mark my words. I can see them coming now, swarms of little men with their cheap cameras and poor pictures. And by the time they are here we must be the concern that society connects with the art of photography.'

'Art?' Rankin snorted. 'What's art to do with it? This here's a new trade and one what's alive with opportunities.'

'Trade? Heaven forbid, Mr Rankin! We might as well be scissors and card men making silhouettes. Do you know what they've called photography, John? Painting with light. A skilled photographist is not a tradesman but an artist. And his aims must be the same as other artists – that's the only way he'll achieve a similar standing.

'In its ideal form,' the older man continued, as John Rankin knelt before him and tugged off a shoe, 'photography should aim at the grand style. I can see no reason why what has been achieved by Rubens and Titian with paint cannot be made with modern methods. That's the stuff to put photography on its proper footing.'

'If that's all we're about we might as well sell the camera and buy brushes and paint,' Rankin said. 'Ain't it obvious that cameras should be doing all that brushes can't? Anything else would be a wasted opportunity.'

'To occupy the position of a modern Reynolds would hardly be that, John.'

'Well, I'm blessed if I can see the point of it all,' Rankin muttered. 'Here we are using painted backcloths and properties to photograph what's outside for free. It ain't natural.'

'You are a good fellow, John, but ill-equipped to follow an argument such as this. Art isn't a mere representation of life. It ennobles and elevates. And that is what will distinguish us from the common picture-taker.'

'Pardon me,' Rankin said, as he suppressed his irritation, 'but that's a waste of time and a waste of a fair chance. You might do things with a camera your artists never dreamed of. Why, what if you was to take a camera to the cuts and courts I grew up in down Seven Dials – not a mile from here, in fact, but where the gents and their ladies never sets a foot? And then how would it be if you was to show such photographs in places they might be seen by them as knows nothing about how the poor has to live in London? It's my thinking that if the charities and the other do-gooders was to see what was happening on their own door-steps they'd find better uses for their cash than sending it to the pygmies.'

'Pie-in-the-sky rubbish!' pronounced Touchfarthing. 'Respectable people don't want that filth thrust in their faces.'

'Mr Touchfarthing, I believe I am a partner in this here business?'

'You are an essential cog in the machine, you know that. But there's more for you to learn, John, before you can have your name written after mine.'

'I sunk thirty pound in this business,' Rankin said. 'And as your partner I say I've no objection to you going all out to get the nobs' business, so long as we keeps our feet on the ground and a roof above our heads with the regular trade. But if you've got plans to be doing other things on top of that, then I'll expect the same consideration.'

'You might do anything except drag photography into the gutter, John. If it's only a matter of using our calling in the service of others, you might assist me.'

'With what?'

'I have my own plans, John. Plans for a series of moral photographs, instructional images which will provide examples for those in need of guidance. Some simple, Biblical scenes. They can all be executed quite easily here in the studio, with only a few properties and the services of one or two persons of suitable appearance.'

'Poor folk don't want moral guidance!' Rankin exploded. 'They want houses wivart holes in their roofs and a hot meal now and then, not framed photies of the baby Jesus.'

'But don't you think that with the right examples before them they would not fall so low as to require the support of others?'

'No, I don't. Pardon me, guv'nor, but if anything sounds like wasting tin, it's this. Properties cost money – and I suppose there would be costumes, and all?'

42

'I thought, John, that as you are so handy at sewing, we might save . . .'

'Oh, your needle-woman as well, am I? And then we're to frame these pictures and give 'em away to folk who will pop 'em to uncle the first chance they has, I suppose?'

'They will not be pawned, they will be treasured, John. My *Accurate Scenes from the Bible* – I think I shall call them that – will have threefold advantages. Firstly, they will be morally efficacious. Secondly, the use of property and costume will be excellent preparation for the grander projects I have in mind. And thirdly – and most importantly from your point of view, it seems – they will make us money.'

'I don't believe it, guv'nor.'

'Mr Rutter assures me it will be so.'

'What's Holy Harry to do with this? That villain ain't settled his account yet and after I was half a day getting a picture of hisself as he liked. And 'is good Lord knows how many prints we did for his congregation.'

'Mr Rutter was admiring the study I did of Mrs Langham, the actress. He remarked how like Jezebel she appeared to him. It was the inspiration for the improving photographs we shall produce. Mr Rutter will provide the themes and the market. If we must continually talk of money, you might see this as a sound investment, John. Safer than reg'lar investments such as the 3d Consols.'

'And what's Mr Rutter want 'em for?'

'He may display them in his meeting house for the edification of his congregation. Or they might be employed as aids to his teaching. There is no saying with a non-conformist. But he has all but promised to buy whatever I can produce. That is the difference. These pictures are already sold. They will not drain our resources which, I regret, would very much be the case if I allowed you to pursue your own plans.'

'Allowed me? To do what I want in my own time, using only as much paper and chemicals as wouldn't be missed?'

'It isn't the sort of thing that the firm of Touchfarthing,

Photographer, should be involved with. Not if it's to be Touch-farthing and Partner.'

'And that's flat, is it?'

'That is as it must be, John. It will be best if you learn to accept my guidance in these matters.'

'I may very well have to review the nature of our relationship, Mr Touchfarthing,' said John Rankin, picking up the tray of tea things. 'And you can warm the bed as best you can tonight, for I'm going to sleep in the shop. I bid you a very good night.'

Rankin picked up and dusted off the costume worn by Touchfarthing that day. In the back of the house, he wrapped it in a parcel of brown paper which he tied up with string. When Touchfarthing was heard to mount the stairs, he returned to the studio and carried away the tray of tea things, which he washed up at the scullery sink. He lifted a great grey cat from a chair and deposited it beyond the back door, where he stood, allowing the cool evening air to calm his mood. He took his pipe from the deep recess of his coat pocket and stuffed the bowl with a little coarse tobacco. The sun had set but a thin grey light persisted. Nearby, hooves clattered and wheels squeaked as broughams and cabs ran up by the house in order to avoid the congestion of Oxford Street. Hard by the back wall, footsteps and laughter were abruptly stilled by the closing of a door. Further off, from the direction of St Giles, a child or a woman screamed and a man shouted a drunken oath. Rankin smoked his pipe, and listened.

When he had finished, he knocked the bowl against the heel of his shoe, muttered, 'Blow you, Mr T.,' and went back inside. He bolted the back door top and bottom and lit the candle that was kept upon the greasy dresser before making his way to the front of the house. From the room above came the creaking of bedsprings as Cornelius Touchfarthing prepared himself for sleep. He checked the lock of the front door and peered over the half-curtain at the arrangement of framed photographs in the shop window. The door, warped in its frame, required a sharp shove to open and it was not unusual for this sudden vibration

44

to topple the lines of matrons and children and clerks and ministers like so many tin soldiers. This evening his regiment was all stood to attention and Rankin was turning towards his makeshift bed behind the counter, a frequent place of resort after a difference with his partner, when his attention was taken by a person beyond the glass, on the far side of the street. The person in question had stopped, retraced his steps and turned to look directly at the shop. He might have been staring directly at Rankin himself had the photographer's assistant not known that he was as shrouded in shadows as the man's eyes were hidden by tinted spectacles. For a moment Rankin was perplexed. He thought he might know the man, though from quite where he couldn't say. Then he snapped his fingers.

"Ullo, old chap. I recall you now, I do,' he murmured. 'And just what is it that you might be arter, I wonder?'

4

An Imperfect Image

The Times, London. August 10th, 1851. Last evening, the bridge at Vauxhall being made an impassable beargarden by a collision between a brick-maker's wagon and that of a corn factor, and this mishap causing a knife-board bus to overturn and spill its passengers, revellers were obliged to look about for some other means of traversing the River. Not only was the bridge blocked to wheeled traffic: the over-turned bus, a dying horse and returning Exhibition hordes tramping over a carpet of fresh grain had stopped access from the Surrey shore for everyone, not excepting some medical men called to attend to the injured passengers.

Great millstones of cloud had been rolling across the heavens since late afternoon, presaging the rain that now fell in glass shards and making the scene by the Thames more akin to a November's night than a late summer's eve. The deep gloom was relieved only by a luminescence emanating from the environs of the Crystal Palace, which reflected faintly upon the river and also on the darkened spectacles of Henry Hilditch.

The day had not been used well. Had he visited Vauxhall Gardens only yesterday instead, he might have arrived at the river in better humour. From a journalist's point of view the expedition should have been a successful one. It should have been no less so from a scientist's: the information that Henry turned into spirited prose for the *Morning Messenger* he prepared in more objective form for his ambitious work-in-progress, an entomological study of the working classes. At Vauxhall there had been sufficient data to satisfy the needs of either case.

Here at noon he had found the army of waiters and workmen who nightly serviced the raffish crowds in their supper boxes or brought watered negus to those who danced. Hard-worked and poorly paid, the views of these men would make compelling fare for a readership whose letters to the editor already betrayed its fear of the volatile mob. But as Henry had sauntered the length of the South Walk beneath unlit lanterns hung from trees, in the wake of a young couple who walked arm in arm, he could not help thinking of the vacancy in his own heart. Once again he had the impression that, for a little while not so long ago, he had been a different man.

He spoke to no one and made no notes. The afternoon had been wasted and, annoyed at his laxity, he wished only to return to his lodgings with all speed. Vexed at the sudden obstruction of his route and ill-prepared for the sudden change in the weather, Hilditch hailed a ferryman whose craft he had spied tethered beneath the iron supports of the bridge.

This broad-shouldered fellow was being addressed by a tall and well-made man, buttoned into a dark uniform. Hilditch explained himself and tendered the ferryman sixpence, more than the fare he might expect and which he offered in the certain knowledge that other frustrated travellers would soon be competing for his custom. The man shook his head and nodded to the gentleman with him. 'I am already commissioned,' he said, shielding a match set to his short pipe.

Hilditch looked upwards to the bank and saw the crowds on foot and heard drivers cracking their whips and yelling at teams of horses as they strove to extricate themselves from the tangle of traffic and turn about. Cold, wet and quite fatigued, he was in no humour to be carried along as part of a swollen mob that flowed like a second river towards the bridge at Westminster and decided instead to wait beneath the arches until the confusion above had been cleared or he could secure a place aboard some river craft. The ferryman offered no further conversation but the man in uniform turned to him and said, 'It ain't that there's no room, sir, but I've a van full of prisoners bound for the Tench stuck in the traffic half a mile back. I'd as soon get 'en safe across before the alarm is raised, so I'm come ahead to secure a boat. However, if you don't object to such company I'm sure Charlie will take your tanner.'

'If it pleases the gentleman,' grunted the other.

Soaked to the bone by the enfilading volleys of wind-blown rain, they awaited the arrival of the prisoners with their own heads hung like the Calais martyrs. The sky was now shrouded in the most dismal grey, the advance guard of a summer storm which was quickly upon them. Now, instants of dazzling illumination relieved the obscurity, flashing upon the turbulent waters and petrifying all movement. Here was a rearing horse ossified as equestrian art; there, by the Middlesex shore and dramatically delineated, a keeling sailboat stopped dead before a many-towered and brooding fortress. A blinding blue streak fixed the ferryman with his pipe pulled from his mouth, his thin lips open as if he were about to deliver himself of some profound observation regarding the river and its part in the lives of men.

Not knowing how long he might have to wait in this miserable condition, Hilditch again attempted to engage the ferryman in conversation. Among the reports already published in the *Morning Messenger* he had several accounts of interviews with those who earn their bread on, or beside, canal and river. He had noted the particulars of lightermen, coal-heavers, bargees and lock-keepers and transcribed the prattle of the scavenging mudlarks who waded in filth as they hunted for scraps of coal and rope, iron and ships' nails or any water-borne refuse with which they might turn a penny.

Recently, the river had invaded his dreams and disturbed his sleep. In a dismal shed by the Limehouse stairs he had seen the ravages it had wreaked on the body of a woman of indeterminate age and appearance. The lighterman who had recovered the cadaver and who was now awaiting its collection and his own small reward had recounted tales of other luckless souls plucked from the depths or discovered caught among tangles of rubbish by the banks. A young boy in gentleman's clothes; a woman tied to her two children; such a number of young girls, most likely ruined, who had come to the river to find their release. Henry Hilditch would as soon leave behind this river and the disturbing thoughts that it provoked.

His eyes were raised towards the Middlesex shore but his mind was in his lodgings at Somers Town, to which he would now repair. He was thinking that he would certainly allow himself a reviving glass of brandy, when the gaoler spoke.

'A fellow might take it for a French fortress,' he observed. 'For I've seen such when I was working the steam packets.' He extended a braided cuff and pointed across the river at the low and massive shape of the Millbank Penitentiary. The Tench squatted by the shore, faint gleams showing in its conical towers which rose from corners like candles on a cake. 'You can't get the compass of it at this vantage,' said the gaoler, 'but there's a thousand cells within those walls. They do say there are three miles of corridors and I believe it. I'm up and down them all day long. Working the Tench goes terrible hard on the feet.'

'I'm sure it does,' Hilditch said. 'It's not a job I should care to do. Nor one that I suppose any man could?'

'Never a truer word spoken, sir,' said the gaoler, with enthusiasm. 'The management of miscreants isn't a calling that suits everybody. It's my opinion that you must be born to it.'

'I wonder how you came to be doing such a thing,' Hilditch remarked, innocently, thinking that he could yet salvage something of this night.

'Ah, sir, now, there lies a story,' he said.

'I should be interested to hear it,' Hilditch said, quickly. The gaoler offered his hand and gave his name as Farrel. Hilditch explained the nature of his own business and Farrel said that he would be happy to oblige him with a full account if Hilditch thought it might be useful. He listened with unfeigned attention as Farrel began to explain the origins of his employment with the National Penitentiary at Millbank.

'I used to think I arrived there by a curious route but now I wonder if it wasn't the most direct. My father was a debtor – never out of debt, nor often out of the Fleet or the Marshalsea gaols. He was an imprudent man, my father, a city broker's clerk who acquired tastes above his station and paid for them every so often in quod.

'He was in and out of gaol like a thief in a pocket. Somehow we got by, but at last he acquired a debt that we couldn't pay off if we lived to be old. He had borrowed a large sum and gambled it upon a very uncertain venture. After that, there seemed no end to our struggling. My mother had been a Herefordshire farm girl before she met my father and wasn't suited for such occupations as might be found here. She took to the drink. She couldn't cope, not at all.

'She beseeched my father to do something. Had he no friends in the city and what about his relations in Northumberland? It seemed that something might still be done for him but the trouble, as even I could see, lay with my father. Once behind a turned key he had no cares nor responsibilities, no need to hide from dunning bailiffs and creditors. You could say that being in prison freed him – all he needed were a few pennies for a glass of grog and he was a happy man.

'He appeared not to care that his family were now in poor straits and there was never enough on the table to feed me and my sister Margaret. My mother ate less as she drank more. We sold everything. Best clothes, second best. Shoes, coats, cooking pots, knives and forks. My mother was the pawnbroker's best customer. One day she went to pop the kitchen chairs and didn't come back.

'I never told no one she was gone. For one thing, I always thought she would come back, but also I was fearful we might be sent to the workhouse, where Mo would go to one place and

51

me to another. So I kept quiet and took it upon myself to bring my sister up. For a half year or so we got by. I fell in with a band of street arabs who scavenged Covent Garden when the costers were setting up their stalls and garden produce was falling from the wagons. We were always chased and sometimes beaten but I generally came home with a cabbage for the pot. Other days Mo and I took potato sacks and went foraging for fuel on the dust heaps. In all this time I never visited my father. I couldn't gauge what he might do – he might report us for our own good. We left the house when the quarterly rent became due and for a while we had a decent enough crib in the basement of a collapsed warehouse. The cellar itself was still sound and it was dry if it wasn't warm.

'However, someone found us out and moved us on. We spent the next few nights under the arches and sleeping in doorways. Mo come down with the 'flu and out of desperation, I resolved to visit my father and to find out the true state of his case. If there was indeed no hope of his release then I would have to set about something more than stealing cabbages.

'I found him in the prison snuggery, drunkenly regaling the inmates with song. He would have made a fine street patterer because he could talk and sing well enough to keep himself in lush, even in prison. On that first visit his mind was dulled to everything but the promise of another glass of rum. I went again and this time I took with me little Mo, hoping that the sight of his youngest child might stir him to his senses, but he quickly disabused me of this hope.

'It was clear he neither expected to be quickly released nor could be counted on for aid. However, as on the last occasion of our visit, he found us a little something to eat and a place by the fire. The company may have been disreputable but it was convivial. There were coiners and embezzlers and men who had never even considered pursuing an honest occupation but there were also those who, like my father, had found themselves in gaol by their own ineptitude. We sat among them as they toasted bread on the fire and passed about a tin jug of rum and water.

52

'With nourishment and warmth Mo recovered quite quickly. The Marshalsea came to mean food and company and we were regular visitors, well known among the prisoners. The prison was also the source of a scanty income. I earned first one penny and then another running errands for the prisoners. Some of the turnkeys took small bribes and others liked me well enough to turn a blind eye when I slipped out to the cookshop for pies and plum-dough or to the taproom for a quartern of gin, or ran with messages to attorneys and creditors. I began to feel at home in prison and so we came to be oftener inside than out. I believe we might have grown up there had not fate taken a hand. My father, whose health had been frail ever since he had once taken a severe chill in his damp room, now became ill and within a few weeks had got worse and finally died.

'I was fourteen years old and still without proper employment. I could no longer go to the prison and make my living running errands. Instead I had to cast about for other employ. For a while I returned to stealing potatoes and cabbages, but they were wise to us now and those boys still working the Market were being taken up daily. That first summer, Mo and I walked to Kent with the hoppers. That was well for as long as it lasted but when the season was over we were back in London, facing a winter on the streets. Little Mo was rising eleven when we saved a few bob and I bought her a tray of things to sell in the street – laces and ribbons and buttons mainly. We found her a pitch on the Strand and she might come home after standing there all day with only five or six pence to show for it.

'I obtained brushes and a bottle of blacking and began cleaning shoes by the steps of the station at Waterloo. Sometimes I did all right, sometimes I made less than Mo but it was sufficient to afford us nightly shelter at a low lodging house in a street called Perkins's Rents at Westminster.

'That place and its noxious atmosphere was the cradle of the ill-fortune that followed. I had met some disagreeable male-factors in the Marshalsea but never such a lot of vicious heathens as was in that padding ken. The place was run by a pock-faced

crone named Mrs Moxon and she did not keep a clean establishment. Roaches and beetles infested the place, which was already
horribly overcrowded. Latecomers slept between the beds and
as many were packed into those filthy, rag-covered flea pits as
could be got. Boys shared with girls and nobody complained at
the awful abominations committed in the night. I sheltered Mo
as best I could and prayed that our luck would change.

'But Mother Moxon wasn't only a keeper of a boarding house,
she was also a fence for two or three gangs of young villains that
brought her the plunder of street robberies and house-breakings.
They were much better dressed than we lodgers and had the
impudence to regard us with some disdain. They were cheery
and well-fed, and entertained all within earshot with accounts
of their crafty larcenies and marvellous escapes from the
clutches of the law; no wonder, I suppose, that their number
was often increased by hungry lads willing to run risks for the
sake of a little money.

'But it was not these young outlaws who blighted my life but
another party. Coming and going at all times of the night was a
varying number of young girls, most of whom managed to look
garishly presentable even though they lived in this lair of filth
and vermin. They usually had money and something to drink
and were loud in their merriment. The boys were forever solicit-
ing kisses and wheedling from them sixpences and shillings. It
was no secret that they were prostitutes. However, for the most
part the girls were good-natured, particularly towards Little
Mo, who sometimes benefited to the tune of tuppence or a
bright new handkerchief. One girl, whom Mo knew as Sally but
others called Hookey Sal, took a special interest in my sister and
when the weather was awful would look after her while I set up
my blacking business in the shelter of Waterloo Station. This
occurred on several occasions: as Mo often got as much given
her by the girls as she might make from her ribbons and laces, I
persuaded myself that it was better to leave her in the warmth
than have her stand a full winter's day in the bitter cold.

'But Mo was young and impressionable. I first saw that

something was amiss when I went to meet her at her patch and witnessed a strange incident. She had not seen me approaching when she stepped out from the pavement and, so doing, put herself in the way of a gentleman who was walking briskly towards me. She screamed as she fell upon the ground, spilling the contents of her tray into the foulest part of the road. I ran towards her but something about her actions arrested my steps and caused me to stay where I was and observe. Mo sat upon the paving, crying so loudly that a crowd had gathered about her and the gentleman, who had picked up her soiled laces and was now offering her a coin. Mo cried louder and someone in the crowd said, "For shame, sir!" and another said it was "a bit thick when a man could knock a little girl down and give her a penny for her trouble". The man was extremely disconcerted and, having seen that Mo was not hurt, now apologised and I heard him offer to buy the entire contents of her tray of wares for a half bull. Mo made no reply, only sobbed. The man looked about him and saw he was surrounded by censuring expressions. "There," he said, reaching deep into a pocket, "there is a sovereign, now do stop those tears!"

'When the man had gone and the crowd had dispersed, I approached Mo and asked if she was hurt. She laughed and called me a great booby and then she bit hard upon the gold coin. Where she had learnt that dodge and for how long she had been perfecting it I could only guess. I should have conceived then how great a danger we were in.

'One evening, on a day when the weather had been so foul I had again left Mo at the lodging house, I returned home and entered the front room to look for her. It was full; old men playing cards on a deal table, the new-come Irish family sweeping out their alcove, two tract-sellers sorting their papers upon the floor, girls upon the benches, supping bowls of soup and, through the open door of the kitchen, Mother Moxon and her woman, who were sorting a pile of clothes. Mo was nowhere to be seen.

'I was about to open the door and look out in the street,

where perhaps she had gone upon an errand, when a smaller girl put down her soup bowl and turned to me. My first thought was that this painted pygmy in bright ribbons and a candy-striped dress was a newly-arrived prostitute, but then her mouth opened and she began to laugh. "What's the matter?" she said. "Ain't you seen your sister afore?" No doubt she saw the shock upon my face because her own was all consternation as she hastened to tell me that "Sal done it all" and I wasn't to worry as she "'adn't charged a penny".

'I think I might have done better than to lose my temper as I did. I'm sure I never hurt a hair on her head, only destroyed the things that had been given to her by her friends, the whores. But Mo was howling. She was shocked by the ruination of her bright new things, by being humiliated before her friends, but also because she had never before seen her brother in such a mad rage. She refused to sleep with me that night and went instead to Sal's bed.

'We made it up after a fashion the next day, but we never got over it entirely. Mo felt she couldn't trust me and that I was for ever denying her a little bit of fun. I worried for her as I worried for us both. We found another low lodging house and went on as before. Somehow or other we got by. I blacked boots and sometimes earned an extra penny sweeping out and cleaning the lodging house. Mo continued to sell her little things, though I thought I marked a new reluctance when I sent her off in the mornings. It was not an ideal life. We ate poorly and we were generally too tired to amuse ourselves in the evenings. On Sundays we went for walks. But we had shelter and perhaps, before long, something better would turn up.

'One night, she failed to return home. I waited and then traced her route to her pitch on the Strand, without seeing anything of her. I returned to the lodging house, thinking she might then be returned and that somehow our paths had crossed. But no one there had seen her. I sat on our bed and I paced the room but in the end I could not remain in the house while Mo was abroad in London. She was young and anything might befall her. I set off again, and with no other idea in my head, once again walked towards the Strand. My route took me to the Haymarket, which at this time of the night was blocked with cabs and omnibuses. The pavements too were swollen and it was all I could do to force a way through the patrons of theatres and restaurants and the innumerable fancily-clad women who got in my way.

'Further down the street was a separate group, a ring of girls making no attempt at circumspection, but who were all sharing some joke and laughing uproariously. I might have taken no further notice but that they stopped their noise when they saw me and then Little Mo stepped from the mob. I recognised the girls as Hookey Sal and some others from our previous lodging house. I took Mo by her arm and told her we must cut along as it was late. This time, however, she was not going to be upbraided before her friends and shook me off. I loudly remonstrated with her and took hold of her once more and began to pull her up the Haymarket. Now she was screeching, but I didn't care; I only wanted to get her safe home again. Then she began to call for help, crying out to all about that she was being abducted. Two drunken young gentlemen stepped in and one of them struck me about my face with his cane.

'I fell in the road, stung with pain and embarrassment and when I got to my feet neither Mo nor the gentlemen were to be seen. Sal and her friends were also departed. I searched high and low that night and did not return to my crib until dawn's light had broken. It was all to no avail so after three full days of tramping the streets and enquiring after her, I took up my brushes again. She was always in my mind and my eyes were sharpened whenever I went up the Haymarket or around Covent Garden or found myself in any place where I thought Hookey Sal and her mob might be. I doubt they had changed their ways but it seemed they had changed their patch, for I never set eyes on them again.

'After a time a fellow whose shoes I had blacked, and who must have taken an equal shine to me, told me there was work at

57

some brick fields outside London. I worked at that for close on two years. That was as near as I came to having settled employment. At the end of that period I became restless and returned to London, where I was for a time on the docks at Shadwell and then I went once more to the hop fields of Kent. On the Kentish coast I fell in with seafarers and took work aboard one of the steam packets that plied between Dover and Calais. I never forgot about Mo, though, and I was devoured by thoughts of what might have happened to her up in London. It came to be that I could not bear to be away from London where the chance remained that some day I would discover her. I returned.

'But there came an evening when, after buying myself a cheap supper from the market at New Cut, I found myself in the Borough, with sufficient funds for a pot of ale. A fellow smoking a pipe caught my eye. We both were certain we knew the other and when he revealed his occupation, I placed him as Jeremy Nedd, a Marshalsea turnkey who had done Mo and I the odd kindness a long time ago. We fell into conversation and I asked after many a mutual acquaintance. We talked of the sudden blow-ups and of the occasion when a man had been found with a knife in his ribs. We drank some more and it seemed there had been good times too. The sad goodbyes when a "Collegian" left, the money given readily to the widow of a man who died in the prison, the warmth of the snuggery.

'He also told me more than I had known before of my father. Distorted by time and not a little beer, that period when Mo and I had food and shelter and were together, now seemed a happy one. It came to me that the Marshalsea, more than anywhere else, had been my home. On an impulse, I asked Mr Nedd how I might come to work alongside him in the prison. No sooner had I uttered the words than I knew for certain that this was what I must do. Nedd shook his head and said they had no need of another turnkey but he thought that he had heard of a position lately vacated at the City Bridewell.

'My mind already made up, I sought that post and secured it. I worked there the best part of a year before going to a better berth at Tothill Fields and after that I watched over the lads in Scotch caps at Pentonville. Lately I have been employed over at yonder Tench. I never did return to the Marshalsea, but that was no matter. I have found honest employment to which I am suited and not everyone can say as much.'

The blast of a whistle caused Farrel to break his discourse and look towards the road. 'Here come my charges now,' he said. He blew upon his own whistle and beckoned the driver of a large dark van which had stopped on the roadside a little distance from where they stood. The gaoler asked Hilditch to wait while he escorted his wards to the ferry, after which he might ride with them to the other bank. Hilditch caught his arm. 'A minute more,' he said. 'What of your sister? Did you find her again?'

'There's no time for that story now, sir. But in short, I saw her again and quite often as it turned out. She went to the bad, was often seen in the worst places, but dressed as fine as money might allow. I tried to bring her to her senses, but it was like talking to the dead. There she was in all her finery and there was me in my dusty, workaday togs. Sometimes she had the effrontery to offer me money. In the end I stopped trying to save her and did my best to put her out of my mind. I don't recall when was the last time I set eyes upon her. It's not an uncommon story, sir. That sort of thing is what can happen all too easily to a girl who is on her own in London.'

He excused himself and joined the men at the van, busying himself with a jangling bunch of keys while he and the others bellowed commands and urged those aboard the van to 'stir themselves or they'd know about it!' While this was going forward, the mind of Henry Hilditch was in turmoil as it turned upon the man's story. He had no fear that significant details would be lost before he came to write it all up the next day. Once seasoned with a little low slang, Farrel's story would fascinate the readers of the *Morning Messenger*. But it was not the history of a man's search for a home and family that transfixed him now, but the little he had said about his sister.

This tale of a young girl sucked into the vortex of London's nether world and condemned to haunt padding-ken and street-corner for ever more struck a resounding note deep within the recesses of Hilditch's mind. A heart long-steeled against softer sensations was stirred.

Such were his thoughts as the rattling of chains and the blast of a policeman's whistle alerted him to the imminent arrival of the boat party. With a prison officer in front and two behind, six closely chained, prison-garbed men shuffled down the bank and halted by the water's edge. The ferryman, seated in the prow, knocked out his pipe and beckoned them in. The first to board were two boys, not above fifteen years old. The taller of the two was doing his best to stem his sobs while his friend, who might have patted him on the back but for his fetters, muttered, 'There, there, old chap. It ain't so bad, you know.' A great brute of a man, full of noisy braggadocio, was swearing horribly, laughing loudly and cajoling the officers as he stepped aboard and took up an oar. The man seated at his side was a sullen cove, but as strong as his neighbour and the gaoler promised a speedy crossing with these two at the oars. Two slighter fellows, in some awe of the bigger men, sat behind, with heads bowed. Henry Hilditch stepped in and installed himself by the stern, where sat another gaoler and Mr Farrel, who had taken hold of the tiller.

A tall and black-mustachioed turnkey, who appeared at least as capable of evil as anyone else aboard, barked a command and the prisoners began to dip their oars. The craft was pulled slowly about and out into the Stygian blackness of the river. The boat was heavy and strong currents made by the funnelling of water through the piers of the bridge forced it from its course and the men struggled to keep it true. Once clear of the bridge they were caught by another powerful current but the ferryman, silent as a mute, left it to Mr Farrel to exhort the rowers. 'Pull together, lads . . . in, out, in, out!' With no little effort, the oarsmen broke free of the current's grip and now began to strike out for the far shore.

It seemed to Hilditch that the turbulent and foul-smelling waters were reluctant to assist him in his passage and the boat was bumped by unidentifiable obstacles and buffeted by the wind. The boy at the prow was now sobbing loudly, his cries heard only in lulls of the wind. Hilditch looked about him, attempting to gauge when this dreadful voyage might be ended. The gloom was infinite. The lightning storm had passed over and the only lights before them now were liverish gleams from slim windows in the Tench. The faint glow that had lit the skies above the Great Exhibition was extinguished.

5

Developments

Now that the photographers had established the couch in a
position that best utilised the morning sunshine, the bright light
fell upon brow and nose and made a flaming halo of the child's
hair and when John Rankin had knelt at her side and opened a
newspaper, enough was thrown back upon her face to annihilate
the shadows. In the comparative darkness of the room and
beneath a sun-struck cloud of whorling dust motes, Mr Touchfarthing assayed his field of view.

'You are too close, Mr Rankin,' whispered the photographer.
'You look like one of the Magi adoring the baby Jesus.'

Rankin shuffled backwards upon his knees as Touchfarthing
now approached the child and smoothed creases in the pillow
on which her head was laid and brushed aside a lock of hair that
was fallen over her eyes. He straightened an unruly fold in her
dress and stood back to admire the effect.

'Such a pretty child,' he said and covered his head with the
black cloth. Upon the glass screen the inverted image was a
masterwork of chiaroscuro. Bordered by darkness, sunbeams
blazed upon the face of the subject, brightly lit her embroidered
shift and gleamed on the tiny buckles of her shoes. The effect
was such as to cause Touchfarthing's heart to race. Properly
processed, he told himself, the result would be worthy of

Caravaggio. He uncovered the lens and counted off the seconds.

In the street outside, the clopping of a horse stopped as it drew up beneath the window. Touchfarthing re-covered the lens. As John Rankin was leaving the room to complete the work, the father of the child, a staid and solemn-looking man, entered.

'I don't wish to hurry you, gentlemen, but the conveyance is here.'

'We are finished,' Touchfarthing said. 'But for Mr Rankin's process. If you would like to make a choice from the selection of frames? I can send for further examples if none suits.'

'I must leave all that to you,' said the father, distracted by the sound of footsteps upon the staircase. Following a soft knock upon the door, two men wearing crêpe-banded hats with black gloves and grey expressions entered the room. A third followed, bearing in his arms a small wooden box.

Touchfarthing waited until the child had been placed in the tiny coffin, the lid had been fixed down and the father had gone with the men and the box to the front door. He watched from the window as the hearse was loaded and the father had escorted his softly-sobbing wife to another carriage. When the cortege had moved off, he removed the lens from the camera and, hands upon his stout hips, he turned a judicial eye upon John Rankin, who now entered and held up a dripping photograph.

'The best frame, John,' he said. 'A work of art deserves nothing less.'

II

A smell of frying liver and kidneys percolated through cracks in floorboards and wainscoting, filling Touchfarthing's senses and stirring him from languorous dreams in which his vast potential was realised, his worth publicly recognised. He pulled on his gown and popped the breakfasting hat on the back of his hairless pate. Downstairs, in the tiny kitchen, he squeezed past John Rankin, fully dressed and attendant upon a spitting frying pan, picked up a handful of leaflets that were scattered upon the

64

dresser shelf and opened the kitchen door. He stopped, turned and regarded the other man. 'Up early?' he remarked.

'I'm taking the camera down the Dials. As it's Sunday and you won't be needing it.'

Exasperation battled with an urgent desire to complete his journey to the backyard privy. 'It's a damnable waste, Mr Rankin. I thought you could see the way forward. Our first commission from nobility only yesterday and today you would have us among the rats in the gutter. I'm not happy about this, not one bit, and I shall deduct the costs from, from . . .' and struggling from his gown as he left the kitchen, he flew across the yard and slammed shut the privy door.

Settled upon the cold seat, he regarded his plump, pink thighs upon which a beam of light was pouring from a large knot hole high upon the privy door. Rankin's annoyance forgotten in a surge of stupendous relief, Touchfarthing grunted his contentment and awaited the next movement of his bowels. The smell of frying onions added to the compound of odours that now composed the atmosphere of the chamber and made him desirous of finishing his business and despatching his cooked breakfast. Sighing heavily, he resigned himself to a prolonged confinement. He affixed two of the pamphlets to a nail on the door and the last he lay across his lighted lap and opened.

A Warning to Young Gentlemen and Young Ladies Who are in Town to Visit the Great Exhibition

Harold Rutter, B.A. M.A. Phil (Oxon)

It is our earnest hope that nothing dangerous or untoward will befall these tourists and that their stay in London will be both happy and profitable. The city offers many diversions of a wholesome nature, but it is regrettably also true that London harbours a multitude of deadlier amusements. That innocent visitors may be cognisant of precisely where danger lurks, we warn them against the following named places.

The Haymarket and Regents Street

There is no more dreadful sight in all London than that of the scores of painted harlots gathered in **The Haymarket** and in **Regents Street**. These pitiable Jezebels ply their awful trade from three in the afternoon until long after midnight has struck and it is hardly possible to traverse the length of either thoroughfare without being made the unwilling subject of numerous propositions of a grossly indecent nature.

This area, inclusive of **Covent Garden**, is alas, not the only place infested by strumpets. **Cremorne Gardens** from late afternoon is transformed from a place of harmless pleasure to a fearsome den of vice. Night houses on **Regents Street** and **Great Windmill Street** are only façades, places where prostitutes may be encountered with comparative discretion. **The London parks** at night are habituated by the most loathsome of creatures, Magdalens too marked by disease to show their faces in God's good daylight.

Despite the best efforts of the Vice Society and humbler crusaders such as ourselves, brothels abound in all areas of the town. Gird well your loins, young passengers, and you shall never find yourself enticed to such dens of terrible iniquity as, for instance, the establishment run by Mrs Newsome, in **Curzon Street**, wherein are said to be courtesans skilled in the arts of Aphrodite who cater to the most depraved of tastes. Beware, too, of a certain address in **Circus Road, St John's Wood**, which is the notorious haunt of flagellants.

Wych Street and Holywell Street, just North of the Strand

Here, in shop after shop, are sold what I believe are called 'warm gems', species of print and literature that will offend and outrage all but the most corrupt of sensibilities. I am told stereoscopic slides of an unmentionable nature may be purchased now at prices that are dangerously within the compass of a student's pocket.

Be not alarmed: most sojourns in the Great Wen are safe and blameless. Remember too that the Church, as ever, offers its sanctuary. In particular, I might mention that young men and vulnerable lady travellers will find safety and solace and good guidance with my little congregation, who gather at the **Reform Chapel, Berners Street**, on weekday evenings at 6 p.m.

The light from the knot hole was extinguished as Rankin's knuckles rapped smartly upon the door.

'Halloa in there!'

'What is it?' Touchfarthing said, shortly.

'I thought you had gone to sleep,' called Rankin. 'Or had a fit, perhaps . . .'

'What in Heaven's name do you want?'

'Just to say as your breakfast is cooling on the table. And that you have a visitor what I've left standing in the shop.'

'Who is it, for goodness . . .'

'I'm off down the Dials, as advertised,' said Rankin.

'Who's in the shop, Mr Rankin?'

But Rankin was already unlatching the back gate and there was a dull thud which might have been anything, including a rosewood camera knocking hard upon an iron gatepost. Touchfathing grimaced and screwed up the sheet of paper into a tight little ball.

III

'I do apologise for keeping you waiting,' said Touchfarthing, drying his hands on a rag as he hurried into the shop. 'I was attending to the process. A tricky business, you know.'

The man before him, back-lit by the window, his face

under-exposed, had picked up a framed photograph from the counter, a picture of an actress, which Touchfarthing had bought as part of a lot from a book-seller's barrow.

'I expect you've seen her at Drury Lane?' Touchfarthing said, using his rag to dust off a larger picture of a man holding a skull. 'We take all the leading players. We're known to be sympathetic to the thespian arts and of course word gets around. Perhaps you yourself are upon the boards?'

As the man made no reply, only held the picture closer to his eye, Touchfarthing looked up, pierced the masking gloom and recognised his customer as the man whose uninvited image had marred his study of the Crystal Palace. 'I've seen you before, I think,' he said.

'Very likely,' Hilditch said.

'I think you considered having your picture taken one day in Hyde Park?'

Hilditch was looking about him, taking in the neat arrangements of family photographs that surrounded a tariff of prices, and his eye appeared to linger upon the bottom line: 'Hair dyed with nitrate of silver, with whiskers, 1/-; Warts removed with nitric acid, 6d.'

Touchfarthing asked himself whether the fellow might be here to take advantage of one of his range of sidelines.

'Have you been here a long time?'

Touchfarthing frowned. 'Long enough to establish our company as the leading photographic firm in this part of London, I think. Might I ask why you make that enquiry?'

'It cannot be a small undertaking, opening a photographer's shop. There would be the lease of the premises, the equipment, the chemicals, your assistant, a tout on the door.'

'I don't use a tout,' said Touchfarthing.

'All told, it cannot be an inexpensive venture.'

'I am in partnership and naturally the junior partner brought something to the table,' said Touchfarthing, wiping his palms with the bit of cloth. 'Though I cannot see how this can be any concern of yours.'

68

'It still seems to me that you would need to be in possession of a considerable sum of money yourself.'

'Well, what of it?' said Touchfarthing.

'I'm just curious about the provenance of such a sum,' said the man.

'This is a gross impertinence,' said Touchfarthing, though he said it with uncertainty.

'If I am not mistaken in your identity,' the man continued, 'then I am right in saying that the money was a gift and that gift was made to you by a gentleman who resides in the North Riding of Yorkshire.'

There was no note of enquiry in his tone and Touchfarthing choked back the expostulation that rose in his throat. Henry Hilditch put down the photograph and turned to face the photographer. 'Forgive me, but I did want to be certain before I touched upon another matter. But you are, I think, the person who held the position of butler at Sibthorpe Hall, near Whitby?'

Touchfarthing's reply was thick with surprise. 'Who are you?'

'My name is Hilditch and I knew you by sight in Whitby. I have no other concern with you than your relationship with a certain woman who was employed as a governess at Sibthorpe Hall. I think you may know something of her sudden dismissal from the Hall and perhaps her current whereabouts?'

'Miss Medworth? You are close with her?' He regarded the slighter man with suspicion, perhaps even distaste.

'I am a gentleman,' Hilditch replied. 'My relationship with that lady need not concern you.'

'These are my premises,' Touchfarthing said grandly, 'and I have nothing to say about her. I have had enough trouble from that direction already. I am respectably established on my own account and that business has long been dead and buried. I've no wish to have it dug up again now. Now, gentleman or no gentleman, I must bid you good day.'

He opened the shop door and Henry Hilditch, his face grim-set, walked out. The small beady eyes of the photographer followed his progress all the way to the street-corner.

6

Illuminations

Henry Hilditch glanced at the two letters that lay on the table before him. Both were addressed to him in the same hand but only one had been opened. The other had only this moment been delivered to him by his unexpected visitor, who now dropped his negligently-attired self into a heavily upholstered chair by the dying fire and rested his street-soiled shoes upon the fender. With a journalist's curiosity, Jabez Flynt, editor of the *Morning Messenger*, gazed about the room, taking in the makeshift shelves stacked with scientific books and journals; his tired eyes rested on works about fossils, varieties of beetles, three volumes of *The Divine Comedy* in English and a single tome with the word 'Medici' boldly tooled in gold. The furniture was of no account: cheap, functional and entirely in keeping with the expected provisions of an inexpensive but respectable London lodging house. He turned to Hilditch.

'I say, but that last squib of yours stirred 'em up!' he remarked. 'Never knew so many people who couldn't spell "outrageous"!'

Henry Hilditch, standing by the leaded bay window, put down the letter he had been reading and averted his face, as if he had found something of interest in the street below.

'If anything, the babble was louder even than for "A Dogfight in the East End". It's coming to something when a boy's only at home in a prison, what? This'll prick the the reformers, I should say! We might get another question in the House. That's not bad at all!'

'I had begun to wonder whether you still approved of my writing,' Hilditch said.

'Well, yes, there you've hit it,' said Flynt, shifting his attention from a dark blue stain on his own shabby waistcoat. He sat forwards in his chair and thrust a poker among the sulky embers of the evening's fire. 'That Great Exhibition stuff was all very well in its way – the souvenir seller, the potato man and all that – but it's this other stuff that's made them hot. These last pieces – the dogfight, the gaoler, the crossing sweeper, the pickpocket – these are what's had 'em writing letters and buying the *Morning Messenger*. I'll be plain with you, Hilditch, nothing I've published so far has provoked such a sensation.'

'Truly? I never thought my scribblings would be controversial.'

'They're more than that. If we get this right, your reports could be just the thing to turn this paper around. You've struck a chord with the readers. You're giving the parlour voyeurs a glimpse of a world beyond their experience.'

Hilditch, mildly surprised, pursed his lips. 'There was a time when I walked and only observed,' he said, softly. 'In Paris, on my return from Italy, I found a breed of fellows there that walk the city for no better reason than that. Some are writers, others philosophers. They walk the boulevards only to observe their city.'

'Well, thank God you've given that up,' said Flynt. 'Go to places the readers never go, meet the people they would never meet.' Flynt stood up and absent-mindedly shouldered his poker. 'You, Henry, must be the eyes and the ears of respectable people in Kensington and Belgravia. People who wouldn't dream of setting foot in the East End, or cutting through the Devil's Acre or Jacob's Island. Give me the underbelly of London – the thieves, the whores, the magsmen and the like – and by Heaven, we'll have the *News Chronicle* on the run!'

'And you think my articles can do that?'

'With my direction, I do. Get this right, Henry, and I'll double your fee!'

'I don't need the money.'

'Don't you, by God!' Flynt looked about the shabby room and said wryly, 'This is for amusement, then?'

'Not quite that.'

Flynt arched a straggling eyebrow. 'Well, no matter. What concerns me is that you make these rough places your fiefdom. There's a voracious appetite for this sort of thing.' Flynt's forefingers made a church spire on which he rested his chin as he said, meditatively, 'It's a safe world on the surface, Henry – modern, progressive, a world that has the confidence to mount this Great Exhibition. We're not at war, the Chartists have been quietened. But beneath the surface perhaps there's trouble brewing, a revolution around the corner. We close our eyes to the beggars and the invalids, the conditions in which an enormous number of our fellow creatures are forced to live out their lives. When will the hungry man see the goose on our table and decide he'd like a slice himself? Who is not thankful that language and salt water divide us from France and the Continent? The most assured and certain of our citizens fears the mob. This is why they are so hungry to know the enemy, to meet the burglar who may attack them in their beds, the man so poor he will steal to feed his children and let no man get in his way! There's a great slumbering guilt in this prosperous world, Henry, and that's what you must confront. I want you to address yourself to our frightened citizens and . . .'

'Reassure them?'

Flynt hesitated. 'Perhaps it will suffice for us to just acquaint them with the magnitude of the problem, to show them in how many quarters and in what form dangers might lie.'

'Is that right?'

'It's good business. Now, I shall need to know where you will go next. Then I can puff it the day before.'

'I hardly know where I shall go. I'm no expert on the East End nor its denizens. I've had a couple of misguided forays in

73

that direction and stumbled across a handful of apparently interesting characters. I'm a stranger there and they know it. It might be a long time before I come up with anything as good again.'

'Then get yourself a guide,' said Flynt. 'A native who knows what's what down there. This boy who took you to the dogfight, perhaps?' Hilditch shook his head. 'Somebody, then. There's money in this for you, Hilditch!'

'If I do, it will be for reasons of my own. When I began at this it suited me to have a pretext for my peregrinations. This occupation is a heaven-sent distraction for a restless mind. Now, though, I have another motivation: there is someone I must find. Someone who may be in poor straits, peril even. And I think this person is somewhere upon my patch.'

'A woman, I presume,' Flynt said, smiling. 'Can the *Messenger* assist you?'

'This is my business,' Henry said with decision. 'You need only know you shall have your copy. I think there is a fellow who might serve as my guide.'

'Why, that's capital! So I can count upon you?' He paused and looked again at Hilditch, who was still intent upon the street below.

'Look here, it's hard to talk to a chap who doesn't look you in the face.'

Hilditch turned suddenly and Flynt, seeing his visage for the first time unclouded by coloured glass, was shocked to see a glaring gash about Hilditch's left eye, a poorly mended injury still livid in colour. Flynt cleared his throat, mumbling an apology as he took up his hat.

'Well, as soon as you have an itinerary, if you don't mind,' he said, and let himself out.

II

Hilditch took up the letters that had been sent to him care of the *Morning Messenger*. He settled himself under the yellow light of the flaring gas and ran his fingers along the creases of the folded paper. The letters might as well have been posted from another part of his life, one to which he had thought never to return.

When the first letter had come, a little more than a week before, he had thought himself proofed against the emotional ferment that he had enthroned and stored away behind glass. He had fondly imagined that his new and very different life, which he had lived in Paris and which he now, in modified form, pursued in London, was one in which the memory of the woman would not signify. He had a new and engrossing occupation, one in which he could utilise the science which had delighted him as a boy and one in which he had found a growing degree of unlooked-for celebrity. He truly felt that at last he was putting the past behind him. And so he was shocked to find how little he knew himself: only days after he had received George Devereaux's initial communication, he had already made contact with the photographer, the one man who might be able to tell him where Mary Medworth was.

And now London itself had become saturated with her presence. He smelled her perfume on Bond Street and half-expected to see her on every street-corner or at one of a million windows, from Westminster to Wapping. He had stayed all day in Hyde Park, on the slenderest of chances that she might come, that she might still have some sort of connection with the man who had been butler at Sibthorpe Hall. Now, his observing of London and Londoners had become more intense and driven by a more singular purpose: it had become an obsessional search. No wonder he had been instantly marked out as 'an odd 'un' at the rat-killing. His objectivity had been compromised.

Hilditch took from the table the first letter from George Devereaux. His eyes listlessly scanned the words that were already etched in his mind.

York, September 1st, 1851

My dear Henry,

I have this hour had conversation with our old

schoolfriend Ralph Atkinson, who has lately been up in London to see the Great Exhibition. You will imagine my surprise when he said he had seen your work in a daily newspaper! He recognised in the prose the same keen and analytical mind that won you the science prize when we were boys under Mr Troutbeck's tutelege – and rod! I have directed this care of your editor and hope it finds you safe and well.

I had until now no intimation that you were returned to England. Rumours had reached me that you had taken a post in Florence; that you had been seen in Bologna or were living in Paris. Certainly, the last I saw of you was in your hospital bed in Florence. You will recall that urgent business necessitated my immediate return to England, otherwise I would, of course, have stayed at your bedside until you were completely recovered. I did think you would have followed in a week or two.

I cannot know what you have been about in the intervening period and so I must give you my own news. As you will see from the letterhead, I am presently at York, where some business I was pursuing looks like failing me. But more of that later. Of course you recall Mary Medworth from Florence. I rather think you had eyes for her yourself! I was as good as my word to the girl and I obtained her a position as Agnes's companion at Sibthorpe. Rather a cushy crib, I thought, and I expected her to be dutiful in return and grateful for it. However, I regret to say she disappointed all of us and left Sibthorpe under a cloud, bound for London. I believe we both had a close escape there, Henry!

The day that Miss Medworth left, Sibthorpe also lost the services of old Touchfarthing. He disgraced himself somehow but I believe he was handsomely paid off. You will be amused to hear that he has turned his hobby to profit and is now sole proprietor of a photographer's shop, off Oxford Street in London. He sent his card to my friend Arthur Vavasour, touting for a commission, but Arthur remembered too well the dreadful photographs he had taken at Sibthorpe.

Of something more serious, I was much grieved to hear of your father's death. He was as much a part of Whitby as the lighthouse on the quay or the abbey on the clifftop. People there were sorry when your agent put up the family business for sale. The counting house and the warehouse still stand, ships still berth at the quay but there is no Geoffrey Hilditch directing it all as ever there was of old.

I'm sure you had the best of reasons for the sale and I'm glad that you will never again want for ready cash. I wish the same might be said for myself. I know that you will believe me when I say that I returned to England fully intending a new start, to put my back to the wheel and make something of myself. However, the fact of the matter is that I have had a run of bad luck recently that has left me in a ticklish position and I can think of no one else in the world who might be able and willing to accommodate me with the loan of £50. I'm sure that after the sale of Geo. Hilditch and Co. the sum will be but a trifle to you and yet it would mean all the world to

Yr oldest friend,
George Devereaux

The first time he read the letter he could think of nothing else but Mary Medworth. To see it suddenly spelled out before him, come unbidden when he was least prepared, was as unsettling as an earth tremor. When, after a lapse of time, he had reread the letter, he reflected upon the character of his old schoolfriend, George Devereaux with whom, it seemed, nothing had changed. The York address inevitably suggested the race-track and Henry was loath to waste money paying off George Devereaux's gambling debts. Florence was to have cured all that. 'I'm sending you away,' Edmund Devereaux had declared in Hilditch's presence, after George had been sent down from Cambridge. 'Somewhere they have never heard of the St Leger or Tattersalls or wherever it is that you squander my money!'

Perhaps when he decreed that George should summer in Florence, Devereaux had really believed that the benign influence of high culture would cure the son of his mania for the turf. He invited his neighbour's boy to join the expedition ('Only fellow George knows that doesn't smell of the stables'). Privately, Henry was convinced that neither the influence of civilisation nor his own quieter nature could do anything towards curing George of his reckless high spirits and thriftless spending. George's first letter bore out his conviction.

What a piece of impertinence it had been. Did George Devereaux really have no idea what had been the cost of his dalliance to his 'oldest friend' Henry Hilditch? And what on earth had George meant, that she 'had left under a cloud'? What could have happened and where was she now? Memories of her pale skin, parasol-shaded under Tuscan sunshine, ousted the bitterness that pricked him still when he recalled that she had left Florence not with him but with George Devereaux.

Henry replied to George's first letter the very same day, asking for details about the circumstances of Mary Medworth's dismissal and hinting that the requested money might be forthcoming if George could satisfy his curiosity. In this second letter, which Henry read now with mounting concern, George expressed mild surprise that Henry should remain interested in the girl. He said that Mary Medworth had made a good beginning as Agnes's companion about the house and had been her guide when she went out. Somehow, though, she had incurred the wrath of Devereaux and one day a dog-cart had appeared at the back door and Mary Medworth and her things had been delivered to the station and a ticket bought for London. George, who complained that his father rarely welcomed him at Sibthorpe any more, had been able to find out little more.

Hilditch put down this letter and recalled the fat face and blotchy skin of Cornelius Touchfarthing with sudden sour repugnance. 'I have had enough trouble from that direction already,' the man had said. What had happened at Sibthorpe that might precipitate the sudden departures of both Mary Medworth and the butler Touchfarthing at the same time? Hilditch had no answer. He only knew for certain that Mary Medworth, perhaps without character, was now very likely in a precarious, even dangerous position. It was too awful. Now he considered the case, he realised that her only transgression in his eyes had been to mistake George Devereaux for the better man.

It was Henry who had found her at Florence and through him she had met George and come to Sibthorpe. Perhaps, because of Henry, she was now ruined. This could not be, it must not be. He dropped the letter and gazed out at the night-time sky, and watched a waning moon become obscured by clouds, in whose silvered cotton he made an arrangement of Mary's hair. Without looking hard, he could see also the delicate features of her face. Where this face was in reality he feared to think. He would approach Touchfarthing once more and if necessary he would beg him for information. It was becoming increasingly clear to him that he had lost something extremely precious and pure, something which he was determined to find before it had been defiled on the streets of London. There was no chance of sleep this night. Better it would be if he were to walk himself into a state of exhaustion and seek out whatever distraction might palliate his pain and confusion over Mary Medworth, to walk until his head was cleared and he had some clearer notion of what he might do next.

7

An Aerial View

John Rankin led the way up a creaking, bird-shit-spattered staircase where soot-grimy and web-curtained windows offered diverse views of South London streets in frames of rotting wood. He swapped the heavy valise of equipment to his other hand and, after mounting one more steep flight, deposited it gently on the topmost step, loudly calling down to his companion to be careful with the camera because 'that last turn was uncommonly tight'. When repeated knocking on the only door on the landing went unanswered, he opened a casement window and stepped out on to a flat roof space.

Skinny as tools in a burglar's bag, John Rankin edged nimbly along the narrow walkway separating a steeply-inclining roof from a low wall that screened a precipitous drop. Henry Hilditch, less cat-sure, faltered as he crunched over broken tiles and held fast to the crumbling wall top. Reeling, he stopped to catch his breath. 'Nearly there, sir,' called Rankin, from about a corner somewhere.

When Henry Hilditch allowed himself to look over the parapet the sheer wonder of the vista before and below him dispelled his vertigo. All about a thousand chimney pots erupted with morning smoke and across the river the dome of St Paul's Cathedral struggled to surmount a low-lying fug of gloom pricked by two dozen sharp Wrennish spires. Holding tight to the flimsy wall, Hilditch peered below him at the ancient tenement sprawl cut through with a maze of narrow thoroughfares and ditches, its various parts communicating with themselves by a maze of courts, man-wide alleyways and roof-high bridges and lashed together by lines of limp, grey washing. A movement caught his eye and Hilditch only now saw the boy ten feet beneath who frowned at him as he processed from one window to another by way of a double row of projecting nails and who advised him sharply that he would 'mind 'is own if he knew what was good for 'im'.

The boy disappeared into an unseen aperture and Hilditch was distracted by a new spectacle: in the street below, great ribbons of foot traffic were threading towards the bridge with unwavering purpose and for a moment his mind flashed upon the insects he had observed as a child, when an ants' nest in a glass bowl and several cases of pinned beetles and butterflies were his special fascination at Whitby. When George Devereaux had introduced a live beetle into the ants' bowl and the ants had set upon it and killed it, they had carried away its tremendous carcase with as little mind as the packman below, who bowed beneath his enormous back-strapped bundle. Or those women bearing full-laden trays on their heads, Hilditch thought, as he comprehended this great diurnal emigration of craftsmen and mechanics with bags of tools, men pulling carts and pushing barrows, street hawkers already crying their wares and a scattering of crazily-weaving children. All were part of a moving stream, save for a few men who leant on corners and a coster-monger who dragged hard upon reins while his donkey dug its hooves into a pile of ordure and refused to move.

Beyond was another stream and the source of a familiar but overwhelming stink. On the river, packed ferries plied through lines of high-masted vessels at anchor in the deepest channels, the waterway itself fringed by busy docks and jetties early-crowded with passengers awaiting the morning packets. Near the bridge, lightermen strolled up and down their barges, sailors cast painters and dropped thudding gangplanks and the whole interesting scene was overlooked and supervised by a great gang of ragamuffin boys whose small heads topped the parapet of the bridge like those of spiked traitors.

The crowds on foot funnelled on to the bridge, feeding themselves into the gaping jaws of the city. This transpontine exodus diminished and disappeared at the high-built junction on the far side, no doubt swelling and congesting the pavements of the streets hidden behind the ramparts of riverside buildings. Hilditch closed his eyes and breathed in the city, the focus of his study, with its street upon street bursting with a swollen population, a hundred thousand faces, legs moving, arms swinging, and above and below the tramping workers the remainder who could not or would not work, the old and the infirm, the day-sleeping prostitutes and crib-breaking cracksmen, the wild spirits lamed by gin and opium, the malingerers and the malcontents. Nausea began to well in his stomach; Hilditch put his handkerchief to his mouth feeling he might retch. Somewhere, he had remembered, down in that almighty and infernal place and very likely at the mercy of Fortune, was Mary Medworth.

'Mr 'ildish! If you please!' Rankin's voice came close at hand and Hilditch carefully edged about a corner and found himself in a wider space, bordered on two opposite sides by steeply angled roofs. Before Hilditch was a cluster of four great brick chimney stacks, and protruding to one side was evidence of some other construction. Hilditch walked around the chimneys and into a flurry of startled pigeons.

'Come in, Mr H., but mind you shut the door directly,' came Rankin's voice from within. Hilditch opened a leather-hinged door and entered a place where darkness was relieved only by the poor construction of the edifice itself. Light speared through ill-fitting plank walls and from gaps in the tar-cloth roof and revealed a thin man sat upon a rough bed. From the man's bony left hand a bird was taking corn. John Rankin squatted by his side, holding something in his arms which, as Hilditch approached, struggled madly until it broke free of Rankin's hold and leapt upon a high shelf, where its dark shape chattered and shrieked. 'What in the name of Hades . . .' Hilditch began.

'You'll see in a minute, sir,' said Rankin. 'Our 'ost Mr Underwood 'as kindly agreed to discover to you all the ins and the outs of bein' a Happy Families man.'

'The blinds, if you will be so good,' croaked the man on the bed. John Rankin hooked up the cloth window-covers. Light flooded through the wire grilles to an alarming fanfare of strange shrieks and squawks and showed Hilditch a gaunt and elderly man, whose wispy grey hair matched and was almost a piece with the multitude of feathers that adhered to his shiny black coat. More strange to Hilditch were his companions. The thing that had leapt upon the shelf was a small monkey, quieter now as it mortared those below with nutshells. High on the window lattice perched a dove and a brilliantly plumed cockatoo while in the shadows of a corner a fierce-looking dog lay panting as a white mouse darted before his nose, watched closely by a softly-purring ginger cat on the man's lap. Before Hilditch could comment on the extraordinary variety of pets the man kept, he had seen the rats in a box at his feet, in which was also a sleek ferret.

The old man shook his head. 'Oh, yes,' he said to Henry Hilditch, 'I dare say you think I keep a considerable number of animals – John, have you seen the coatimundi? – but it isn't nothing to what I had in the old days, when there wasn't more than four chaps showing a Happy Family in all London and mine was the best of them all. Ah, but times have changed and it's new novelty the public wants now and chaps like me can barely make enough to feed our animals. There was a time when people paid well to see the hawk and the dove living peaceably and sometimes I took a pound a day. Not any more – last time we set up by the Monster Globe in Leicester Square, we come home with two bob flat. How are the creatures to live on that?'

'I have heard of these entertainments but I never saw one myself,' said Hilditch.

'In my best days, of birds I had a pair of magpies, some jackdaws, a great many starlings and a screech owl. I also kept guinea pigs, tortoises, rabbits, hedgehogs, cats, dogs, rats and mice. When I had saved a little money I bought my first monkey. The monkeys was always very popular.'

'Surely so many animals cannot share a single cage?'

'Bless you, sir, but I've shown as many as fifty at once. I built a big cage for the purpose, which I mounted on springs so's that the animals would not be jolted and frightened by the holes in the road. And when I set up and raised the blinds people might be five or more deep before the cage. There were those that came just from a love of animals and others who drew a moral lesson. But there were always some who watched hoping to spot a cat quietly take a mouse or a hawk kill a bird though they never did. Some ridiculous fellows maintained it was the Devil's work or that it was at least against the natural order. Of course I got my share of doubters too, who believed that some trickery was involved and that it was all done with opium. I might tell them how it was done but the explanation wouldn't be to their taste. You see it's only kindness I use. Careful coaxing and taking everything just a small step at a time is what does it.'

Hilditch, making marks on paper: 'Might I ask how you came by your skills?'

'It was like this, sir. I was never brought up to a trade and as a younger man I turned my hand to any little job that came my way. I kept out the workhouse but that was all. As a diversion, I bred mice. I kept cats too and, of course, the mice was always getting killed but when the she-cat littered I saw how alike was the new-born kitten with my new-born white mice and the notion took me to introduce one o' my young mice to a young cat and try and make 'em get on and that way maybe I wouldn't lose so many mice. I kept 'em together, watched 'em for trouble but there was none. This cat and the mouse became the best o' pals and folk marvelled to see 'em together. Sometimes I put the mouse upon the cat's back and he took a ride. She, the cat, was always gentle with the mouse and let the mouse sleep with her and the mouse looked like it was a suckling kitten.

'People talked about it and some said I might have a special talent and so I tried it with other animals. I found as by similar means I could get another o' my cats to make friends with a sewer-rat. It must have been about that time I discovered that I wasn't the only chap about this lark. A fellow from Nottingham had started showing his Happy Family there and making quite a go of it. He took a tour of the country and exhibited his animals by invitation or on speculation. I saw him and his animals when he was visiting London and it struck me that I might do such a thing and do it a little better, too.

'I collected my animals slowly. When I got a bit of work I bought another animal, if I thought I could afford the cost of his food. When I had collected together a respectable number and had got them all to live in peace with each other – even the ferret – I started showing the animals in Piccadilly, but I discovered that a Happy Families man had already established himself at Regents Street and so I moved my pitch to Tower Hill, where I found I could make a tidy living amusing the folk visiting the Tower. I had that pitch for nine year and was another full ten year set up before London Bridge. I tried my luck at New Cut market at Lambeth, and was lately in Leicester Square. I've made my living as a Happy Families man the best part of my life and mostly it's done me proud but in the last few years it seems that the public wants new sensations and ain't content with the amusements of old.

'I'm not sorry that I won't live to see the day the Happy Families all shuts up shop and I pray that my lungs will last me long enough to see my little friends pleasantly disposed of. How that is a care for me!'

Underwood looked about the room with despair in his eyes.

'When I built this place it seemed like the ideal home for my animals. There was space and air and the pigeons might take a turn in the sky before coming home for the night. It took me long enough to take each down in a cage to load the van in the street but I was strong and didn't mind the stairs overmuch.

Now my lungs is going I find it beyond me. I kept it up until last Christmas but as I have told my friend John, it's been all I can do lately to get myself down into the street where I might beg sufficient halfpences to feed them.'

'And 'ardly feeding yourself, I suppose!' said John Rankin.

'Oh, I don't mind going short commons if I can see the animals fed and there ain't so many of them now, as you can see. It has broken my heart to sell so many of them, but otherwise the others could hardly have survived.' He turned to address Henry Hilditch. 'So you see, sir, that rather than having a lot of animals here, I have in fact got precious few and soon I won't be here to look after even them.'

The man stifled a sob while John Rankin sat at his side and gently patted his back. 'Now, then, surely it ain't as bad as all that. That ain't what the doctor said, surely?'

Mr Underwood smiled through his tears. 'Don't think I'm not very grateful to you,' he said. 'Paying for the doctor and sending me food too – that was handsome of you, Mr Rankin. But a time comes to us all when neither physicians nor better fare will do any good and we have to accept the inevitable. It won't be long now and I might be ready for it if only I knew that my little friends were to be well cared for.'

The man's breath whistled from his lungs and he gripped Rankin's arm. 'I'm a little tired now, John,' he said, 'and might take a sleep.'

Rankin lay him down upon his bed. 'You take your rest, old fellow,' he said. 'We'll do that portrait another time and there won't be no cost to you, neither.' The man dropped into a troubled sleep with the cat purring on his wheezing chest while a rat moved about under his blanket. The monkey now leapt from its shelf and sat upon John Rankin's shoulder. Hilditch slipped the notes he had taken into his coat pocket and prepared to leave but John Rankin lingered, shaking his head as the monkey chattered and pulled at his hair. 'Don't you go worrying about your friends,' he said as he opened the door. 'I'll find something to answer.'

Upon the street again, Hilditch shouldered the camera and cast an upwards look. 'All that work,' he said, 'for so small a reward. Surely he should have got rid of his animals when he saw there was no profit in it?'

'I think he continued for the love of it,' Rankin replied. 'For the love of his animals. Money don't come into it, when there's love in the case.'

'Yes, but surely...' Hilditch began, and then broke off. 'No, you are right, I'm sure.'

II

Later that day, as he searched Seven Dials for unusual stories to fill his newspaper column, Henry saw Mary Medworth sweeping into a gaudily-lit gin-palace upon the arm of a fellow in yellow chequered trousers whose appearance struck him immediately as being disreputable. Heart pounding, he followed the pair into the saloon, lost himself amid cigar-smoking swells and rubicund no-hopers, and fetched up by accident behind the very person he sought. He coughed and mustered no more than a whisper to breathe, 'Mary!' The woman – dark curls softening an angular, rouged face – turned and paralysed him with consternation. 'We've not 'ad the pleasure – 'ave we?' she said, 'but charmed, I'm sure.' The fellow on her arm gave Hilditch a look that might have said, 'I was here first you know, old man,' and placed his shoulder between Hilditch and the woman.

Henry Hilditch, softly cursing his error, made a clumsy, awkward exit and, once released by the crowd inside, took several deep breaths before continuing his journey. Rattling bird-cages and tangling with gibbets of second-hand clothes, he escaped the cramped by-ways of Seven Dials and emerged upon St Martin's Lane and so to Trafalgar Square, where the monument to Lord Nelson towered over the National Gallery and evening strollers promenaded on the piazza below. Then, coalescing with a great group of men whose only claim to sobriety was in their dress, he started down Whitehall, skirting pubs whose patrons over-spilled upon pavements, passing Horseguards without a glance. He peered into Downing Street before marking the Prime Minister on the other side of Whitehall, heading a knot of noisy men walking towards the Houses of Parliament. By Westminster Abbey his passage was obstructed by choristers arriving for evensong as black-skirted clergymen dodged omnibuses to the last reverberations of the summoning bells.

Upon Victoria Street, the doubts and fears engendered by the return of Mary Medworth to his consciousness began to seep away, to fade like the colours of the clothing and the faces of passing pedestrians. In their place was only the steady beat of his footfalls. His legs moved with a calming rhythm, his arms swung to the same silent tempo. His breathing, after his shock in Seven Dials, became just as measured; walking, for Hilditch, was the universal panacea.

His attention was free to wander. He walked on. The red sails of a distant yawl caught his eye. In his imagination, hard paving melted into springy tufts of long grass as he swallowed air fresh-washed by the spume of rolling ocean waves. No longer upon a London street but tramping a coastal path in the North Riding of Yorkshire, from Whitby to Robin Hood's Bay, with the North Sea spread before him and the wind blasting through scalp and cloth, Henry Hilditch was again upon the clifftops, shaking off the dust of the family counting house, blowing away the stupefying torpor of his mother's parlour, freed for a time from the tyranny of his father's overpowering nature.

How long ago was that? Not long by the scales of Ned Peatty who sat upon the quay mending nets, day after day and no time at all, perhaps, in the mind of Joss Boythorpe, who had smoked Whitby herrings for forty years. But for Henry Hilditch, that same period was a bubble of time that had swollen and distended, expanded until it had accommodated a superabundance of novelty and experience: a journey to Italy and the acquaintance of art, the blossoming of some hitherto-unknown part of himself; the awakening of love and such hope as he had never known. These few years had also brought him the hideous mortification of disappointment and failure and a new life lived on the streets of Paris and London. On the ordered, tree-lined boulevards of Paris he had learnt to walk and observe and to read the city. And after that, amid the chaotic and curious streets of London, he had walked and talked and written about the sprawling metropolis that had come to dominate the Age. Only on the unchanged clifftops of Whitby had he walked purely for the pleasure it gave him.

For the first time since he had left the place, Hilditch wished himself back in Whitby. Now that his father was no longer to be encountered around every street-corner, the town of his remembrance took on a pleasing aspect and at that moment nothing might have better delighted him than to be strolling in its narrow streets or embarking upon one of the long moorland walks he had taken as often as his duties and the weather allowed. Sometimes he had gone as far as Scarborough and even Flamborough Head before returning across the high heathered moors with bags full of fossils and jet. In these places, much more so than in his room at Ryedale House, he had found his asylum.

His father, safely dead, was also undergoing a transmutation. Once the incarnation of success writ as large as the great white capitals upon the quayside warehouses that spelled out HILDITCH, he appeared now a smaller figure, whose loud bombast and wrath might be excused as the outward signs of impending failure. The man Henry had most feared was now no more than a tombstone in St Mary's graveyard, a plaque on a church wall and a topic of conversations in Whitby pubs. The name, though, would persist in the life of the town, whether or not Henry himself lived there. It was as synonymous with Whitby as Caedmon's the poet: Hilditch and Whitby, Hilditch and whaling.

Henry's grandfather, Christian Hilditch, had built up the fleet that had brought whale-oil and work to Whitby. To be a Hilditch in Whitby was to work the whalers. It was also to be an eminent figure in the life and society of the town. Each Sunday a Hilditch had preceded the vicar in the procession up the two hundred steps to St Mary's Church, and almost as often a Hilditch had read the lesson to a respectful congregation, huddled in the high box-pews carved from the wood of Hilditch ships.

Henry's walks were respites from his father's vociferous disappointment in a younger son who would never replace Josh, who had been swept from a deck into the icy Arctic. His father would have had him studying charts and learning navigation, understanding the nature of ocean fishing and of sharp business too, but although Henry was daily to be found at a clerk's desk in the counting house, it was clear to everyone that he could never take his proper place as head of the business and scion of Whitby society. The boy, who preferred to closet himself in his room with his cased and classified insects and beetles and his labelled drawers of ammonites and bits of jet, remained an unfathomable mystery to his father. Whether it was his grief, his mother's early death or the growing irascibility of his father's temper or some latent, innate quality that had made him what he had become, Henry would not have been able to say.

Lately, he had allowed that his father had reason for the bleakness of his temper. Josh had drowned on the Hilditch fleet's last whaling voyage. Over-fishing and increasingly ice-bound whaling grounds and new replacements for whale products had slowly crippled the family business. Geoffrey Hilditch sold some boats and refitted others to catch herring, but the success of Christian Hilditch's whaling venture was never to be repeated. Geoffrey Hilditch was too old to start anew and his surviving son would be no more use than a simpleton. His father raged and became ill. When his neighbour Edmund Devereaux suggested that Henry accompany his son George and daughter Agnes to Florence, Geoffrey Hilditch had readily agreed, muttering, 'And good riddance, too!' Had been, in fact, as agreeable to part with his son as Sir Edmund with his own.

Henry Hilditch, almost without thinking, turned off Victoria Street and on to Strutton Ground. His walks about Whitby had often been as directionless as this and certainly as rudderless as his voyage through life at that time. Vague, airy plans had filled his head as he walked upon the cliffs. He would go away, become something other than a Whitby Hilditch, but precisely what was never settled. To go away had seemed enough, the invitation to Italy an opportune solution.

And this evening, in London, he would walk with as little purpose as he had done in Whitby. He would not seek out the lying beggars and the petty thieves; the spongers and the cheats; the unreliable witnesses who might say anything for the price of a drink, the very subjects that Jabez Flynt declared sources of unquenchable fascination for his readers. Nor would he approach the honest but unfortunate, whose strivings Flynt said might be left for the pen of Henry Mayhew. Tonight he would leave aside the occupation that these days passed for his business.

He crossed Duck Lane and so avoided the low lodging houses packed with street musicians and pickpockets whose exploits, slightly exaggerated by Jabez Flynt, had filled a *Messenger* column the week previous. He hastened along Pye Street, lest he should re-encounter the vicious band of coiners who defended a garret apartment above a dollymop's premises and whose look-out, taking Hilditch for an officer of the law, had tried to pitch him back down the stairs. Very shortly he was upon Horseferry Road, a broader thoroughfare, walking only for its own sake.

The light, however, was failing and, deprived of the literature of the streets, its signs and puffs in shop windows, the hoardings and the handbills, distractions upon which he would fix unwarranted attention, his mind was inevitably repossessed by its obsession of recent days. He was still wary of reviewing the whole nature of his relationship – if it might be called that – with Mary Medworth, and was not yet ready to linger upon their acquaintance in Italy. What exercised his mind now was the problem of locating this girl in the enormity of the brick and timber, flesh and bone that was London. With only one line of enquiry so far open to him, it would not be an easy task. If, indeed, this was what he had decided to do.

Upon Millbank, he laughed. It would be clear to anyone else that his mind was made up. He saw himself days before, interviewing the fat photographer as if he were a person suspected in a police enquiry, saw himself the same day making arrangements with John Rankin that would provide him with a guide to London's darker places and permit him, too, to observe at close quarters this Cornelius Touchfarthing. Hilditch could no longer deny it to himself. He knew now that whatever the result, whatever wounds might be reopened in the process, he would scour London until he had found Mary Medworth. Thus resolved, he walked along the riverbank in the direction of Vauxhall Bridge.

8

High and Low

The Reform Chapel on Berners Street, with its stuccoed front and tall sashed windows, appeared to be only another town house, a brother to its short row of neighbours. Only the sign erected beside the compact Ionic portico identified it as a place of worship, which activity occurred at the times there listed, under the auspices of Mr Harold Rutter, BA MA (Phil) Oxon.

Its polished panes, through which might be admired an austere yet pristine interior, sparkled with respectability. The pair of steps were regularly scrubbed and the pavement swept. John Scraggs, the surviving constituent of the local builders Scraggs and Son, whose wagon-loads of wooden-scaffolding, bricks and Portland stone now more often trundled the streets of burgeoning Belgravia, might tell you that the edifice was a sham, and that the frontage was a fashionable addition to a much older, timber-framed building and that anyone with any knowledge at all would know that just from the uneven lie of the floors and the disposition of the chimneys and the upstairs rooms. The ground floor was more radically altered. Here, walls had been removed to create a large reception chamber, whose corniced ceiling was supported instead by grand plaster pillars and whose new fireplace was as fancy as might have been purchased at the time of the alterations, within the limits of a reasonable budget. With a sprung floor, the room had done well for Monsieur Auguste Roquefort, who had there presided over the premier dancing academy of the North West End of London.

After M. Roquefort's precipitous return to France – the newspapers intimated *un scandale* – the house, which had already only the teetering respectability of an institution of this kind, fell from its eminence and became The Juno, a middling sort of club in which the elderly colonels and half-pay pensioners who played slow rubbers of whist for penny stakes in the ground-floor saloon were for the most part unaware of the real money changing hands faster than telegraph signals in the illicit casino below.

While his luck lasted, the owner, Galileo Godfrey, was as successful as could be. Poor but respectable gentlemen arrived at the front door; rakes, and other makes of dissolute gent, came and went at the rear and no one was the wiser, unless it were the police, for whose discretion he paid very handsomely. Godfrey could not help but make an untidy fortune until he broke his own golden rule and took to the game himself. His luck refused to accompany him to his own tables. Though he made every reasonable attempt to weight the odds in his own favour, he lost repeatedly and lost so heavily that the establishment itself passed, on a single hand of cards, to a new owner, who was already sufficiently wealthy to forget about it altogether and on his death the neglected property was advertised for a song and bought by Sarah Malone, who was on paper a milliner employing five hard-working hat-makers, but was in practice a well-known madam employing a fluctuating number of industrious prostitutes.

For above a decade the house was a riotous and widely infamous address. It was such a magnet for sin that when Mrs Malone retired to Ireland a rich woman, a non-conformist sect who were looking for premises in that neighbourhood saw that two birds might be despatched with a single stone. They would buy the premises and thereby stop up another cess-pit of corruption and in its place install a church, a centre from which evangelising ministers might radiate righteousness throughout the neighbourhood. Mr Rutter was the first incumbent to be installed in the chapel and the great care he took of the renovated and rededicated building indicated his huge pride in the place and also, perhaps, that his past appointments had not been as salubrious.

Cornelius Touchfarthing, resting an elbow on his tripod-mounted camera as he stood by the door at the back of the meeting room, regretted that there wasn't more to distract the mind of a fellow who hadn't come here to listen to the minister. Unconsciously mirroring Mr Rutter, who stood before a congregation mostly of women with his own elbow at rest on a lectern, Touchfarthing's gaze arced over the brightly white-washed walls and the plain and unadorned windows, took in the nine rows of hard forms on either side of a central aisle, the long table covered with a cloth that served as an altar, the very emptiness of the place, and reluctantly returned his focus to Rutter himself who was, he was forced to admit, the most interesting thing in the room.

It came to him as a minor revelation that perhaps the startling bareness of the chapel was not so much an expression of the faith, but a marvellous background against which to show to best advantage the minister himself. Though in itself his attire was plain and no one would accuse Mr Rutter of being the Beau Brummel of Berners Street, his every garment fitted him like silk; his shoes were shined to a patent gleam and his thin wrists protruded from the sleeves of a grey frock-coat that was neither frayed nor even shiny at the elbows. His thinning auburn hair was sleekly groomed and smelled faintly of pomade. The perfection of his turn-out made the most of fifty-year-old features that were at best ordinary.

That he practically mesmerised his female congregation was not to be accounted for by his heavily-lidded pale blue eyes, nor by his sharp bill of a nose and small chin that disappeared behind a whisper of a beard, nor by the histrionic adroitness of his performance. Rather, it was the aggregate effect of a man who dressed and talked to be admired. Such were the accusations levelled at him behind the coloured glass of neighbouring churches, and his own congregation did not deny and even revelled in the vanity of the man. When it was known that Mr Rutter was to have his photograph made for a *carte de visite*, he received so many petitions for copies that he ordered in total one hundred, which he was known to have resold at a shilling apiece. Touchfarthing, though he shrank from such base wrangling, resolved that he would bring up the matter of the money owing him for these *cartes de visite* before anything else.

As Mr Rutter addressed his flock, the rows of variegated bonnets nodded and small notes of assent rose from beneath their brims but only the occasional phrase permeated the consciousness of Cornelius Touchfarthing. 'Gird our loins, we must, and fight the great fight not only on the streets where vice and temptation positively abound, but within our own breasts, in here!' Touchfarthing gave an involuntary nod at this profundity and let the sibilance of the speaker's faint lisp lull him into a state of stupefaction until his attention was awoken by Mr Rutter striding down the aisle towards him.

Before Touchfarthing could open his mouth and perhaps broach the business on which he had visited the chapel, Mr Rutter clapped his hands before the face of an elderly matriarch who had begun to snore softly, turned upon his heels and marched to the front again, where his wiry frame suddenly inclined over a tiny mop of ginger curls whose owner might have disappeared under her seat had she not been wedged in place by stout neighbours. 'You, Sally Deakin,' said the minister, 'stood upon the brink of the abyss. On Tottenham Court Road. For there it was that I found you, alone and friendless, without a penny nor a crust. Happily, Providence decreed it was I to whom you offered yourself that night and not some beast of baser appetites.' The little girl nodded furiously. 'And you, Moll Sargent' – Rutter picked out a tall twig of a girl in a grey and many-patched dress – 'were like to have drunk yourself to your ruin, had God not directed me to you at that dreadful den in

Wapping.' Miss Sargent, seventeen years or less, covered her face. 'And Jane Pipkin of Putney, seduced by her master and quick with his bastard child.' The mob-capped girl who sat at the front, the better to accommodate her swollen belly, began to sob quietly. Rutter sucked in his cheeks and shook his head. 'Was there nothing that any of you might have done to save yourselves?' The bonnets shook their response. Mr Rutter patted the sobbing girl.

'There, my child. Not one of us here can claim to be pure of sin. Not even I. All we can do is to truly repent and seek our salvation. And you are most fortunate, for you have been given a chance; a place of refuge and a guide who shall direct your feet until they are safely set upon the right road.' A change came over the man. His face became troubled, his voice deep and low. 'Do not, at your own peril, reject this God-given opportunity!'

A shudder rippled along the lines and Mr Rutter paused to allow for emphasis. Jane Pipkin wailed and clutched her belly. A girl before Touchfarthing trembled as Rutter's gaze swept over the wide-eyed assembly. It occurred to Touchfarthing that had Rutter a scourge in his hand he might have launched himself among his miscreant flock like Christ among the money-changers; the minister was holding fast to his lectern as if it might restrain him from just such an action. Now he stretched over his opened text and craned his head towards his quailing congregation. 'There you sit before me now, as damnable a lot of sinners as ever was assembled in one place. Heed me closely, for I am your only chance for salvation.' Touchfarthing shifted uncomfortably as the finger was again pointed, it seemed, squarely at his own person.

Rutter dabbed away a droplet of spittle from the side of his mouth. 'But the Lord in His Mercy has sent you another sinner, poor Harold Rutter, and if you cleave to me you shall, with my guidance and His Grace, be saved from temptation and harm and shall be so instructed in the evils and ways of this vicious world that you may walk abroad with a fearless heart and sure tread.'

'Thanks be!' came the united rejoinder. As the minister approached the end of his lesson, the little responses of his congregation had become more resonant. He had frightened them but he had carried them with him, far from the cares of their daily existences. Flushed cheeks and flashing eyes suggested that Mr Rutter's severe admonishment had been as productive of exhilaration as it had of terror. Even Touchfarthing, whose father had been a brimstone Baptist from Wakefield, had been caught up in the rise and fall of his oratory and was not at all surprised when some of Mr Rutter's convocation had given way to an outburst of enthusiasm and had begun to applaud. Mr Rutter stilled the commotion and took up a piece of paper. 'Until tomorrow, then,' he said. 'Tread wisely in the ways of the Lord.' As the women stood and one or two were making for the doors, Rutter held up a hand. 'A moment, please. Tonight I would select for special Bible study, let me see, Elsa Bowring. Is Miss Bowring here tonight?'

The service over, Touchfarthing began to make his way towards the preacher, but found himself obstructed for several minutes by ladies requesting interviews with Mr Rutter himself. When at last the crowd had dispersed with much rustling and sweeping of cotton and crinoline, only one remained, a young girl with a face full of freckles within a mop of ringlets and a dress that told of a country seamstress ignorant not only of the new town fashions but most of the old ones also.

'Please sir,' she whispered, 'I'm Elsa Bowring?' and waited at Rutter's back as he addressed the photographer.

'Ah, Mr Touchfarthing. And how did you like the lesson?'

'There was much to ponder upon,' Touchfarthing said.

'That's as it should be, of course. Are you aware, Mr Touchfarthing, that within a slingshot of where we stand are some thirty brothels? Did you know that in the very next street are printing presses turning off the most terrible types of literature? You can hardly have failed to notice that little girls are selling themselves for pennies – pennies! – on every street-corner. Why there are probably more fallen sinners between Oxford Street

100

and St Giles' Church than in any thoroughfare outside of Sodom and Gomorrah.'

'Is that so?' said Touchfarthing, who frowned and scratched his nose. 'I suppose, Mr Rutter, that it is your business to notice such things. And all credit if you can alleviate the suffering caused by these people. But the higher mind, sir, sees not the gutter but the great sky above. Some of us must set our sights on better things. How else are we to have beauty in the world? How Art, how Architecture? Why, only this afternoon, I walked here from St James and I saw much to raise the spirit, not dash it underfoot.'

Mr Rutter sighed. 'Unblinkered eyes cannot but see what is all about them, Mr Touchfarthing. There is a corruption at the core of things that we ignore at our peril. Base instincts and unbridled passions are the root cause of so much misery. What is it that causeth the inveterate drunk to squander his family's dinner money in the ale-house? That lures a fine young man to dissipation and disease?'

'But these people are weak and without character, Mr Rutter. I can tell you that I never had my head turned by a pretty pair of eyes.'

'We must be aware of the temptations that abound, though we ourselves are proofed against them,' Mr Rutter said. 'Can you imagine what a pernicious effect the sight of unclothed flesh can have on a man?' He looked about him and then took from his pocket a piece of paper, which he unfolded before Touchfarthing's eyes. 'Do you know what only a few pages of this filth can do?'

Touchfarthing looked as if he had suddenly been shown a deadly snake. He had barely the time to establish the nature of the act depicted before the piece of paper had disappeared into Rutter's clothing.

'Is it any wonder that young men have come through these doors enervated and drained of their spirit?' the preacher said. 'That is why my crusade is so important, my little refuge for lost souls here at Berners Street, so invaluable. And you see why the pictures I have in mind to execute will provide a much-needed moral paradigm. What I have planned will suit us both, I'm sure of it.'

'Mr Rutter, sir?' the little girl implored. 'The Bible study?'

'We'll start for your studio before we lose the light,' said Rutter. 'Follow along, Miss Bowring, no Bible study tonight. There is something else we might do which will be just as profitable.' The minister rolled up a sheaf of papers that lay on his lectern and tied them with a ribbon. With uncertain steps, the little girl followed in the shadow of the corpulent photographer as he and the sleekly-made Rutter stepped out of the chapel and turned the corner on to Oxford Street.

II

John Rankin, sitting cross-legged on a bed of long crushed grass, heard the back gate creak on its hinges and saw the dark figure of Henry Hilditch steal into the yard. Rankin watched through shading branches of the old pear tree as Hilditch, shielding his eyes with a hand, peered through a cracked pane in the studio window. At the back door the visitor tried the handle and was on the point of stepping over the threshold when his name was called aloud. He turned quickly and, looking about him, descried a figure amid a tangle of untended plants and rubbish at the end of the yard. Pushing aside low drooping branches, Hilditch discovered John Rankin, head bent over some small bundle in his arms. He did not look up.

'There was no reply at the shop door. I presumed you would be in the studio.'

'Little fellow's half starved,' said Rankin, who was giving morsels of food to a small animal wrapped in a cloth. The creature, a marmoset, was using up Rankin's attention and Hilditch was left to look idly about him and to perceive that the stack of boxes he had taken to be discarded crates were in fact rudimentary cages and that in all but one an animal of some sort was prowling, sleeping or gazing back at him with sharp black eyes.

'This is the Happy Family? Belonging to that fellow Underwood?'

'What's left of it. No one knew he had died 'til a fortnight had gone and by that time a lot of his friends had gone with him.'

'Surely you can no more afford to keep them than he could? It would be kinder to kill them.'

'What a thought,' said Rankin. 'I made a promise and I intends to keep it. I've found homes for some and I'll do as much for the rest. Though there's one or two I should keep if it weren't for the guv'nor.' Rankin held out the monkey. 'Would you like to hold it, Mr Hilditch?'

'No, no, not I,' Hilditch said, as he shrank from the proffered bundle. 'So Touchfarthing knows nothing of your managerie?'

'Not as yet. I almost think I might keep an elephant in this yard without him noticing. His mind ain't always here with us mortals.'

'He's an odd sort of fellow, I think,' said Hilditch, carefully.

'Wivart doubt,' said John Rankin, with a chuckle. 'I think you understate the case.'

Hilditch touched his temple, his eyes quizzing the other man.

'Oh, he ain't mad, Mr Hilditch. He's a 'umbug, for certain, but that's only his way. Underneath it all he's the best of fellers.'

'Really? And that's your honest opinion?'

'I know that for a fact. It's 'cos of him that I'm where I am and not down in Botany Bay with my back striped by a whip.'

'I should like to know more,' said Hilditch. 'You fascinate me.'

Rankin frowned. 'You, and not the newspaper?'

'I am only curious, I assure you.'

The creature appeared to be sleeping but Rankin still cradled it gently. 'I don't mind telling you about Mr T. There's a few too many has the wrong idea about him. It's his own fault, I own. His manner is too singular for most folks. But underneath, he's a proper gentleman.'

103

'Then might I ask, John, how you come to know this gentleman?'

But Rankin was suddenly upon his feet and peering through the studio's glass panes. 'I thought I heard the shop door,' he said.

'Touchfarthing is returned?'

'Yes and with visitors too. Should you like to meet 'em?'

'We'll not disturb them,' said Hilditch. 'I should rather learn the nature of your connection with Mr Touchfarthing.'

'You'll not mind me feeding the family,' Rankin said as he began to open cages and distribute scraps of leavings and handfuls of grain to the caged animals. 'And mind this, I can't tell you everything without revealing something about myself. What I will tell you I don't tell everyone, Mr Hilditch, so I would take it as a kindness if you would keep it to yourself.'

'I hope you don't mistake me for someone who would betray a confidence, John.'

Rankin, shooting the bolt on a rough-made hutch, said, 'I was born and raised in the Dials. My mother was still a child herself when she had me. Unwed she was – I never met my father. It was just her and me to begin with. Years later, she married a cove called Horkiss, who was a coster with a pitch down at New Cut and she bore him two children. This 'Arry Horkiss was a drinker and when he was in his cups he was the life of the party. It wasn't until arter they were wed that his drinking become a problem and he was more often in the Blue Cow than he was with his donkey in Lambeth. He weren't never gay arter the drinking had taken a tight hold of him. He niver touched my mother, but he took it out on us kids instead. If I knew what was coming I would hide my sisters, sometimes in the chimney or in the midden and let him blow his temper out on me. What kid hasn't had a lick of the belt or a swipe with the rod? But the furies that took 'Arry Horkiss were something worse. It was like he put all his failures and his frustrations, the blackest part of his soul, into each kick and clout.'

'Your mother never intervened? Never said anything?'

'O' course not – it wasn't her place. Whatever else he was, he was the man o' the house. Half the time she niver knew what was going on about her. He'd say I got my cuts and bruises falling down the stairs. And she'd make out she believed him.'

'Was there nowhere you could go to escape this Horkiss?'

'And leave Rose and Sarah? How could they have stood what I had to? Well, as it turned out, I didn't have to stand much more of 'Arry Horkiss.'

'What became of him?'

'Drink did for him in the end and not too soon neither. He was found one morning face down in a gutter, 'aving cracked his poll upon a cobble. I can't say any of us was unduly sorry, even my mother. We was free of him but none the better for it. My mother was never a strong woman and now she was often sick and Rose and Sarah was always hungry or wanting something I couldn't give them. I had used to help Horkiss down at New Cut but with his passing I had no reg'lar occupation of my own. I was too young for a pitch at the market and for a while we lived off scant charity from neighbours in the court. We was all hungry with nothing to burn in the grate and I was shamed that I could do nought to help. But I was young and didn't know how a penny might be turned. But one day I found out.

'I had a pal called Jack who would give me the loan of a penny here and a half-penny there. I asked him how he come by the cash. The next day he took me and Sid Dawkins up West and I done my first bit of star glazing – we broke a shop window and made off with a handful of second-best jewellery. We took it to a fence in Cheapside who give us next to nothing for it. What I got that day fed the family for nigh on a week, so I couldn't afford no scruples. I joined the gang and became quite a reg'lar shoplifter. I'd chuck my cap into a shop so if anyone was there I might say I was only retrieving it. If the coast was clear I'd strip that shop as bare as a boy might, with only a minute to spare. I was good enough at that game to keep us in vittles. Mother knew what I was about but she never let on. She preferred to believe what I told her, that I earned it selling fruit at the New Cut. Perhaps it was because I had gotten used to sneaking about to avoid 'Arry Horkiss that I was so good at shoplifting. But good I was. Too good for the Dials, where they all knew me anyway and I soon had to move my operations up West. Just as well, too, as I was beginning to see as how I was robbing from my own, from people with little more than we had. The West End was a different matter but the shopkeepers were up to all the dodges and I stuck out like a horsefly on jelly.

'I didn't know that the thieves up West got themselves fancy-suited so they might pass as gents. They could breeze into any shop on Bond Street, jist as long as they kept their traps shut. The long and short of it is that I was soon taken and spent a few weeks behind a locked door. That was bad enough for a young first-timer but what hurt me most was knowing I wasn't there to help my family. When I got out I resolved to be more careful in future. Arter that, I cased every shop, watched and waited and gin'rally was successful.

'We was all having a little luck at this time; I suppose it was our turn. When my mother popped a half-hunter I said I'd found, she met a watch-making cove called Simmins. He was a meek little feller and I niver thought anything of him until one day she informed me that her and Mr Simmins was getting hitched and the family was off to Greenwich. I suppose that if I'd been as straight as I'd supposed myself and really was only filching for the family, I should have gone with them. They didn't need my support now and the money I got arter that, I generally saved. I stayed because I was accustomed to this new life and even liked the excitement. But without my family to provide for, my heart wasn't entirely in it and many was the time I was nearly taken up.

'About this time, as I watched the shops, I began to mark the pickpockets. You never see them as a rule, so practised and polished are they. Some work in twos: one chap distracts you while the other filches your pocket-book – or the patterer stuns you with fancy talk while t'other has his fingers in your every pocket. It looked a lot easier than the work I was about and I set myself to learn the trade.

'Sid Dawkins did a little in that line and he showed me how to lift a coat-tail and swipe a handkerchief as he brushed by his mark. I managed a few easy picks but many more times I was chased up the street. It was beginning to look like I was too clumsy to make a good pickpocket and I was reconsiderin' my future when I spied a portly gent peering into the window of a photographer's shop. The corner of what I judged to be a nicely-stuffed wallet was showing from a pocket. It was much too good an opportunity to pass up. I stood aside him at the window and I 'fected to be inspecting the photies too. He stood up straight to look at a shelf of Daguerreotypes and the tail of his coat fell over the pocket-book I was after. Sid had shown me what to do but I allus found it a deal harder when I couldn't see what I wanted to filch. I wanted the gent to bend over again, so the tails would slip off his pocket, but he persisted in staring up at these poor Daguerreotypes.

'Arter a while he says, "Lovely!" and I 'as to presume he's addressing me as there's no one else there. "Noble likenesses," says he and tells me that this one is Lord someone and that one's Lady something. The gent talks like 'Arry Stockrussy, but that don't stop me saying I've seen better pictures – which I had – and tryin' to direct the fat gent's attention to the Calotypes on the floor o' the window. "Whoever took them's the better photographer," I tells him. I'm hoping he'll bend low to look at these pictures. "Well, really!" he says. "Paper prints of coal-porters and costermongers. These are low in every sense!"

'He laughs at his little joke and I'm a piece provoked as I suppose I know a decent picture when I see one. "Begging pardon," says I, "but you ain't seeing them in the proper way. It looks to me that this here photographer ain't just taken their faces, he's exposed their characters too. Look closely at that coster there and then you'll find the chaps in the Daguerreotypes appear no more'n dummies."

'Mr Touchfarthing does me the kindness of comparing the two pictures, one above and one below but he just says I have not the trained eye. He looks me over and winks at me. What I need, he says, is takin' under the wing of someone who knows about these things. But he continues to admire the Dags and tut at the Calotypes and as his head is bobbing 'twixt one and the other, I'm glimpsing his pocket-book. Finally, I make a grab for it but it's not best-timed and he tumbles to me. I niver saw a cove look more shocked. I wasn't too sharp that day for he'd no sooner turned around and shouted "Stop thief!" than I was nabbed by two peelers who come out of the ground, I think, and took me up.

'This time I thought I was for transportation. I'm hauled off to Bow Street and the gent comes along with the peelers and me. I've been to Bow Street before and my mind isn't on the proceedings – it's somewhere down in Botany Bay, when I see Mr Touchfarthing looking at me peculiar. Then I hear him telling the peelers he's Lord Sibthorpe and that it's all been a mistake and that he would take it as the greatest kindness in the world if they would release me to his care. He says they must know of his philanthropic mission to set villains on the straight and narrer. He 'spects they have also heard of what he gives to police charities and I don't know what else he said but the next thing I know is that he and me are sprung and out on the streets again.

'I'd had the wind knocked out of me and hardly knew what was occurring. I remember walking with Mr Touchfarthing and him saying something about me being a perceptive young man who only wanted a bit of directing and would I do him the honour of takin' tea at his lodgings? I couldn't fathom any of this. What's he arter, I'm wondering? You don't get a feller off the peg once he's robbed you wi'out wanting something, do you? I was imagining all kinds of horrible things. There had been some terrible murders in the neighbourhood and I was wondering if I wasn't going to be the next carcase the police found in pieces. I can see now it was no way to show my gratitude, but the first chance I got I hooked it down an alley and out of sight.

'I niver thought I'd set eyes on the strange gent again until one day I saw there was a new photographer's shop in this here location. The last I saw, it was a flower-shop and I was curious to have a look at the photies in the window. I never could pass by a photographer's wivart givin' it the once over. In fact, I considered myself a bit of an expert in the science, which was how I had come to dispute with Mr T. Well, I had a proper gander at the window, saw there was quite a lot of rubbish up front and one or two good photographs hidden away at the back. I was so interested in it all that I didn't hear the shop door open nor anyone step out, 'til I felt a hand on my shoulder. I didn't recognise Mr Touchfarthing at first, as he wasn't dressed like a toff but had on his work clothes and was something more approaching what we recognise as 'uman.

'One way or the other we got talking and I concluded he wasn't no mad butcher and rather that he was a stunning gent. I had a bit of tea with him and before I knew it I had told him all about myself, about my thieving and even about the thirty pounds I had saved up. I'd been keeping most o' my spiles in a boot. I sort of hoped that some day I might find a honest use for the money – maybe start up a little business, though I had no precise idea what.

'Mr Touchfarthing again complimented me upon my eye and said it only needed directing and I might be of some use in the photographic business. It 'appened, he said, that an opening had arisen in his firm for a small investor. I think he was a little short of the readies if the truth was known. But I didn't 'ave to think long before I agreed to go in with him. Here was a chance to make a new start and in photography, too. The arrangement also suited Mr T.: he was new-come from the North and didn't know a soul in London. He appeared as much in want of a companion as a partner. And, it turns out, a cook and a cleaner and all that goes with it, but I don't mind that.' Rankin smiled ruefully and looked into the soul-shading dark glasses of the pensive Henry Hilditch. 'Now, you might take him for a strange fish, Mr T., but I ask you, what other cove would have done that for me?'

'It seems to me,' replied the other man, 'that if, on top of your professional duties, you perform also those of a domestic, then Mr Touchfarthing has the best of it. You'll forgive me, but when I saw vases of flowers and curtains on the windows I thought that Touchfarthing must keep a maid or had perhaps a wife somewhere.'

Rankin snorted. 'Mr T. take a wife? What woman would have him, I should like to know?'

Hilditch's face betrayed a keener interest than his voice pretended. 'Then you have never seen him in the company of a woman?'

'I ain't sure what you are saying, Mr H.'

'I mean a particular woman. Not above twenty-five years old. She might have accompanied him from Yorkshire.'

'I niver heard of Mr Touchfarthing keeping company up there. That would have been such a singular occurrence I should have known of it, I'm sure.'

'Ah. I am to be disappointed, I see.'

'Was there a particlar reason you asked?'

'Yes.' Hilditch resolved some contention within himself with a clicking of tongue and teeth. Quietly, as if speaking to a part of himself, he said, 'Perhaps if you know my quest you can be of some aid to me, John. I shall need a guide, someone who knows London much better than I if I am to find the person I seek. I can give you something for your trouble.'

'A few bob would be useful, for sure,' said Rankin. 'As you say, the more of the case I know, the better I might be able to help.'

In a faltering voice that sometimes ebbed away altogether, Henry Hilditch revealed to John Rankin the nature of his disquiet while Rankin sat in silence, sucking upon a blade of grass. When at last Hilditch had finished, John Rankin surprised the other man by promising his assistance without reservation. He would help find this Mary Medworth though they had to scour all London to do it. But what he couldn't tell Henry Hilditch then was just where they should start.

'It's been my idea that Mr Touchfarthing himself might help

us there,' said Hilditch. 'And that he knows more of Miss Medworth than he is prepared to tell me. Before we spoke I had thought him the root cause of these troubles. Perhaps I was wrong. But some part he has played, I am sure.'

John Rankin was again vouching for the character of Cornelius Touchfarthing when a short, high shriek burst from within the photographic studio. 'God blind me, what was that?' he exclaimed and his eye was at the glass in a moment. Henry Hilditch tore away a rag that stuffed a broken pane and both men peered into the old glasshouse. The sun was low in the evening sky and beams of russet-gold speared through the sloping glass and silhouetted two male figures, one notably tall and of prominent *embonpoint*, the other making a less substantial vignette. To one side, standing before a painted scene of indeterminate Eastern appearance, was a third figure. There, to John Rankin's astonishment, was the quivering white body of a young girl, whose wide eyes met his. Her small hands did what they might to cover her nakedness.

III

Henry Hilditch held back by the studio door but John Rankin entered the studio with such violence that he knocked over the standing camera into the big hands of Cornelius Touchfarthing. The girl, shielding herself with a crumpled cotton shift and seeing no escape from a predicament which promised to become more alarming by the moment, emitted a second screech and looked from one man to the next as if she were cornered by slavering wolves.

'For the love of God, pray silence, Miss Bowring! Have you gone mad?' said the Reverend Harold Rutter as Touchfarthing, his hands pressing his temples, expostulated, 'I warned you! You've gone too far!'

'She mistakes our intention, that's all,' said Mr Rutter.

'After this, I'm not sure I comprehend it myself,' said Mr Touchfarthing.

'It seems clear enough to me,' said John Rankin.

'You said Bible study,' the girl sobbed. 'You didn't say nothing about taking my clothes off.'

'I told you as plainly as I could what was required of you,' Rutter said.

'This was not what I had in mind,' said Mr Touchfarthing.

'I ain't that sort of a girl. Not like Jane Pipkin or Nell Vesey.'

'I agreed that the shift might fall from one shoulder,' Touchfarthing explained to John Rankin, 'thus suggesting the loss of innocence. I never agreed to this!'

'Come, Mr Touchfarthing,' Rutter said. 'You cannot have Eve dressed for a walk on a winter's day.'

'But naked, Mr Rutter, naked!'

'I wish I were back in Hemel, I do indeed,' the girl declared.

'Whatever was you thinking about, Mr T.? This could be wery bad for trade.'

'You have your business these days, Mr Rankin, and I have mine.'

'I think I have a say in what goes on in this studio,' said Rankin.

'This is a poor start, Mr Touchfarthing,' Rutter said. 'Bad enough we pick the wrong girl. Worse that we must suffer intrusions like this.'

'I'll intrude if any more o' this goes on. You can count on it,' Rankin said.

'John, I almost think you choose to misunderstand. You know about the photographs for the edification of the poor.'

'Edification's going to be very popular if you carry on like this,' Rankin muttered.

'What you witnessed just now,' said Mr Rutter, with a glance that sought strength from above, 'was our progenitress of trouble, Eve herself. The first of a series of depictions from the Scriptures. These won't be ordinary moral pictures, Mr Rankin. They will bring the Good Book to life.'

'Mr Rankin understands though he might pretend not to,' said Mr Touchfarthing. 'You see, John, that you are not alone in

112

extending a hand to the less fortunate. And not only do I confidently expect my ventures to keep us afloat, but they will, I think, be my first steps on the road towards creating real photographic art.'

'I don't know much about art,' said John Rankin, pointing to a wobbling screen behind which Miss Bowring was reclaiming her modesty, 'but I 'ope you don't think that's it.'

'I agree that a line was inadvertently overstepped on this occasion. But . . .'

The young girl, still snuffling, emerged from her screen and trembled with an admixture of fear and rage. 'All these people 'ave seen my all,' she quivered. 'What you going to do about that?'

'All these people are here for the sake of Art,' said Mr Rutter, patiently. 'This is the professional photographer without whom we cannot accomplish our aims. And this man, though he came uninvited, is entitled to be present by virtue of his trade. He is the photographer's assistant.'

'Partner, if you please.'

'So we shall be a little less hysterical in future, shall we?'

But the girl stamped a tiny foot and pointed beyond the Reverend Rutter and the commodious bulk of the photographer. 'Who's that?'

'Mr Rutter has told you. He's my assistant,' said Mr Touchfarthing, complacently.

'Not him,' breathed the girl. 'Him!'

Mr Touchfarthing turned and followed her pointing finger to the dark figure stood in the doorway. He came forwards as John Rankin whispered into the ear of Cornelius Touchfarthing. 'What with all of this, I forgot to mention it. Mr 'ilditch is here begging a moment of your time. He would be indebted if you would kindly furnish him with some information regarding a Miss Medworth, once of Sibthorpe Hall.'

9

Positive and Negative

'I say, this saves Mohomet's cab fare to Somers Town! Come in, Henry, come in!'

The inky-fingered clerks looked up from their table and two men who had obstructed the office door with their turf-talk and cigar-smoking abruptly made way for Henry Hilditch. Jabez Flynt beckoned the visitor over to his desk, where galley proofs and newsprint and dishevelled pyramids of correspondence competed for the available space. Some of this detritus fluttered to the floor as Flynt stood up and shook Henry Hilditch's hand.

'Here he is,' Flynt announced to four or five sub-editors at their tables and a checked-suited man drinking from an amber glass. 'The saviour of the *Messenger*!'

'Direct from the dust heaps,' muttered the suited gent, but nodded with as much cordiality as the clerks.

'Don't mind Treby,' said Flynt. 'He thinks as much of you as we all do. Ain't that so?' The audience had resumed its former occupations as Flynt, clasping Henry's shoulder, waved his free hand over his cramped domain. 'How do you like the *Morning Messenger*?'

'I suppose I imagined something larger,' said Hilditch, glancing idly at a wall papered with scribbled messages, lists and rosters and a crudely defaced photograph of an elderly sprat-seller. 'And perhaps a little neater.'

One of the seated men punched a bell upon his desk and a boy – who had bulleted past Hilditch on the stairs – grabbed at sheets of paper waved aloft by the men at the table and shot off again. The sub-editors, stationed at tables laden with more paper proofs and marmalade jars tickling with pens and ink, continued to move their rules slowly down columns of type, managing all the while to keep up their conversations with each other. The reporters by the door went on loudly broadcasting a discourse flagged with the names of politicians, murderers and race horses.

'Tell me Henry,' said Flynt, in softer tones. 'What can you smell?'

Hilditch frowned. 'Smell? Fried food. Tobacco, of course. And hot lead, I imagine?'

'Ha, yes! But I'll tell you what I can smell, Henry, and that's money! I wouldn't share this with them' – he pointed out the other reporters – 'but I can tell you that sales are positive. Very positive indeed! We're levelling with the *Chronicle* – and that's if we ain't already overtaken them. There's money in truth, Henry – it's a rare commodity. Look at these letters! They're fish on the hook; the bait is taken. Why, there's some here who are afraid to go out of doors because of your reports!' Flynt laughed loudly and flicked his lank hair back into place.

'I hope they are not all so serious,' Hilditch said.

'Do you know, we started our series with the very poor, the crossing sweepers, the costermongers, the street traders and so on. Then we introduced the sellers of horse turds, the scavengers on the dung hills, the toshers fossicking for pennies in the sewers – and that went better. But once we started to rub shoulders with the criminal classes, well, Henry, that's when we began to make a real difference! Make no mistake, this is what we must give *Messenger* readers now: the thieves and the street robbers, the pickpockets, the cracksmen and the prostitutes – especially the prostitutes, Henry! Perhaps even a murderer or two, hey?'

'As long as it diverts me, I shall do your bidding, Jabez.'

'You really must, Henry. I'm paying you twice what Treby gets.'

'You know that's not my motivation.'

'So you say. But if you're as rich as they say, why put up with those dreadful lodgings in Somers Town?'

'Where I live is of no concern to me, Jabez. In any case, I think rumours of my wealth are probably much exaggerated.'

'You're a quiz, Henry. I should like someone to write you up for the *Messenger* one day. Is this the new piece?'

'Notes for one, perhaps,' said Hilditch. Flynt scanned the two pages of closely-written manuscript while Hilditch, seated by the editor's desk, gazed out of the window at the spire on St Bride's Church.

'Promising,' Flynt muttered. 'What are star glazers?'

'Young shop thieves. They apply treacle to the window and knock it out.'

'Do they, by George? I'm learning a whole new vocabulary. What the devil is a bluey hunter?'

'He strips lead from roofs.'

'And a drag sneak?' Flynt's interrogation barely interrupted his concentration on the pages before him.

'Steals luggage. You might meet him at a railway terminus or a coach inn.'

'A noisy racket man?'

'Takes china from the bins outside shops.'

'Snow gatherer?'

'Snatches washing off hedges.'

'Smatter-hauler?'

'Handkerchiefs.'

'I think you might work this up, Henry, I really do. Damn me, if a run of such reports won't sink the *Chronicle*! Readers won't chance the other paper in case they miss a sensation in this! Treby couldn't do it. Your trick, it seems to me, is to instil a sensational story with the spirit of scientific enquiry. There's no mawkish sentiment with you, Henry. It's as if you were nailing misshapen butterflies against a newspaper background.'

'Well, I confess that these creatures fascinate me. We know so little about them and yet they swarm about us every day, outnumbering us ten to one. Look at the hordes in the street down there. We know no more of them than we do of the Hottentots in Africa. And they may be dangerous, as Europe is discovering. They should be studied, categorised, labelled, and . . .'

'Exhibited in glass cases? Not quite that, but they should entertain and sell newspapers!' said Jabez Flynt. 'Bring me more of this, Henry. I want the real villains. The sort of blackguards my readers will lose their sleep over. I want you to take them by their sweet-smelling scruffs and rub their noses in the real filth! Can you do that?'

'I'm not sure,' Henry said. 'But I have been spending as much time as I can in the East End. I am sure to come across something that will suit.'

'You are still searching for this enigmatic woman, then?'

'And will be doing, until I find her.'

'Well, Henry, if it's she who keeps you in these interesting places, I almost hope you may not find her. Here is your cheque. You will see that I have increased your fee.'

Henry pocketed the payment and had turned to leave when Flynt said, 'Oh, by the by, I nearly forgot. There is a fellow waiting for you. He turned up yesterday insisting to see *Enquirer*. I told him to come back today when you might be here. It was that or direct him to your lodging. You don't mind?'

A boy escorted Hilditch down the stairs and led him into a small ante-room off the entrance way. As the door was opened, a tall man in a threadbare frock-coat and a shabby hat looked up from a *Morning Messenger* and blew out a coach wheel of blue smoke. For a moment, Hilditch was unable to place him.

'Remember me, I suppose? Ratcliffe of the Life Guards?'

'You're out of uniform, Captain.'

'My uncle has the loan of that for the nonce.'

Ratcliffe appraised Hilditch's own appearance with a judicial eye. 'Odd to think that you are *Enquirer*. Of course, I knew it as soon as I read about the ratting at the Black Swan. I suppose I was the *sham military man*?'

'What is your business, Captain?'

'It's none of mine. I'm doing a favour for another. William Saggers.'

'Why doesn't Mr Saggers come himself?'

'Ho, that's ripe! There are those up West would love to have sight of William Saggers. He knows he's safest in Whitechapel and that's where he stays.'

'What does Saggers want with me?'

'I'm not a confounded oracle. He wants me to take you to him. If it's convenient.'

'It's not. I have business today; I must know why.'

'He says he has something that will interest you. I don't know nor much care what that something might be; my commission is only the message.'

The name of William Saggers returned to Hilditch the memory of his awkward departure from the rat pit and his impulse was to bid his visitor good day and turn upon his heels. But it occurred to him that this Saggers, surely a font of local knowledge, perhaps knew something that might lead him to Mary. When Hilditch had talked again to Touchfarthing, he had learnt that Miss Medworth had sent her baggage to an address in Shoreditch, which Touchfarthing was able to supply, along with his low opinion of the area. Henry had arrived in Shoreditch the same evening, only to be told that the lady had quit her rooms the day after she had taken them. She had boarded a cab with her bags and had given the direction, 'Whitechapel'. If he was relieved to hear that Mary had seemed in good health and spirits, he was as perplexed at her strange behaviour. Now someone with many confederates in Whitechapel, such as William Saggers, seemed the likeliest source of information. If nothing more, he could no doubt provide the sort of story Flynt was demanding for the *Morning Messenger*.

'Well, what is it to be, Mr Enquirer?' said Ratcliffe, coolly. 'You'll find him at Kelly's Yard, Moorgate, if you won't come with me.'

'You may tell Mr Saggers that I will wait upon him tomorrow evening,' Hilditch said, and leaving Ratcliffe to finish his smoke, he closed the door. From a balcony above, Jabez Flynt peered down with a quizzical eye.

II

Dear Henry,

I hope that this finds you well – and I hope also that you can make some sense of my hand. I have had made the strangest contraption that enables me to write along straight lines but whether the result is legible I can only guess!

It has been such a time since last we corresponded that I hesitate to begin now with a petition for help. However, as that help is for another, I trust you will overlook my presumption. Henry, I have to say that I am concerned for my brother George.

You might not know that it was I persuaded Father to send him to Italy, rather than away from home altogether. I had hoped to show him a world made of something other than port wine and horseflesh. Though brother and sister, we are very different people.

In those first weeks in Italy I even thought there was reason for supposing I had been right. Do you remember how you took my arm in the Uffizi and tried to describe the paintings, though I remembered each almost as well as you could see them? And how George condemned Donatello and praised that brute of a horse by Giambologna?

I had hoped that once we had returned from Italy things might be different. George had been so optimistic in Florence, so full of plans. Perhaps it was the accident,

120

or perhaps I was unable to see what was happening in our little group, but when we got back his plans seemed to dissolve in the damp Yorkshire air.

I think he suffered some severe disappointment. George isn't one to speak of matters of the heart and I can only guess its nature. I didn't know what was happening at first – only that he for ever cursed his luck and smelled strongly of brandy and horses. He spent his time and more money than he had at the races. Father and I hardly saw him from one month to the next.

Our news of George came through the most unpleasant channels. Tailors and wine merchants presented accounts in George's name; notes of hand were flying hither and thither. You may imagine my father's terrible choler when he learnt that George had been borrowing heavily against his expectations. He swore to cut George from his will and receive him no more at Sibthorpe. When George knew he was found out, he did stay away. He continued to write letters to me, but these always ended with requests for money. You might like to know, though, that he asked after you.

After you wrote to me, I told George that you were returned to England. I thought it would startle him to know that you were become a journalist and not the natural historian we had so certainly predicted. His last letter to me was dated in London. Perhaps he has already written to you or even visited in person? If so, you must tell him that his sister frets for him and that if he will only return to her, she shall find some way of melting his father's cold heart and of making things right again. If you have not encountered George, might I depend on our old friendship and ask you to draw on the resources that you must now have at your call, to find George and send him safely to me?

Tell me everything. Eliot can be trusted to read me

your reply without fear of my father knowing anything
of it.

Your good friend,
Agnes Devereaux

Agnes. It was long indeed since he had spared a thought for her.
The perfunctory note he had despatched to her when he had
arrived back in England had been a poor reward for someone
who had always tried to be his friend. Even so, it seemed wrong
and that he had been remiss. His mind retained few childhood
pictures in which Agnes was not featured, if only as a figure at
the edge of the frame. On the occasions when George had
dragged his neighbour from his hermitage of beetles and rocks
to join in high jinks at Sibthorpe, Agnes had so often made the
experience more bearable. While George showed off a new gun
or his fishing flies, or fought on the hearth with a slavering
terrier, there would Agnes have been, by a window with an open
book or her box of water-colours.

George had been overpowering, impossible to resist, but
Agnes had many times sat and listened while he explained to
her the life-cycles of beetles, the significance of trilobites and
the fantastic worlds he had discovered through the lens of his
microscope. Her brother thought Henry an odd fellow and
regularly wished aloud to have another neighbour, but if Agnes
thought him strange, she never showed it, unless such an opinion
was manifest as the wry smile that so often played about her
lips. In return, she showed him her paintings and talked to him
of her books and her studies and of an oft-projected visit with
relations in Italy. Agnes had been his defensive buffer against
the marauding good-will and exuberant vitality of the young
George Devereaux.

He should not have expelled her so peremptorily from his
mind. But to have thought of Agnes would have been to conjure
other, sourer memories. Even so, he knew he had been wrong.
He would write to George at his last-given address and ask that

the letter be forwarded to him. Irresolution cleared from his brow: in this letter he would promise – at the very least promise – to pay George the £50 he had begged of him and so bring him out from the shadows. Even the man George Devereaux had once likened to a staring dead fish could do no less for poor, blind Agnes.

Other lodgers were returning from their day's business; 'Halloa!'s and hearty greetings, slamming doors and boots thundering on staircases told Hilditch that he might as well bring his business of the afternoon to a close. He wrote a brief note to Agnes, not the 'everything' she asked, but a few friendly lines asking after her health and promising to watch out for her brother. He began to make notes for a piece he planned to write under his *Enquirer* pseudonym and so put Agnes once again from his mind. He was anxious to return to the East End.

III

The fog that made sickly halos of street lamps might as well have been a viscous slime through which bodies might percolate only with the patience of gasteropod molluscs – 'Commonly, snails,' Hilditch said aloud.

The omnibus had moved so slowly that Hilditch had begrudged the fare. He might, he thought as he alighted, have saved the money and enjoyed a warming nip of gin in the shop on the corner, not very far from Kelly's Yard. Once, he would not have taken a drink while upon his investigations, fearing that his objectivity might be compromised. Now, however, he recognised the value of a tot of brandy or a glass of hot gin and water. It loosened not only the tongue of his subject, but his own as well.

But it was late already and he passed by the brilliant entrance from which sounded the hullabaloo of loud and careless conversation – not so quickly, though, that a voice did not call after him, 'Hoy, Professor! Comin' in for a drain of pale?'

A boy sprang from the doorway and into his path. 'Now,

then, Professor,' he said. 'What you gone and done with Dan'l Saggers? I an't seen him since he was took up wiv you.' He turned to wink at his rag-tag following. 'Hey, you in't that cove what's doing away with young fellers, are you? Cutting up kids as neat as a Smithfield butcher? There's another 'un found at Limehouse Stairs.' The children, mostly unshod Hilditch noted, and wearing filthy, rent and almost comically ill-fitting garments, screeched with laughter and a girl, saucy-faced and gaudily made-up, asked Hilditch to stand them all a drink.

'Garn, you won' get a penny outuv 'at tight-arsed skinflint,' Pineapple Joe said. 'Not wivart you gives 'im your soul fust!'

Unperturbed, he continued on his way. It was strange how accustomed he had become to his new milieu. On recent forays he had experienced an exhilaration when he found himself again among the sweatshops and the brothels, the squalid tenements and the black alleys of Shoreditch and Wapping, Whitechapel and Spitalfields. Whether or not Flynt asked it of him, Hilditch increasingly had been haunting the public houses, cheap musical theatres, dancing rooms and street markets of East London. He had enquired assiduously after Mary, and had followed information that had led him into places where his very dreams had not trespassed. But of one thing he was certain. The more he was upon these streets and among these people, the sooner he would achieve the object of his quest. With such a thought in his head, he turned into Kelly's Yard.

IV

'You found him, did you, Captain? We had all but given up on him, eh, lads? But 'e don't look so well?'

'Give a hand there, damn you,' Ratcliffe growled as he and another man hauled Henry Hilditch on to a wear-shiny settle.

'Did you mace 'im, Captain? Taking him for another jintleman, mebbe? Anyone might do the same.'

Ratcliffe put a tin mug to Hilditch's lips. 'No one's maced him,' the soldier said. 'He's only knocked his head falling over some of that cursed clutter you fill up the yard with. Barrows, kennels, nightsoil. It's worse than a damned dust heap.'

'Looks a bad business,' observed Saggers, pointing to the unsightly scarring. 'That's old. He's had a bad knock but it's nothing that rest and little laudanum won't put right.'

'So speaks the medical man,' sneered William Saggers. 'Tell us, Ratcliffe: was you actually finished larnin' the doctor's trade afore you was dismissed the Army? I'm damned if I can remember.'

The thin man who sat beside him with a small dog at his ankle strangled a laugh as Ratcliffe looked up.

'Oh, you want to be careful of him,' Saggers announced to the two other men present, "e ain't one for a friendly joke.'

'What did you want with him anyway, Saggers? Some damned vicious piece of foolishness, I suppose.'

'Stay and find out or go now, it's all the same to me,' Saggers said. 'Don't keep the duns on your doorstep waiting. You're safe from the sponging house here and should be grateful, I'm thinking.'

'I wonder which is the worse place!' Ratcliffe snapped and stalked into an adjoining room, where he could be heard uncorking a bottle and spitting out the stopper. Hilditch took his bearings. The apartment was lit only by a great fire of broken wood that threatened at any moment to overspill its grate. Around it, on chairs of some antiquity and probable value – which were of no piece with the other poor sticks of furniture, the rags that blinded the windows and the dirty, bare floor – sat the thin man, who looked at William Saggers with the same expectant eyes as he was regarded by his dog; also a thick-set fellow in a wide-awake hat who clutched a bottle of spirits which the fleshy young woman beside him had evidently shared: she swayed on her seat, softly humming the tune of 'Lillibullero'. The stocky fellow said, 'Well, Bill? Shall we have at 'en, then?'

William Saggers looked at Henry Hilditch and gravely nodded his head. 'We're obliged to you for keeping your appointment,' he said. 'We've been waiting this last hour or maybe two, ain't we, mates?'

His head had begun to pulse with a dull pain and Hilditch cursed his own carelessness. He saw that his spectacles, presumed lost outside, had only been taken off him when Ratcliffe inspected his wound. He replaced them and said, shortly: 'I think you have something to show me?'

'I've that all right. But fust we have to talk, you and me.' The man's eyes squinted in the light of the guttering candle that stood between them on the table, amid the leavings of old cheese, hard bread and some overripe pears, as if he would pierce the opacity of the shading glass discs before him. 'You recollect the night you was a guest at the fancy as was organised and administered by me?'

The man with the dog scraped his chair towards Hilditch and said, 'I was there, Bill, I remembers it.'

Saggers' fat head rocked on its bearing. 'We took you for a regular sporting gentleman, come for the fancy. But that wasn't you. You wasn't like all the rest. You was there only to watch, you said. To hob-serve. And not the rats, neither. You was there to hob-serve us!'

The man with the dog nodded vigorously. 'Like freaks at the fair.'

'You come to us under a false flag,' Saggers said, in a low and studied tone. 'But now I think I've got your measure.'

'We all got that,' said the man in the hat, whose voice woke some memory in Hilditch's mind.

'You know my friends here, I believe,' said Saggers. 'Though I mark you don't greet 'em as you should. Are you denyin' the acquaintance of Abe Owen here?'

Saggers moved the candle so that the flame flickered in the bone-sharp visage of the dog man. His own face glowed with a lunar effulgence.

'I'm not sure,' began Hilditch, 'I can't remember everyone I . . .'

'Not sure?' said Saggers. 'Can't remember? Why, accordin' to

Abraham, you spent the best part of two hour drainin' him of his valuable larnin' and special experience.'

The man in question bit into a soft pear and wiped his mouth. ''E took it all and didn't give me nothing.'

'Just so,' said Saggers, in a judicious tone. 'And I believe you know this man and all? Tom Clute here was the gentleman whose time you took up in the Three Tuns, I believe. And what was it you told this here cove, Tom, out of a gen'rus desire to oblige him?'

'I let him into the thimble-rig lay and I told him how we sells the rotten fruit from Covint Gardin. Now that's knowledge worth money to some, but much good it did me.'

'Just as I thought,' said Saggers, rocking back in his chair like an over-dined judge. 'And what about you, Jen? Don't you have a 'plaint agin this gentleman?'

Tom Clute nudged the fat girl, whose attention to these proceedings had been scant.

'About the jintleman here,' Clute said. 'Tell Mister Saggers what he done to you.'

The girl laughed shrilly. ''Im? He didn't do nuffin', not in no normal way.' She laughed again and pinched Tom Clute's thigh. 'I tole 'im everythink he axed. 'Ow I'd growed up in Essex and got abused as a sarvin' girl and how I come to be working the gents in the Saracen's Head and all the time he's saying "Yes? Yes?" and axing to know the sort of things I wouldn't tell no one. Behind the bedroom door stuff. And I thought,' she winked at Tom Clute, 'he's biling as hot listenin' to this as my regular jints does when I . . . well, you know, Tom.'

The girl's hysterical laugh was drowned in a long pull from her bottle of spirits.

Tom Clute said, 'She give 'im her life and her good name, she did, for a rum and cloves and nothing more.'

'Not a penny he give me,' the girl spluttered. 'And now Willum here says my very secrets was all in the newspaper.'

'Every bit of 'em,' said Saggers. 'And I showed you what he writ about you, Abe, did I not?'

'You did, Bill, and it's been precious hard coming the cripple ever since.'

Tom Clute said, 'That's the problem, ain't it?' He pointed a dirty finger at Hilditch. 'You're giving the game away for nothing. Folk will get fly to the dodges, you see. For myself I find they ain't playing the peas like they was. And only a sennight past, I was marked in a public house as "that willun in the papers".'

Saggers knitted his fingers and exhaled a long and sickly breath. 'You done a lot, for a observer, it seems,' he said. 'Ruined lives, it seems to me.'

'Preposterous!' said Hilditch. 'I changed the names. They could not have been recognised.'

'You can come off your 'igh 'orse now, I think,' said Saggers. 'You listen to us for hour on hour, watch us all day long and now you say you don't believe us? I call that a affront, hey, mates?'

'If this is all you want with me, I'll be taking my leave,' said Hilditch, but Saggers obstructed his path with his chair.

'Mr 'Ilditch,' he said. 'You can see how we are fixed. We don't have money. We live from day to day, hand to mouth. Why, I shall most likely have to pop these chairs tomorrow – though it will break my heart.'

As Hilditch looked at his interrogators, he was conscious of a sickening fear mounting within him.

'We're honest folk who get along the best way we know how,' Saggers continued. 'And you've stolen from us. You've taken what was said on trust, posted it for all to see and got handsomely rewarded, I'm told. Now, it can't be right and proper for a chap to have his living taken away and his life exhibited in the newspaper and receive nothing for it.'

'That can't be right at all,' agreed Tom Clute. Abraham Owen nodded vigorously.

'I should say that something was owing to us and that you should be glad to pay that something. I think five pund for each of these would be about equable.'

'Five sovr'in. That's only right,' Owen said.

Hilditch's anger overcame his fear. 'I owe you nothing!' he exploded. 'I explained that I was engaged in research and that the exchanges might form part or all of some future publication. No one here demurred at that and no one refused the drink that I paid for.'

Ignoring this, Saggers said, 'As for me, I should be letting you off very lightly indeed if I was to accept only twenty guineas as a beginning.'

'The Devil you would!' exclaimed Hilditch. 'Just what makes you think I owe you a penny?'

'I see that I'll have to show you,' Saggers said, regaining his feet with some trouble. 'Come with me.'

'I've had enough of this, Mr Saggers. I think I will be cutting along.'

Saggers nodded at Tom Clute. 'This way, matey,' said Clute and pulled Hilditch's chair from the table.

Saggers, candle in hand, preceded Hilditch, Clute and Abraham Owen up a narrow, rotten staircase and along an equally treacherous passageway whose boards creaked and cracked under their weight. He unlocked the door at the passage end and beckoned Hilditch. As he stepped into the small chamber, sudden nausea overwhelmed his senses, the vilest stench filled his nose and his head and he whipped his handkerchief to his mouth.

'You've left it too fucking long, Saggers, too fucking long by half!' said Tom Clute.

'You're right at that,' Saggers murmured. He gripped Hilditch's wrist and pulled him towards a low bed on which was a tarpaulin-covered bundle. 'You look here and you look close,' he said as he unwrapped first a corner and then more of the tarpaulin cover. Saggers looked closely at the contents but Hilditch had to be pushed hard by Tom Clute before he was near enough to recognise the blond hair and lifeless, damaged face of Daniel Saggers.

Saggers shuddered. 'I thought it was cold enough to prevent him becoming so blessed maggotty.'

'You'll bury him now he's seen it, will you?' demanded Tom Clute.

'O' course I will,' said Saggers looking up at Henry Hilditch's white face. 'You 'ave seen it, an't you?'

Hilditch, trembling with an aggregation of confused emotion, struggled for breath and tried in vain to tear his eyes from the horror before them. He had seen death before, seen bodies pulled from the Thames and dead fishermen laid out at Whitby, but he had encountered these with cold objectivity. An icy dread told him that he was somehow personally linked with this dreadful spectacle. Blood at his temples pounded and as he spoke, he felt his guilt must be noticed by all. 'Why show me this? Why is he not buried?'

Saggers held the candle so that it burned brightly in the dark glasses on Hilditch's face. 'Because that is all your fault,' he said. 'All the fault of your interfering and your observing. I would never have dropped him into the ring again, not after the way he was the time before. But I was provoked by you with your ob-servations and your damned de-tachment. I would involve you yet, I thought. And the rats scratched him all to hell, they did and the wounds went bad. Oh Dan'l, what should have been my crutch in my old age. How is he to do that now? It's down to you, sir, to make up that loss.'

Hilditch looked once more at the dim face on the bed, at the awful wounds dried by death and the eyes closed with half-pennies. Tom Clute, his own face masked with a handkerchief, said, 'You'll pay for this. You'll pay for it all.'

Saggers turned the party towards the door. As they creaked along the landing, he said, 'I've been talking to a gent at your paper, name of Treby, who says Henry Hilditch is a gent of means. Money, Mr Hilditch, that's what we want, that's what you owe us. You can't make exhibitions of people without paying for the privilege.'

'This is monstrous, monstrous,' Hilditch choked, his mind full of the fair-faced boy who had shown him across London and the same boy overrun by rats, now dead and unburied.

Hilditch pushed past Saggers but the tallow candle held by Saggers was too weak to show the turn at the top of the stairs and Hilditch knocked blindly against the newel post and lost his footing. Clutching at posts, he crashed head over heels, down the steep flight of stairs to the floor below, where he lay senseless and still. Saggers stepped over his body as Captain Ratcliffe flew into the room. 'Get him on your bed, Saggers,' he said. 'Unless you want a gentleman found dead in your house. Blankets, my laudanum!'

V

'Mr 'Ildish! If you please!'

The guide, tireless and deaf to Hilditch's protestations of thirst and heat, hunger and fatigue, beckoned him on, down steps and steep hills to burning streets. Through fantastic Italianate arches they ran, pursued all the while by ravenous animals and great oscillations of fluttering moths. Packs of dogs chased numberless rats where children erupted from chimneys and shit-slimed toshers rose from steaming grates clutching pennies. Carpets of beetles crunched underfoot, human hands grasped and clutched and called out for his mercy. At last, his head throbbing and his legs giving way, Hilditch saw that he was arrived at the jet-black heart of the city where the winding river caught flashes from the light that was at the centre of all things. There the boat crossed and recrossed, bearing load upon load of prisoners bound for the Tench.

Now he could see it all. Great avenues radiated from the place where he stood like the spokes of his soul and each teemed as far as he could see with dead-eyed men all tramping relentlessly towards him yet getting no nearer. Drums beat insistently, tricolours waved from their poles and a voice at his ear hissed, 'What do you want with us, Mister Hilditch?' Another, louder, voice shouted through the din of the wind, 'It's you what wants obsarvin!'

And now the women had found him, harpies that pinched at

his cheeks and tore at his clothing. He screamed that his body must not be touched – and then a sudden gust sent a pink parasol spinning about a corner. 'Mary!' he shouted as loud as he might and began to run. His glasses slipped from his face and were trampled underfoot. Faster he ran, sliding on wet cobbles, through Whitechapel and Montmartre, tumbling down the hill from Fiesole, past laughing faces packed in upper-storey windows shouting for the snail or the caterpillar, the panther or the wolf. He circled the Campo twice, cheered on by the frenzied crowd, calling 'Mary! Mary!' but he had no sight of her nor her fine parasol. The mob was at his heels again, yet their faces were before him, accusing, pointing, jabbing, crying always, 'What is it that you want with us?'

The faces faded into swirling black smoke, the wind rose to a deafening blast. The guide was gone, no one to direct him now as he ran blindly, oblivious to hazards and also to the one small voice that sounded clearly above the hullabaloo, 'I can save you. Only let me save you.' Now as he approached the source of the fires, the palls of smoke began to dissipate. Before him, rising from it all and looming over everything else, was the top of a huge orange ball of fire, that shimmered and ossified, sharpened and defined itself until it finally resolved into a pin-sharp image of the enormous dome of Santa Maria del Fiore at Florence.

10

Interlude: Florence, 1850

Beneath an ultramarine sky from which the morning's rain clouds had been chased by a blustering southerly wind, Henry Hilditch was being guided through the streets of Florence by a blind-woman.

'No, Henry, you misread your map. If the Duomo is at our backs and this' – she tapped her cane lightly on smooth stone-work – 'is the Palazzo Rucellai, then turning left here will take us to some very lovely places – but not, I fear, to the Piazza Santa Maria Novella. Come along, Henry; you had better follow me.'

Henry frowned, thought better of his reply and stuffed the small paper map into his pocket. Agnes Devereaux, maintaining the brisk fearless pace which alarmed Henry and also anyone who got in her way, flicked her cane from side to side and marched on ahead.

'For Heaven's sake, be careful!' he expostulated. 'These streets are Bedlam!'

Henry took her elbow as he gazed in consternation at bullock carts, careening coaches and the overspilling pavements. He stopped her at the corner as a pair of cabs chased off down the Via del Purgatorio.

'I am careful, Henry. Only I'd like to get there before this place crumbles like Ancient Rome.'

With apparent prescience, she stepped deftly around importuning beggar boys and hungry ragazza. Henry shut his eyes for seconds only, curious about Agnes' perception of this wonderful place. He heard a whip crack and metal-rimmed wheels grind over a rutted road, Italian-speaking voices shouting in a room above him and, behind, some braying English tourists. When he opened his eyes Agnes was nowhere to be seen. He ran ahead and, turning on to the Via dei Palchetti, beheld Agnes in conversation with an olive-skinned man in a wide-brimmed hat. Taking him immediately for another of the local Lotharios who had marked out Agnes as easy prey or, charitably, had seen more in her pale complexion and petite form than a sightless woman of plain aspect, Henry was instantly at her side. But still the man talked, as if oblivious of his arrival.

'It would be an honour,' he was saying, 'to show you my city, though of course my knowledge of the painters and the builders will never compensate for your . . .'

Henry touched her arm, to show that he was there.

'I am extremely grateful, Signor Landini,' Agnes said. 'But today I have my protector in Mr Hilditch.'

'I beg your pardon,' Landini said, raising his hat to her companion. 'I wished only to put my little experience at your service.'

'I know,' said Agnes, as they parted. 'And I do thank you. But today I should like to be the guide. I have bored Mr Hilditch year upon year with my fond memories of Florence. Now he shall see everything for himself. But, Signor Landini, if you would like to wait on me at the Pension Vittorio on Wednesday, say, I should be happy to renew our friendship.'

They turned a corner and, crossing the piazza, approached the squat green and grey marble façade of Santa Maria Novella. The spring sun was hot on his neck and steam was rising from great puddles left by the morning's sudden downpour as they entered the great cool space of the basilica.

'Take me to the Masaccio,' Agnes whispered. 'I should like you to see that.'

As his eyes became accustomed to the obscurity and the dark chapels gave up their fading treasures, the hours Agnes had spent setting her cherished memories in granite paid dividends. Rarely did she enter a chapel whose name she did not know and whose contents she could not describe with exact and affecting accuracy. As she talked about the remembered frescoes or the carved sepulchres over whose cold stone she ran exploring hands, few of the tourists who stood with them would have taken Agnes for the party whose sight had been lost. She was tireless and refused to quit a place until every detail of every fresco had been reported to the best of her companion's abilities. Hours passed and then Henry, to whom all of this was entirely novel, conveyed without saying so much that his legs ached and that a man might enjoy a certain amount of this and no more. They found a cold seat before a great and gloomy fresco.

'I think I shall have to call on the skills of Signor Landini,' Agnes sighed. 'You were to be my eyes, Henry.'

'My eyes are more used to squinting into a microscope,' Henry said. 'It's all very pretty, of course, but just now I wonder whether there is only so much painted piety a man can stand.' Agnes' unusual silence prompted Henry to redouble his critical efforts. 'What this great thing here is supposed to be, I can't imagine.'

'Is this the Capella Strozzi?'

Without waiting for Henry to go off and enquire, she said, 'Then that will be the Inferno. Nardo di Cione, mid-Trecento. You read Cary's Dante at school, Henry?'

'I have some faded memory of it.'

'Well, look now and see if you can't find the shade of Virgil, guiding Dante through Hell. And on that wall must be Paradise. I don't remember that so well – is Beatrice there, Henry?'

'I don't know. It's all a confusion to me. The simple truth is that I don't have the language.'

'Ah, I was foolish to think I could enjoy this vicariously. I've made you suffer enough, Henry. Landini shall be my cicerone.'

After a moment in which he too became silent, Henry said, 'Who is this fellow?'

'A friend. Signor Landini is a sculptor – quite a fine one.'

'I thought he was taking a liberty.'

'When I came first to Florence as a girl of sixteen, I stayed at the Jennings'. They were dear people who introduced me to other dear English people. Signor Landini appeared to be their only Italian acquaintance. Had he not taken me under his wing I doubt I should have seen more than the English community here: I shall always be grateful to him. He has a studio on the Oltrarno. Should you like to see it?'

'I don't know. I promised to spend my time with George, too, you know.' A whiff of petulance hung in the air like altar smoke.

'Blow George, Henry. Unless he finds a horse-race or some other filly he's going to be kicking his heels this next six weeks. Come with me – Landini is excellent company.'

'More so than me, I suppose. Well, of course, you should not go alone.'

Why the Italian had got under his skin Henry could hardly fathom. It was his responsibility – and George's too, of course – to see she wasn't mown down by cabs on the Borgo San Lorenzo or accosted by ruffians in the backstreets by the river. It must follow that he should also protect her from the advances of ill-looking and questionable men. Whatever the reason, it could not be jealousy. Agnes was always only a good friend.

II

Henry Hilditch's appreciation of art began on the day that he joined Signor Landini and Agnes on their tour of Florence. Landini had kept his assignation with Agnes at the Pension Vittorio and had greeted her warmly and, in the tenderest fashion, had expressed his astonishment and his pain at her blindness.

On meeting her earlier, he had suggested they go again to the places they had enjoyed when, five years before, he had introduced Agnes to the splendours of his city. Now he regretted his own deficient sight – he had not immediately perceived that she was blind. He suggested they change their plans. They must visit Boboli and enjoy the scented evergreens. She would come to his studio where she might trace the fruition of his inspiration with her fingers. Smiling, Agnes had firmly declined. It had been her intention to revisit her favourite places and to take whatever pleasure might be derived from a second-hand experience. She would be indebted if she might count upon Signor Landini's practised eye.

Henry, who agreed as a matter of course to be of their party, had spent the preceding days in the company of George and so was the more eager to partake of sedate pleasures. George's amusements, beside nocturnal card games with the English fast crowd that he had located only days after their arrival, had included racing Henry, for a five-shilling prize, to the top of Giotto's campanile; frightening him with an exploration of the massive dome of Santa Maria del Fiore and joining a rat hunt by the river. The painted saints of which he had tired after their first few days in Florence appeared very agreeable after George's hectic pursuit of distraction.

Landini was, as Agnes had said, 'excellent company'. With Agnes on his arm and Henry at his side, he described in critical detail the paintings of annunciations and crucifixions, feasts and last suppers. He led them before carved pietàs and depositions, which he alternately derided and applauded with infectious enthusiasm.

His own work, which he created in his studio below the hillside church of San Miniato, was lithe and graceful, his figures slender and smooth to the touch. But, Henry had thought, as he stood alone upon Landini's loggia while the artist and Agnes sat within and talked softly to themselves, anyone might make beauty in such a place. From the church above, evensong filtered through the trailing honeysuckle and bougainvillaea, which was all that obstructed a vista that comprehended the Arno, the Ponte Vecchio, the Duomo and Bargello and, raggedly fraying towards the distant hills, the city of Florence in its entirety.

To Henry, Landini was polite and answered his visitor's every question with careful consideration. He was solicitous of Henry's well-being and enjoyment, and the sculptor's knowledge of the city, its art and its people revolutionised Henry's experience. Once, Landini had begged a restorer cleaning a Heaven-crowded ceiling to allow them a closer view of his work. With Agnes safely seated down below, Henry and Landini had scaled a succession of ladders until they attained the precarious perch on which the man dabbled with his brushes and cloths. Gazing from this panoply of Heaven upon the sprinkling of tourists below, Henry could not but feel favoured. Among disporting cherubs and angelic hosts, he looked down upon the succession of frescoed chapels, on the ornately-decorated font and pulpit, the intricately carved arches and capitals of the edifice itself. As Landini talked about the patrons and the power that had made all this possible, Henry was overpowered at last by the wonder of it all.

And yet he was anything but grateful for Landini's attentions: the more the liberally-educated artist quoted from Petrarch, discussed the philosophers or discoursed upon art, the more Henry felt keenly the bounds of his own learning. The schooling that had been sufficient for closeted entomological studies and social interaction with Yorkshire townspeople was proving an inadequate preparation for the wider world. No wonder Agnes seemed to prefer the company of her worldly friend. He made it his business to know and understand more of Landini's world and was gratified when Agnes expressed her great pleasure at his new-found interest.

After a Thursday morning on which they had visited Santa Croce and Santa Spirito and had picnicked on cold chicken and ham and a full red wine in the Boboli Gardens, they had, tired and hot, drifted in desultory order into the shade of one more church. Landini was talking to Agnes of his family at Siena and in his turn was asking after Agnes' life in England. Henry, strolling among the piers and pews, was also turning his thoughts to home, in which direction they would be starting in a fortnight's time. It hardly seemed possible that he should shortly leave all this behind, consign this brilliant experience to his memory and become once again the unremarked drudge of his father's counting house.

When he had first come to this other Byzantium he had felt conspicuously foreign, had thought it obvious to all that, a single flying visit to London apart, the furthest extent of his peregrinations had been to Leeds and Harrogate. Yet after only a short time, he felt himself hungry for wider experience. He felt incomplete and unfinished, that something was missing from his life. He thought that perhaps he wished to travel further, to widen his appreciation of art, to be filled again with the sense of wonder that had imbued him here in Florence. George Devereaux too had enlarged his own expectations. Drunk with wine and passion, he and Henry talked a night through about what they should do upon their return. George, whose father despaired of his son's future, was certain that he only needed a little capital to come right in the world. 'Give me some money and I'll show them all, by God,' he had declared, spilling red wine as he shook his glass at the world. While George held forth, Henry had sat quietly, pondering the emptiness at his core and wondering what in the world might fill it.

Only days later he had the answer. Agnes and Landini out of sight and whispering in another chapel, Henry had stopped before a fresco of a lambent Madonna and Child. The Madonna was striking. Unfaded or perhaps retouched, the blue eyes shone out from a face that shed love upon the child lying peaceably in the folds of her indigo robes. Henry compared it in his mind with Madonnas he had admired by Duccio and Cimabue and found them wanting. He made an effort to objectify the work as Agnes had taught him, to appraise its use of space and colour, the composition of its elements – but found it useless. His response to this was purely emotional, the feelings aroused within him revealing. Curious, he sat down, but now his view of the Madonna was obstructed by another figure – a young woman, sitting directly before him. He shifted his position, the better to admire the fresco, but found himself looking at the woman instead. She was lit by a blaze of light entering from the clerestory, which ignited auburn curls descending from beneath a small and pretty hat. The effect was striking, almost theatrical. Sensing his movements, the woman turned and bright eyes greeted his surprised gaze.

III

'I beg your pardon,' she said. The light above and behind, her face was in shadow, yet he knew she was smiling. 'I'm in your way.'

She began to gather her skirts. Henry, so often at a loss for words with strange women, said, 'Please – don't move for me.'

She thanked him and turned her slender neck to the fresco and her face into the light.

'It is beautiful, isn't it?'

'I think so,' said Henry, but he was thinking really of how like the Madonna's was this face: bright, clear; beautiful, in fact. It appeared that he had swallowed his powers of speech and he had to cough into his hand before he could add, 'Though some pass it by.'

'Oh, I could not do that,' said the woman.

'Nor I,' said Henry. 'Though I'm struck by the discovery that I have no idea who painted it.'

'No more have I,' said the woman. 'And I'm glad of it. We should ignore the names and reputations and let our own tastes decide what is good, don't you think?'

Henry thought for a moment, looked again at the Madonna and laughed. 'Well, perhaps I do now,' he said.

They made their own introductions and he discovered that her name was Mary Medworth; that she was visiting with distant relatives; and that Florence was a wonderful place but might perhaps be a little more so if one's only company weren't one's

140

great-aunt and uncle, a couple of well-meaning but essentially dull chaperones. Henry watched her lips moving without attending to all she said. She noticed his distraction and asked his own business in Florence. Leaving out his role as a kind of chaperone himself, he stumbled through an alternative explanation for his presence.

Much later, he recalled that he had told her something of his family; had said rather more than he meant about their local standing; and had declared that it was the duty of a man of sensibilities to broaden his horizons. Never before had his conversation with a woman been so effortless. He sat at his ease in a nearby pew and talked about whatever came into his mind. She nodded and agreed, flashed her pretty smile and laughed. He saw Agnes and Landini waiting for him at the church door and waved them off: he would see them later.

Miss Medworth watched the couple depart. Surely that was Signor Landini, the sculptor? She had seen Landini at an exhibition and dinner at which he had been the guest of honour. Her guardians had attended at the invitation of a minor official and their party had not merited an introduction to the great man himself. Henry made some offhand remark about Landini's work and Mary, pretending to be shocked, had laughed loudly enough to bring a tall and gaunt woman scuttling from the shadows of an adjoining chapel. Invisible strings drew after her a shorter, older man.

'So there you are, Mary,' said the woman, briskly. She lifted a cracked lorgnette and peered questioningly at Henry Hilditch.

'This is Mr Hilditch, Aunt,' Miss Medworth said. 'Mr Hilditch dines with Mr Landini this evening.' The woman peered more closely at Henry, as if she had mistaken his species. She straightened her back and nodded.

'I haven't had the pleasure of Signor Landini's acquaintance myself.' She appeared to address Miss Medworth. 'Met others; never Landini.'

'My aunt is a dilettante,' Mary said. 'She collects.'

'I have an eye,' the aunt said, turning the same on Hilditch.

'Landini's beyond my purse, I regret. Though I imagine the man himself is a fascination?'

Miss Medworth looked to Henry for authority. 'Mr Landini is,' he began and faltered, his gaze transfixed by the pink luminescence of Miss Medworth's throat.

'A foremost Florentine artist,' the woman snapped. 'Or Sienese, I suppose I should say.'

Miss Medworth took this moment to introduce to Henry her guardians, Mr and Mrs Fenwick. 'And do you know Signor Landini intimately, Mr Hilditch?' Mrs Fenwick sniffed.

'Well enough, I think. He has consented to be our guide throughout our stay in Florence.'

'Well, well, an honour indeed!'

'I don't know about that,' Henry said. 'But if it would please you, I should be happy to arrange an introduction.' On an impulse, he added, 'Why not come to tea at his studio on Wednesday?'

'Oh, yes!' said Miss Medworth. 'That would be just the thing!'

'I'm not sure that would be proper,' Mrs Fenwick said stiffly. 'Would that be proper, Charles?' She seemed to take Mr Fenwick's blank and blinking look as a mark of assent.

'He would not object?' Miss Medworth asked.

'Landini always is obliging. My friends are welcome, I assure you.'

'Well, if you're quite sure,' Mrs Fenwick said. 'Come along, Mary; Simpson will have our tea on the table. We must bid Mr Hilditch adieu.'

'Until Wednesday, then,' Henry said.

The girl smiled and nodded. When they had gone and the last shimmering vestiges of Mary Medworth's pink dress were dissolved utterly in the white brilliance of the sunlight beyond the doorway, Henry sat down again, his heart beating so loudly that passers-by must surely hear. He was lost in wonder that the world could change entirely in an instant.

IV

For the best part of a week, an ill humour had possessed the vital spirit of George Devereaux who sat now with his shoes upon a chair, stirring idly the cold contents of a china cup.

'It's all very well for you, Aggie,' he said, and then remembered himself. 'No, of course it's not all right. But you do at least have old Landini to talk to. Someone who shares your passions. Really, this is your sort of place, not mine.'

'I wish Father might have condemned you to another banishment, Georgie. But you will be back in Yorkshire soon enough.'

'Back to being his unpaid land agent. Back to the ditching and the coppicing, the disputes with the tenants, the crumbling East Cliff. I wasn't made for all that, Aggie.'

'Father can't run the estate on his own any more,' Agnes said. 'If you do nothing more to anger him it will be yours one day. You should be helping him to husband our resources.'

'What is the point of that? Each year the sea eats away more and more of our land. The east pasture has gone – the lawn is going. At this rate there will be nothing left to husband.'

'Father is seeing what might be done. He has been talking to Mr Short at Scarborough.'

'That projector? We would lose more shoring up the East Cliff than we would to the sea. We can't afford to get into all that. And where would be the money?'

'He means to sell off Widow's Wood.'

'He'd do better starting me in life. I've a head full of ideas – I only need a decent stake.'

'Now that really would be like throwing his money away,' Agnes said. 'You are profligate, George. How are you to keep any money if you will gamble?'

'Gambling is something I am good at. If he won't give me the money, then I'll get it at the tables and the race-tracks.'

'He will cut you off without a penny if you persist.'

'There will be nothing to be cut off from at this rate. He should let me have capital now while he still has some left. How am I to get ahead otherwise? I tell you, Aggie, it goes hard.'

Henry Hilditch entered at this moment, whistling a popular tune. He slipped on a coat which had been tossed upon a chair and straightened his hair in the over-mantel mirror. George opened an eye and watched him with interest.

'I can't join you for dinner,' Henry said as he fastened a cuff. 'I have an appointment.'

'Another?' George said. 'And when shall we meet her, this mystery of yours?'

'Wednesday. At Landini's, if you like. How do I look?'

'Good God, I don't know, Henry,' George said. 'Dressed, for a change.'

'Good,' Henry said. He tugged a crease from his waistcoat and stole a final glance in the mirror. 'And now I really must go,' he said. 'A man should show himself on such a fine day.'

When Hilditch's steps could be heard no more and the cane he had bought that day had ceased to click upon the flagged yard outside the Pension Vittorio, George broke the silence.

'Do you detect some small change in Henry?'

Agnes laughed. 'A revolution, you mean. Why, only this morning he bought me a great bunch of the sweetest-smelling violets. With money from his own purse, too!'

'And not a murmur when I found myself without lira yesterday. Overnight he has become open-handed, optimistic and debonair. Well, it was high time he kept female company. He was becoming as dry as a stick.'

'I should give much to see Henry in his new clothes,' Agnes said, and smiled as she set her chair gently rocking.

V

Henry, paying for a small decorative bowl on the Ponte Vecchio – the tone of the gift would be just right – was pleasantly surprised by his own image in a shop mirror. Encouraged by Agnes and spurred on by his recent meeting with Mary, he had, after some procrastination, bought an off-the-peg but highly fashionable suit of clothes. Beguiled by the reflection, he admired the cut of the cloth, the highly-polished shoes, the silver-topped cane and concluded that Landini himself was no better turned out. Henry had never spent so much money in his life and yet, he thought, as he looked again at the dandy in the glass, it was probably worth it.

Minutes later, as he crossed the Arno and mingled with the Florentines who promenaded in the yellow light of the setting sun, he no longer felt marked out as an ungainly alien but joined the *passagiata* with confidence and in such colourful company arrived at the Palazzo Vecchio where Mary Medworth, twirling a pink parasol, was in conversation with a young man of dark complexion. She saw Henry and waved.

'I've been having such an adventure,' she told him, as the young man disappeared into a crowded narrow street. 'That man offered me jewellery. Stolen, for certain!'

'Whatever next!' Henry said, his momentary apprehension dissipated by her smile.

Henry had not had to wait for the Wednesday to see Mary Medworth again. Such were the rails on which tourists ran that they met outside San Marco the very next day, where Henry talked to Mr and Mrs Fenwick about Savonarola and Mary attended his every word.

They saw each other the next day near the Duomo, both intending to examine the Baptistery doors. This time she was alone and a discussion of Ghiberti's metal-work quickly gave way to a more intimate conversation about their private lives. They had stopped on a corner, below a niche in which was installed a plaster Virgin. He found in Mary the best of listeners. Encouraged by her rapt attention, he talked of anything and everything: of himself and his philosophic interests, and of his friends George and Agnes, even of Hilditch and Co. Now, as they walked slowly through narrow streets, she remarked how becoming were his new clothes.

After hesitating the length of a street, he offered her the bowl. She was delighted and promised to cherish it for ever. She made him feel worldly, interesting and brimful of confident optimism for the future. A future that might, dare he think it, include this extraordinary creature whose fragrance overpowered his senses and whose delicate fingers now touched his wrist. Her brown eyes looked up into his own as she told him that above all things she hoped they would be able to continue their friendship after they both had left Florence.

Miss Medworth, he learnt, was from a place in Derbyshire, no great distance from Henry's North Riding. Her father had been a successful man of business but – she would not keep the truth from him – he had suffered a terrible reverse in his fortunes. A venture in which he had invested heavily had failed and he had lost not only his own capital but also that of the townsmen who had gone in with him. Threatened with prison, Mary's father had been obliged to decamp to the Continent until he could make good their loss. As if that ill-stroke were not enough, her ailing mother, no doubt weakened by the cataclysm, had succumbed soon afterwards.

Mary had no wish to share the life of a penniless émigré at Boulogne and her father had agreed that she might take up a long-standing invitation to visit with her great-aunt in Florence, but her guardians, who had last seen Mary as a girl of seven years, found themselves unequal to the care of a young woman of twenty. Mary herself could see no future in this gilded sponging house of poor relations, distressed gentlefolk and, though she stopped short of saying so much to Henry, ineligible marriage prospects. She touched a handkerchief to her eye. 'Oh, whatever shall I do?' Henry, with no clear idea in mind, nevertheless told her not to worry, that something would be found to answer.

They had got only as far as the Uffizi when he knew what that answer would be. It was impetuous, perhaps foolhardy. He had known her only a matter of days and yet each one had seemed a little lifetime in which he had grown like a dry plant after summer rain. Withered buds miraculously had blossomed and borne fruit. Never in his life had he considered such an audacious action but, prompted by the pyrotechnical experience of first love and chilled by the dread that this chance might pass him by, he decided there and then to make Mary Medworth his wife.

VI

Landini, to whom Agnes had explained and apologised for Henry's presumption, had welcomed Mrs Fenwick and Agnes to his atelier on the appointed Wednesday. Mrs Fenwick had left her snappish demeanour at home and, with Landini at least, was calf-meek as he explained to her his work in progress and exhibited his own collection of art and artefacts. Agnes, sitting in a wicker chair on the loggia where the sun warmed her face, smiled broadly as Henry introduced Miss Mary Medworth.

'I should like to say he has told me all about you,' Agnes said. 'But Henry is often very closed.'

Henry frowned and said that if they were to talk of him in such a way, he would go off and see about some lemonade.

'He has not been so closed with me,' Miss Medworth said. 'He has told me so much about you that I knew I should love you at once.'

Agnes smiled at such pretty flattery but as she made no immediate reply, Mary continued, 'I understand you were here before, Miss Devereaux, when you could . . .' She stopped.

'When I could see, yes. After the doctors had told me that I must soon go blind, I was determined to see all I loved here one more time. I should have been here two years ago, but my sight failed much sooner than they predicted.'

'How terrible for you,' Miss Medworth said.

'I confess that in the beginning I was desolate. Before, I used to paint – only pretty water-colours, nothing grand – and I read a lot. To be denied both pleasures was a devastation. And of course, my expedition to Florence was not to be thought of – not then. I had all to do contriving ways to get along in the house, never mind the wide world.'

147

'And yet here you are.'

'Here I am at last, though supervised by a pair of philistines who would rather be anywhere else. Though Henry, I think, may be reviewing his opinion.'

'Have you known Henry a long time?' Mary asked as she gazed out over the city.

'Since we were children,' Agnes said. 'George and he were thrown together by geography and snobbery. My parents were very selective about their children's playmates. Henry was the only child nearby whose family was of sufficient standing.'

'The Hilditches are prominent in Whitby?'

'Oh, yes. Although Mr Hilditch's misfortunes in recent years have not been without their consequences.'

'The Devereaux sound equally grand. More so, I think?'

'It's hard to be grand under a leaky roof. We have the house and the estate – so I suppose we have standing. At least among those whose accounts aren't still stuck on spikes on my father's desk.'

'I'm sure you are very well thought of,' Miss Medworth said. 'But what for your future, if I am not too bold?'

'I shall return to Yorkshire where I may be of some help to my father. Henry will come as he always has, and he shall read to me as we take the air along the cliff walk. I think sometimes about opening a school for the children of the tenants on the estate. Would I make a believable school dame?'

'I think you might be anything you wanted,' Mary Medworth said. 'There is much to do on such a large estate?'

'Too much for my father. He is getting on. How George will manage it when he succeeds, I don't know.' She sat up as a loud laugh rang against marble and plaster.

'There's George now,' she said, and the laughter grew louder still as George and Henry stepped out upon the loggia.

'Good Lord, who is that dreadful old harridan with Landini in there?' he asked of anyone at all. 'I didn't dare say anything for fear she might bite me.'

'That is Miss Medworth's great-aunt,' said Henry. 'George,

this is my mystery. Miss Medworth, may I present my friend George Devereaux?'

Mary, who had remained by the parapet, gazing blindly towards the distant hills, turned and smiled. George, quickly dabbing wine from his thick moustache with his pocket handkerchief, himself beamed broadly as he pressed her hand to his lips. 'I am truly enchanted,' he said.

VII

There was no question of Landini remaining in Florence during the first week of July; he had to return to Siena as he did each year, like a nesting bird.

If Henry and his companions knew little or nothing of the Palio before they set off from Florence, they knew a great deal more by the time Landini gave the reins to the ostler in Siena. Landini had driven the hired gig with Agnes at his side while Mary Medworth sat behind, between Henry and George. 'Above all,' Landini was calling over his shoulder, 'you must understand that the *contrada* is everything. To be born into the *contrada* is to be a caterpillar, a snail, a giraffe or a panther all of your life. All the honour of the *contrada* rides with your horse at *il cencio*.'

'Il what?' George shouted, his apathy of recent days vanquished entirely by the propect of the horse-race.

'The rag,' Landini called back. 'Our name for the Palio. When our *contrada* wins there will be celebrations such as you never saw.'

'And if it loses?'

'It is unthinkable,' Landini said as he cracked his whip. 'Especially on the day before the race.'

'We have to reckon with the possibility,' George shouted. 'Should I bet on it being placed instead?'

'Placed?'

'Coming in second, say,' George said, hanging on to Landini's seat, the better to enjoy his turf talk.

'To finish second is a disgrace,' Landini said, spitting on

149

the dust. 'We might as well be a *contrada* like Il Bruco, who never win.'

'I say, this sounds just the thing,' George said. 'What think you, Miss Medworth?'

'It must be glorious – where do they race?'

'Around the Piazza del Campo, the town square,' Landini said. 'I thought everyone in the world knew that. The dirt will be down by now and already the trials will have been run, the horses chosen. Ten out of the seventeen *contrada*s enter a horse.'

'What are the odds on your *contrada* this time?' George asked.

'This is not a horse-race like any other. *Contrada*s ally themselves to beat rivals, deals are done all year and by the jockeys right up to the rope. The result is hard to predict. You should know much more before you venture your money.'

'I'll know enough before I make my wager, you may be sure of that!'

Henry was watching Mary out of the corner of his eye. He followed the fall of leafy shadows on her pink skin and the movements in her throat as she laughed, as she did now, saying something about 'so much trouble for a bit of cloth!' For the moment Henry was content to say nothing. He was happy, immeasurably so, just to listen to Mary chatting with the others. Later, he would talk. At some carefully chosen point that day, he would ask her to marry him.

He was not concerned about what might come after. Just so long as she said yes, which, given her position relative to his own, she must surely do, he would be happy. For a while they would remain at Whitby, but he would return to his desk with a new heart. When they had a little money they would make their way together in the world. Anywhere, it didn't really matter. He settled back in the seat and let the balmy air wash over him.

Landini's *contrada* was reached only after they had passed through several others – and at each, some *contradaiolo* in parti-coloured clothing had invited them to drink to the success of the unicorn, the eagle or the dragon. By the time they had alighted in one of the narrow winding streets walled on both sides by towering ancient houses, the sun had set and they joined the ragged procession climbing the hill by the golden light of countless flickering torches. Landini, who in Florence had sometimes appeared aloof, now surprised everyone by bursting into song, his fine bass voice finding an echo from antique stone. Hastened on by those that followed, they entered into a small square.

'Oh, look! George, Henry, look!' Mary Medworth cried. She clapped her hands as she beheld the packed refectory tables that ran almost the length of the square. Lanterns swung from windows and trees while a thousand candles illuminated perhaps as many diners. They were drowning in noise: a song begun at a far table had been taken up by the next and was spreading like fire all about the square. Henry held Agnes back as a man pushed past bearing dark bottles and plates of food.

'Luco!' Landini blocked his way and shouted above the clamour. 'Where is my family?'

'The same place, Marco,' the man said, hurrying on his way. 'At the top of the middle table.'

Landini joined the singing as he led his guests up a long narrow aisle between the tables, and caused a bow-wave of recognition as he went. Some slapped his back, others grabbed his hand, while an anonymous voice laughed loudly and called him a cursed Florentine. Behind him came George, also shaking hands with people he had never seen before and could barely see now, and then Mary, smiling broadly, accepting the compliments of strangers, and Agnes, Henry doing what he might to protect her from accidental blows and buffeting as they went. Finally they were roughly accommodated, all squeezed on to already crowded benches and introductions were made to Landini's father, a fat, grey-bearded man dressed in the *contrada*'s colours, and his mother, a dark and beautiful woman arrayed in medieval style. Only when the singing had died was the excited chatter audible; it was made comprehensible to the English party when Landini could decently interrupt his conversation with his parents and translate for them.

'They are talking Palio history,' Landini told George. 'Of our last victory ten years ago. This year we are very pleased with the horse we were allotted.'

'Don't you pick the nag yourself?' George said.

'It is done by lots,' Landini said. 'But the Virgin has blessed us and we have a good horse and a great Sardinian jockey, who will surely bring back the Palio tomorrow. That is what they are saying.'

'Ask the fellow there about the horse,' George said. 'Ask about its form.'

But George's neighbour answered himself, in broken English punctuated with alarming gesticulation. When it became clear that the Englishman knew his horseflesh and was almost as fanatical about the race as they, his glass was kept full and his ears rang with a thousand stories surrounding the event. Landini was thus allowed to continue his talk with his parents.

While George was attempting to convey the importance of his big win at the last St Leger, Agnes sat alone in her darkness, looking anything but comfortable in this loud and strange mêlée. Mary Medworth raised her cup and when she said to Henry that this evening was so very wonderful, he knew that his moment was come. He must ask her now or lose the moment. He had no ring, but she would choose something beautiful and unique herself on the Ponte Vecchio later. He took a draught from his wine glass, cleared his throat and turned to his intended. But Mary was up on her feet, singing. She smiled at him as he too stood up and he was on the point of putting his arms about her and whispering their future in her ear when he felt a sharp urgent tug at his coat and was aware of Agnes, her voice unusually shrill, calling his name.

'Henry, please,' she said. 'This is too much. I'm frightened. So many people falling into me, it's like Hell. I'm sorry, but will you please take me home?'

VIII

On the morning of the Palio, Agnes begged to be allowed to stay at the hotel, claiming that she would be just as content to sit upon the small balcony and listen to the sounds of the bands and the passing merry-makers. She was, she confided to Henry, much too frightened of the noisy crowds that were already milling in the streets. He had knocked on George's door an hour earlier and again a half hour later and now stood in a block of sunlight at the entrance, awaiting the appearance of his friends. He had hoped to be about earlier than this, that he might find the chance to be alone with Mary, and then to issue his proposal. But he spent a long time shuffling about the lobby while the doorman strained to see the happenings in the street as the joyful people passed by.

When Henry turned from the spectacle without, Mary was there. He excused himself for withdrawing from the dinner so early. She understood entirely.

'George is keeping us waiting,' Henry said. 'How very vexing on such a day. But perhaps it will be for the best – come and sit with me on the sofa there. I have something to ask you.'

But the small sofa occupying a discreet alcove was never attained; just then the quick tread of leather soles sounded on the stairs and George entered at a clip.

'There you are, you two! Have you breakfasted? No, well never mind, we can eat something later.' He beckoned them into the brilliant sunlight. 'Let's be away – we must not miss a thing.'

By early afternoon, after a morning spent mingling with a press of spectators from the various *contrada*s, and every town in Tuscany and beyond, and hearing the many musical bands and watching the flags twirled and coming across knots of *contradaioli* in urgent argument and drinking from jugs of water and eating sticky confections bought from vendors' trays, they arrived at the chapel where Landini had said he would meet them. It was full already and only with difficulty and by whispering Landini's name was some room made for them at the back.

Landini was nowhere to be seen, but his father's bulky figure was easily distinguished through the haze of incense.

Henry felt George tug his sleeve. 'God in Heaven, Henry, look!' he said.

A whinnying snort and the plack of hooves on marble announced the entrance of a horse into the chapel. The congregation, rippling with loud excitement, startled the horse and the small, dark and immaculately turned-out rider checked a moment of equine indecision with a sharp tug upon the bridle. The horse, groomed to a gleam and bedecked with colours, was now coaxed up the aisle, with pats and caresses from all, to the altar where the priest stood with arms raised ready to give the animal his blessing.

When the service ended, Henry, whose attention had been all upon the horse as it was ridden down the steps of the church to the crashing applause of those standing without, turned to communicate his joy and excitement to Mary Medworth but found himself addressing instead an elderly Italian man and his wife. He peered over countless heads, through gaps in feathered caps, hoisted himself upon a railing to gain better vantage but could make out nothing of Mary nor George. Annoyed at this unforeseen brake on his plans – he had only awaited the right moment to ask Mary to be his – he dropped down and allowed himself to be carried along the streets and around corners where more flags waved from windows and bands blew up the songs of the *contrada*. This was an irritation. Today, the day of the Palio, this day would be such a special day on which to plight his troth. It would signal an auspicious beginning. With his hands to his mouth he called with all the breath within him, 'Mary!'

The multitude swelled as they stopped before a financial institution where others were already assembled and some ritual of obeisance was enacted.

Henry, no time for such things now, looked about him for the Landinis, but slowly and inexorably, the procession was moving again, taking him along with it. Again and again, like adherents at the Stations of the Cross, the pageant halted and some business was gone through that was the focus of all attention. In broken Italian he asked the man at his side where Landini was, but the man only grinned widely, clapped him on the back and began with his friends to chant Landini's name.

His hat had been knocked from his head as they left the chapel and the heat of the midday sun was scorching his neck. The stifling crush was becoming unbearable. Henry felt faint, but walked onwards. Where was she? What was she about? Where was George? And Landini? At last, up ahead, where the road rose, he made out the substantial figure of Landini's father – the smaller man at his side might be Landini himself, and if so, Mary must surely be with them. With gathered strength he forced his way forwards, but sheer will and whispered '*Scusi!*'s would not permit him to advance any quicker than those about him. A side-street sloping steeply to his right gave a glimpse of the Campo itself. Henry had never in his life seen so many people. A great cheer arose as white bulls pulled a chariot across the square. It would begin soon and then he would never find her. The middle of the Campo was an island of people, as densely packed as the fringes of the surrounding buildings, whose every window was a frame tightly filled with craning heads. He looked again at the crowds with dismay. Earlier, drugged with Mary's scent, his ears ringing with her musical, 'Oh, isn't all this such fun, Henry?', he had screwed his courage to such a point he was sure he must ask her that day or never again. But now, as perspiration coursed down his body, he felt the burden of too much heat and exhaustion, and considered whether another plan of action might not be better after all. In the cool stillness of the perfumed evening, upon the hotel's loggia – perhaps that would be the better way. He fell against a doorway and sat there and might not have risen again until all was over, had not a voice close at hand loudly called his name.

'Henry! You will miss the race! We are late already! Do not lose a moment!'

It was Landini, offering him a bottle of warm, brackish water.

'Where is Miss Medworth?' he gasped.

'Never mind that. Come along, to the Palio!'

'No, I must find her!' Henry said, shaking off Landini's helping hand.

Abstracted, Landini looked ahead to where his *contrada* was already descending towards the Piazza del Campo: 'I saw her not a moment ago.'

'She is safe!' Henry exclaimed, choking with relief. 'Where is she?'

'Just up ahead. Not far.' Landini frowned and touched Henry's shoulder. 'She is with Signor Devereaux. Henry, I cannot stay. You must do as your heart bids. Goodbye, my friend.' And he was gone, joining the remaining stragglers who were running pell-mell towards the Campo as a bell tolled and horns blew. Henry ran with them. Something was wrong. What did Landini mean? Was Landini set upon causing trouble even on such a day as this? It was possible that he had overtaken and missed her and he sought to turn around but the crowds closed about him and like a stick in a flooding river he was carried down the street and into the great shell of the Campo itself. And now, just when all hope of marking her small form should have been extinguished, he caught a flash of pink among the dark motley of *contrada* colours. She was only yards ahead. She was following George, who was making his way with unlikely alacrity towards the starting line, where skittish horses were already being marshalled before the rope.

Henry's attempts to follow them were checked by angry *contradaioli*. He could only watch as Mary's pink bonnet marked her course among a thickening crowd until, with sinking heart, he lost sight of it altogether. At the same moment, all about him, everyone he could see rose as one, sinews stretching, throats roaring, all eyes upon the tightly-banded horses that had shot away from the dropped rope and were already fast approaching the place at which Hilditch stood, at the San Martino curve.

Now the horses were upon him, bared teeth and flying foam, the riders' whips lashing horses, hooves thundering, and dirt flying up as the pack rounded the curve and were followed around the arena, past the Palazzo Pubblica and through the Casato bend where two riders were thrown and a horse careened into the wall and lay struggling upon the ground. A minute or two of speed and violence and the race was over and Henry was able to extricate himself and make his way quickly down to the judges' stand, where the horses and riders were assembling and where he had last seen Mary. The first riders were already dismounting as he neared the centre of the excitement. He stopped suddenly. Amid the shouting he heard the distinctive voice of George Devereaux, crying out, 'Damn my eyes, we've won, we've won!' Henry slipped between two quivering horses and came upon George and Mary at the moment that George scooped Mary Medworth into his arms, lifting her off her feet and swinging her about so that her petticoats showed and at the same time kissing her on her lips. Henry could see her face was lit by pure joy. His first thought was to disappear back into the crowd before they saw him, but he could not move. Petrified by shock and bitter disappointment, he could only watch as George began to waltz Mary out on to the course of the Campo. A cannon boomed and Henry saw a startled, riderless horse cantering towards them and shying at the flurry of whirling pink satin and lace suddenly in its path. George was oblivious to the danger as the horse reared high but Mary saw the animal before them, saw the hooves lashing the sky and screamed. Henry, calling out her name, launched himself over the barrier and saw no more of the world for something above a week.

11

The Subject is Foxed

The thing was, God love him, he was not a naturally tidy fellow. John Rankin had realised that much the minute he had crossed the threshold. Orderliness hoisted its skirts and flew from a room the moment that Mr Touchfarthing entered. Objects designed to live together sprang apart like opposing magnets. His progress through the house was recorded in muddy boot-prints, rings on tables, spilt tea, scattered snuff and a trail of items picked up in one place and deposited in another. The shop at the front was a perfectly preserved illusion, a stage set that never hinted at the chaos which a pair of black curtains concealed but not always contained. Rankin collected a waistcoat from the bedroom mantel, a huge and greying shirt from the floor, Touchfarthing's parti-stained unmentionables from atop the chest, where they had knocked down his little framed photographs of the ladies and gentlemen at Sibthorpe, and other items from amid the dust and broken springs under the big brass bed. Dust was the worst of it. Rankin had never known a place like it for dust. It wasn't as if Rankin had all the time in the world, especially while he was building his collection of pictures of the poor that would one day open the eyes of the world; however, he did what he could. But the dust returned, piling on bookshelves, coating ornaments, fogging photo frames and coating his drying prints. He adjusted the bolster against the bed-head. Pulling straight the hillock of tangled sheets, he revealed his own night-cap and a crumpled copy of the *Morning Messenger*. Last night, as soon as Touchfarthing had begun to snore, Rankin had taken his newspaper and carefully scanned it, looking for *Enquirer*'s column with a beating heart. He should never, never have trusted that Hilditch with such personal information. What would the guv'nor say if he saw it? It might ruin the business. And what of his old mother if he was shown up as a thief and a pickpocket?

Hilditch had assured him that his story was safe as houses but very probably he told all his informants the exact same thing and they all lived to regret it later. But once again Hilditch's work was nowhere to be found. It was two weeks or more since he had poked his nose in at their door and asked Rankin if he would take him to some places he particularly wished to observe down the East End.

Mr Hilditch was a queer fellow and no mistake. And yet, Rankin thought, as he collected Touchfarthing's laundry and medicine cup and descended the creaking stairs, it seemed very likely that once reunited with this woman of his, one would probably see a different kind of fellow altogether.

Humming quietly, John Rankin upturned a flat iron from the range and watched a gobbet of his spittle evaporate from its underside. It was to be hoped that the guv'nor appreciated what he did for him. It was to be hoped that he even noticed. Perhaps he thought the fairies did his washing and ironing and raked out the fires and got on their knees with a brush to sweep the old carpets. Food was different. He appreciated what was put before him.

The clock in the parlour whirred, clicked and struck noon and, with a similar degree of automation, John Rankin put away his ironing and took the pan from its hook and a cup of fat from the shelf. The food safe contained a nice pair of pork chops he had bought only that morning, while Touchfarthing still slept. He dropped the meat atop the sizzling fat and let the appetising odour feed his senses, and was roused from this pleasant reverie by a knocking on the back door.

'Reg'lar, is it?' said the little man, whose barrow blocked the back gate and who proffered a newspaper parcel. Rankin felt the grey cat winding itself about his legs as he searched his pockets for a penny. 'He's getting old, bless 'im, ain't he?' said the cats' meat man.

'Not so old he didn't have one o' my white rats when I left the cage ajar,' Rankin said.

'Life in him yet, eh?' said the cats' meat man. 'Well, you'll let me know when he's had enough, won't you? He's got a fine pelt on 'im, that one.' And as if the cat's mortality had reminded him of something else, he asked Rankin if he might be down Newgate on the Monday morning. 'They're hanging that young feller as was murdering the kids. Can't be more'n a week since he were convicted but everyone wants a cove like that to be dropped quick and quite right too. You might do a mint o' business there.'

'I might be there at that,' Rankin said. 'But not for the business you mean.'

When the squeaking of the man's barrow was no more and the cat itself was loudly purring over a plate of horsemeat, a sharp smell of burning alerted Rankin's wandering thoughts to his cooking. Hurrying inside he was able to toss the chops from the pan before their immolation was quite complete.

'Almost ready, old man,' he thought, turning his attention to the glasshouse where Touchfarthing had retired to plan a big picture, his debut, he was calling it, into the world of High Art. Through the glasshouse's chequerwork of clear and white-washed panes, Rankin thought he saw the movements of two figures and now, as the sizzling of hot fat died, he heard raised voices and was about to investigate when the yard door was flung open and Harold Rutter sprang out, bearing a stack of large framed photographs. Now Touchfarthing's bulk filled the doorframe. He was grasping another framed photograph, which he hurled into the long grass by the pear tree. The men were arguing loudly and Rankin opened the back door a little wider so that he might better hear the substance of their debate.

'Why did not I see it at once? I took you for a good man, Mr Rutter, a man of God, a man whose advice I might trust above all others.'

'How dare you impugn my calling, sir! You are making a grave mistake, Mr Touchfarthing, a very grave mistake!'

'The mistake I made was to listen to you! You might have ruined my reputation!'

'Reputation? That's coming it nicely! It's a fine reputation you've got, or don't you know it?'

'Paradigms in pictures, you said! Admonitions for the young and the vulnerable – that's what you said! And what do I find we have we produced? Low erotica for the masses!'

'So the Bowring girl says that one or two of our pictures turned up for sale in a shop in Holywell Street,' said Rutter. 'She is too young to know that there will always be the errant few who will pervert a good intention.'

'You know as well as anyone what Holywell Street trades in. And it gives credence to a monstrous rumour. I heard, Mr Rutter, that these pictures are to be seen on the walls of a notorious meeting house in Chelsea. The Good Lord knows what you have done with the remainder. This will get abroad and when it ruins me I shall see it ruins you too, Mr Rutter!'

'Mr Touchfarthing, do please compose yourself,' said Rutter in a placatory tone. 'You are paying undue heed to one silly girl who misunderstood our intentions. I'm certain that once the series is completed and you can see the wholeness of my design, even you will be fully satisfied with the purity of my intentions. In the meantime I will forgive you for this misunderstanding.'

'None of that gammon now, as Mr Rankin would say! He had your measure. He tried to warn me but I wouldn't listen.'

Touchfarthing, kneeling before the stack of pictures, looked at each in a new and horrible light. 'Jezebel. Salome. Mary Magdalen. And who was this trollop?'

'The whore of Babylon, I think?' Mr Rutter offered.

Touchfarthing pointed to a girl whose face was a picture of

piety, but whose general state was one of complete dishabille. 'I must know. How many of these have you sold?'

'This world has many sinners, Mr Touchfarthing. There are countless misguided souls who are crying out for guidance. We have been supplying that need. Your costs will be more than covered, Mr Touchfarthing, much more than covered.'

Mr Touchfarthing, speechless with rage, pointed a stubby finger at the garden gate. 'You know your way out,' he exploded. 'And take your damned warm gems with you. I shall deny any connection. I tell you, Mr Rutter, from this day forth I shall be known only for my Art. Good day, Mr Rutter, good day.'

'I'll come back when you are more like yourself,' Mr Rutter said.

When the minister had finally backed through the gate with his clutch of pictures, Touchfarthing sat down heavily in the doorway of the glasshouse and sank his heavy head into fleshy hands and loudly sighed. He looked up as John Rankin's head popped out from behind the kitchen door and informed him that his chops were unfortunately a trifle on the burnt side.

II

'I wish I knew, Lord knows I do. No one wants to find Henry Hilditch more than I do, I can assure you of that. *Enquirer* is missed, very sorely missed.'

Jabez Flynt addressed the chaos of papers on his desk. Ink-stained fingers swept lank and greasy hair from eyes that advertised a long want of sleep.

'I shall confide in you, sir. The recent success of this news-paper rested squarely on his writing. Would that it didn't and I own I was foolish to let it be so. But I did. And now...'

The visitor moved a chair before the desk and sat down. 'He was missing once before,' he said. 'We had no sign of him for months.'

'What happened?'

'It hardly matters. The point is that, in normal circumstances,

163

he is hardly the man to do a thing like this. You have enquired of the police?'

'Of course, but what can they do? He's not a child. If he wishes to vanish then what is to stop him?'

'I went to his lodgings in Somers Town. A Mrs Minton last saw him boarding an omnibus bound for the City. It's short odds the reason lies in his work as *Enquirer*. You have retraced his recent investigations?'

'My people have had no success. Only Hilditch himself knew where to locate his subjects and he wasn't free and easy with such information.'

Flynt gazed idly out of his opened window and watched an omnibus driver feeding his horses while just below him the passengers folded newspapers and avoided his eye.

'I can only wait and hope that he will reappear as and when the fancy takes him, God damn him!'

A woman on the omnibus below shuddered.

'When, precisely, did you last see him and what was he about?'

Flynt considered. 'I last saw Henry, let me see, somewhere above a fortnight ago. At these offices. He was . . .' He stopped abruptly and pointed at something beyond the omnibus, on the far side of the street. 'He was in the company of that fellow there! Hoy, Treby!'

The brightly-chequered suit of the reporter Treby appeared in the doorway of a public house across the street. Treby, smiling as he wiped his lips, held open the door which now framed the conspicuous scarlet uniform of Ratcliffe. They shook hands and Ratcliffe strode off. Treby, preceded by a crossing sweeper, was traversing the street towards the doors of the *Morning Messenger*, appearing not to hear his editor's cry. 'Damn you, Treby, bring that fellow to me!' Flynt shouted, causing consternation aboard the omnibus. 'Now perhaps we shall learn something!' he said. With a face lit with excitement he turned to the stranger but saw now only a vacant chair and heard the sounds of the *Messenger*'s stairs being taken five at a time and Treby loudly expostulating, 'I say, have a care there!'

III

There were times before the fever had broken when he fancied that all he heard and all that passed before his eyes was real. In such a moment he had perhaps heard a spittly exchange above his fiery brow.

'I say we kick him out of doors now. Gypping the observer for dog money was one thing. A vindictive judge might take this as kidnapping.'

'Treby wants him out of the way a little longer. And here he'll stay, for as long as Treby pays.'

'I ain't the one to refuse money, and mayhap we should squeeze him for extra. But it's a risk, Captain, and I was never one for a risk. A fellow like that could lead us to Newgate.'

'Rot! He's so pickled in laudanum he'll never know what has happened. When it's time, we'll bring him round and tell him he's had a severe concussion and fever. And we'll bill him ten pounds for his nursing.' At which the other laughed until he coughed, admitting that the captain could be a fly one.

Hilditch himself had no sense of time. There was day and night and sometimes night succeeded night, or so it seemed. He haunted a world of weird phantasms and lurid dreams. Memories and fantasies blended seamlessly with visions that might or might not be more real. He saw men come and go. He saw the ornate chairs taken away at night, saw silver pots and candle holders and a heap of spoons upon a table. Ratcliffe and the fat man drinking, paring cheese, playing cards, arguing over a small, muscly dog. He saw the soldier sleeping in his chair with his boots upon the end of Hilditch's bed, which was a box stuffed with malodorous rags. But mostly he saw only the empty room. Though the captain fed him milk and sops of bread and rendered him irregular and unsteady assistance to the awful midden across the yard where he might leave him for heaven knew how long, and Saggers tried often to rouse him for the sake of some diversion, mostly he was alone. Whenever the fog cleared, Hilditch was left too weak to move and with little else to do but gaze at crumbling plaster and broken lathes and to consider the awfulness of his position. Sometimes he thought himself at the bottom of a deep well, whose sides were worn so smooth that to climb back up them would be impossible. He imagined Mary Medworth, at the top, calling down to him but was unable to form his reply. He had not thought it possible to fall so low. Stripped of his self-respect, Hilditch wondered if he might loathe himself.

He counted on Ratcliffe for his food – though rarely was he hungry – and for the bitter-tasting medicine, which was so often the prelude for vivid, sensual dreams that offered deep and embryonic comfort. For this ministration he was grateful and awaited the soldier's return to the house like a faithful dog.

There were nightmares, too, but more often the medicine brought moments of strangely beautiful peace and pleasant dreams, in which Mary sometimes appeared. After such a dream, in lucid moments, his thinking of her was unusually objective. She had kissed George in the Campo. There was no getting about that. He suspected strongly that she had known George, had met and kissed him before. He confronted the thought that she been in his room the night before the race. He was familiar, too familiar, with all that thinking, had fled from such vile thoughts. But other memories were proving more potent: the piquancy of her scent, the quickness of her smile, her petite and dainty shoes, her tiny nose and the eyes like lemons, the way she blew a single stray curl from her face. What a prize he had lost. Might he not have been too severe? After all, she had been so young and as unworldly as he was. It was even conceivable that he had been mistaken and that she was innocent of all his mind had charged her with.

He would keep to his resolution. He would find Mary and know the truth. With only this thought in mind, he gathered his strength and tried to rise from the bed of rags but overpowering nausea cast him down again. After another such attempt he was found by Ratcliffe on bare boards by the door and was put roughly back in his bed and given another long draft of the potion that brought on the dreams.

If Ratcliffe was late home, Hilditch quickly became anxious, even vexed. On a night when Ratcliffe did not come and Saggers had also gone, locking the door behind him, Hilditch had awoken bathed in a chill sweat, his heart thumping out irregular beats, his throat dry as desert sand. With strength born of desperation, he rose and searched the apartment high and low, looking for the stoppered bottle of reddish-brown liquor from which would come his release. He thrust his arm through cavities in the crumbling walls, blackened his face in the chimney, from which he had seen Saggers retrieving other bottles, pried loose floor-boards, all without making the vital discovery.

He had picked up a piece of coloured glass, which he ground into his palm as he stared through a musty window. It was late evening, a bank of black cloud threatening rain. He became aware of his blood dripping and wiped his cut palm on his shirt-tails. In the yard below appeared a donkey pulling an empty barrow, led by a man who might be a costermonger. The man upended the barrow against the wall and then took a pipe from his pocket and vanquished the shadows with a flaring Lucifer. He puffed with evident contentment, oblivious to the pale face at the window above. Hilditch raised his hand and rapped on the glass. The man did not hear him and disappeared into his own bolt-hole. A cry for help formed in Henry's throat but no sound came forth. It flashed upon him that beyond the glass he would find only cold and a great emptiness. What he yearned for more than his freedom would be supplied by Ratcliffe, if he would only return, God damn and blast his soul!

It was black night when a key was fumbled in the lock and Ratcliffe entered and dropped drunkenly into his chair. Hilditch, able to stand no more, fell at his feet. 'Where is the medicine? I must have it now.'

And waited: he must be patient if Ratcliffe was not to exploit his despair. The soldier brought out the stoppered bottle, which had only been under his chair, and settled it upon his lap. 'A man who needs medicine is still sick. You must be our guest a little longer.'

Hilditch said shortly, 'Let me have what I need.'

The soldier, wearing his familiar scarlet tunic and street-scuffed boots, poured a small measure of the liquid into a dirty glass and Hilditch threw it off. 'You must stay until you are fully recovered,' Ratcliffe said. 'Bad concussion. Can't have you falling under a cart.'

'More.' Hilditch took the bottle and liberally recharged his glass. The craving remained, though its edges were softened. He made himself comfortable amid the mountain of rags while warm and languorous relief flooded his senses. Some moments passed before he identified an insistent droning as Ratcliffe's voice.

'That's not apothecary's laudanum you've got there. It's a tincture made to my own receipt. Two and a half ounces of powdered opium – the only decent stuff is from a Lascar sailor in Shadwell – mixed with two pints of spirits and macerated for fourteen days. I was famous for my tinctures. Newsome's Lotus Water, they called it in Bengal.' He took up the bottle and himself took a long pull from its mouth. 'I wasn't always as you see me now. There was a time, seems a damned age ago now, when I held the Queen's commission. Was a doctor with a fine regiment. But commissions don't come cheap. Nor do uniforms and horses. A fellow has to borrow just to maintain himself in that life. There was a problem. A man to whom I owed money died while I was treating him. Awful things were said. That I'd poisoned him. Nothing was proven, nothing. I was exonerated. But I couldn't stay on. What's that?'

The door swung ajar and the sound of heavy breathing punctuated by whispered curses announced the return of William Saggers. He hurried in and quickly locked the door behind him.

'There's trouble.'

Hilditch, relieved of the need to attend Ratcliffe's discursion, sank deep into his rag bed, oblivious to the doings of the other two men. Saggers took a ragged newspaper from a deep pocket. 'You're the better reader,' he said to Ratcliffe. 'Run your eye over that and tell me if it's true. They're talking of nothing else at the Swan.'

When Ratcliffe had read all he wanted and his face reflected its import, Saggers said, 'So it's true? Everyone is looking for him?'

'So it seems. It's Flynt and the *Morning Messenger* that's behind this hullabaloo, mark me. Mr Flynt needs his *Enquirer*.'

'There was police at the Swan after the *Enquirer* today. Wuss'n when that baronet was found dead in Soft Moll's bed in Bow. Rumour's got it the gent here's been done away with.'

'The *Messenger* has far too much influence,' Ratcliffe murmured as he turned a page. 'All this for a scribbler.'

'A famous one, they're saying. And there's even been whispers in the 'Ouse, they say?'

Ratcliffe grunted and read aloud. ' "The Right Honourable Member for Barnet trusts that nothing untoward has befallen the celebrated *Enquirer*, especially as his recent reportings drew much-warranted attention to the government's incapacity to control crime and make these streets safe for respectable folk to walk upon. We would indeed be sorry to hear after the event that the two factors were in the least way connected. The Prime Minister replied that he bitterly resented the maligning of the government's character and that spurious and unfounded allegations were the province of newspapers and tittle-tattlers, etc etc." '

'What's all that barrikin mean?' Saggers asked.

'It means that this little affair will assume an importance it hardly deserves. We must consider what we do next with care, my friend.'

'What'll happen to us?'

'Nothing; not if we act promptly.'

'Let him go, get rid of 'en now?'

'And have him turn us in? It's you they'd have for kidnapping, Saggers: this ain't my place. Remember, it wasn't me he came a-visiting and I've witnesses to that.'

'But you was with me, you'll be the accomplice in this. You and Mr Treby.'

'They want me for a little more than being some oaf's accomplice,' snapped Ratcliffe. He took a short pull from the stoppered bottle.

'So what do they you want you for?'

'It don't matter.' He filled the sticky-rimmed glass to its brim with the rust-coloured liquid and lifted Hilditch's head. 'Drink it up, drink it all,' he murmured. Saggers watched his tenant with new-found fascination. 'So what's to be done, Mr Whatever your name is?'

IV

Saggers took up the handles and the barrow squeaked out of the court and down the narrow alleys, the soldier's boots splashing through puddles as he followed on. The covered bundle might have been a large sack of potatoes were it not for the fingertips of a hand that showed from under a frayed edge. Saggers shook his head as he pushed, his brow furrowing with new thought. Then he stopped, let down the barrow and cocked his head like a dog. 'There's someone there, I'm sure!' But Ratcliffe only poked him with his cane, told him shortly to get on with it and off they went again, leaving the courts and coming upon cobbled by-ways in which the mist was thicker. They saw no one as they crossed the yard of a soap factory, but as they passed a row of poor lodgings a door opened and the liquid contents of a bucket were poured into the drain. The smell of frying fat and the clatter of tin plates disappeared with the slamming of the door. 'I told you it was too late for this,' hissed William Saggers. 'There's folk abroad!'

'Look at the fog,' Ratcliffe said. 'They won't see us in that.' The nearer they came to the river, the denser it had become, the early-morning kitchen fires thickening the opacity like stock in a soup. Now they saw ghosts, not people; figures drifted in and out of the haze, faded blue coats and white faces assuming solidity and colour only when they passed up close. Here were families laden with boxes heading for the morning steam packet; a knifeman wheeling his rattling grindstone over worn cobblestones; a couple of groggy sailors, arm in arm, who lurched and fell heavily against the barrow; a policeman who saw them on their way; the nightsoil man returning from the shore; a vagrant curled in a doorway with a child in his arms. Too many folk altogether for such work as this, Saggers reasoned.

'Let's just leave 'im here and have done with it. This is too hot for me.'

'There's no other way. It's as hard to go back now.'

'He's waking. I saw him move!'

'He's only dreaming. It's all the laudanum.'

'I done some things in my time, Mr Ratcliffe, but I never done nothing like this. It ain't right in daylight. They'll drop us at Newgate, I'm telling you.'

Ratcliffe took hold of a half-belt on Saggers' old coat and yanked the fat man backwards, deftly spinning him about until his jowly cheek grazed up against a brick corner. 'Listen, you old fool,' the soldier breathed. 'You'll do as I say or you'll be dead a lot sooner than a judge at the Bailey could arrange it. It's the only way, can't you see that? Everyone knew he was a queer one. He'll have no marks, no knife wounds. The police will say it was just another suicide. Now go on, get along there.'

They had turned down a steeply-inclining passage and were now following the course of the river, whose far banks and moored craft were cloaked by the pervading fog. They found themselves at a landing stage for packet boats and Saggers was alarmed to be driving his barrow through a crowd of passengers bearing bundles and bags, all pushing to board the berthed steamer and some cursing the blasted costermonger who was in their way. When they were at last free of all such entanglement, Ratcliffe pointed to the dark adumbration of a distant bridge.

'It will be easier among the warehouses on the Surrey side.'

They began to cross the bridge and were passed at first by a succession of other pedestrians. Then, suddenly, they could see no other passengers upon the bridge. Saggers stopped again and peered into the mist. 'What now?' Ratcliffe snapped, turning to his paralysed companion.

'I heard it again, I know I did!'

'Keep your nerve, Saggers, or I'll make an end of you now, I swear it,' the soldier hissed. 'This is our chance – we won't have a better.' He began to untie the fastenings of the tarpaulin. 'Help me heave him up on the balustrade and we can roll him off. Into the strong currents. Take a hold now – what's the matter?'

'I won't 'ave none of this!' said Saggers, pointing into the barrow. 'He'll come back, that one. Look at 'im, all white, like death already. He'll come back one day and serve us out, I'm certain of it.'

'You're a dangerous fool! Now, lift his legs before you get us both taken.'

'Not 'im. I ain't the man for that,' Saggers said, backing away behind the barrow. He turned smartly and, in a moment, he was gone, the sound of his feet falling flatly on the bridge as he disappeared behind a curtain of fog. Now Ratcliffe was left alone with his burden, which had begun to groan. 'Don't you worry, Mr H.,' he murmured as he took fast hold of Henry Hilditch beneath his arms and dragged him heavily from the barrow. 'You'll be asleep again before you know it.'

And then he too stopped and frowned into the greyness. 'Saggers?' he called hoarsely. 'Is that you?'

Then, being sure he heard no other sound but the loud chugging of a steamboat engine, he dragged his load towards the wall of the bridge. The man was heavier than he had anticipated and Ratcliffe propped him against the wall so that he might catch his breath before the final exertion. At that moment a party of drunken young men, returning after a night's spree, passed close by, laughing. They slowed and stumbled to a halt.

'Fellow here's retching worse'n you was, Edward,' one called. 'That's it, into the river with the Marsala, Captain!' And the party stumbled past, leaving the bridge quiet once more.

Hilditch complained again when Ratcliffe grasped him

roughly, and as he attempted to heave at his limp and weighty body, he distinctly heard the sound of running footsteps. It might be anyone, someone who would most probably pass on the other side, but Ratcliffe had made his choice. He hoisted hard and, the point of balance being overcome, he was able to swing one leg up on the high ledge. As he reached for the other, Henry Hilditch opened his eyes and asked what was happening and, in twisting about, he slipped down from the wall. 'Get up there, help me, you fool,' Ratcliffe said. 'Get up on the wall there, look alive!'

Hilditch regarded the wall with puzzlement. For a moment he thought he might be in the studio of Mr Touchfarthing, who had a similar-looking stage property, made of papier mâché, and he doubted it would take his weight. But now there was shouting, louder, louder, and footsteps clattering, and the blast of a steam whistle somewhere near. He felt the furious urgency of the soldier's actions as, with one great heave, he was thrown up on the wall and found himself lain flat upon cold stone.

The soldier was breathing hard and quickly, preparing for some further endeavour. But now someone else was there. There was a scuffling, two figures grappling, and blows exchanged. He raised his head to see but his mind was too cloudy to make sense of the violent drama being played before him. The men were locked together, straining, shoving, every breath blended with a profanation as they stumbled, now away and across the bridge so that they disappeared completely into the fog. A moment, and then the soldier emerged first, the red of his jacket-back looming large as his adversary pushed him hard, knocking him over, against a barrow, was it? And then they were upon the road, rolling in the gutter, and yet still Hilditch could hardly tell if he were watching a melodrama or only suffering another fevered dream.

The players were up again now, circling, stabbing, grunting like animals. Mesmerised by the strange ballet, Hilditch lay upon the stone and watched dispassionately as the men struck out and made rents in cloth and dark streaks on skin. The dull

173

grey flash of a blade flying over his head seized his attention. Now he could see clearly enough that one man had the other by the throat. A twist in the dance and balance was lost and now the two were falling heavily towards his own person.

Instantly awake to the danger, Henry Hilditch rolled over to avoid the calamitous collision and suddenly felt himself unsupported, moving, it seemed; his stomach turning over as cold, moist air rushed past his ears, and his long locks clove to his cheeks. Questions scrambled for precedence in a mind that was possessed of a single surprising, quite incredible thought: that he was falling, down and down.

12

A Seascape

Agnes Devereaux, eyes closed and arms outstretched for balance, leapt nimbly across a chasm of three feet and landed safely upon the next stone. Henry Hilditch dropped the handkerchief of fossils and abruptly stood up. 'What are you about? You'll hurt yourself! Why do you do such things?'

'How else am I to know that I am still alive?' Agnes called with a short laugh. 'Throw me my cane, will you?'

A hand was reaching out for the stick Henry now passed up to it. 'See this, Henry!' And before he could climb up and follow, she had crossed to the far side of the granite block, had run her stick all along its edge and was now leaning dangerously as she described the form of a neighbouring stone. She took a sharp breath and leapt across another black void, landing unsteadily but keeping her feet beneath her. She turned, and said, 'Well?' to a vacant space some feet to the right of Henry's person.

'Come down at once,' Henry said. 'You will certainly do yourself an injury!'

'La, Mr Hilditch, you care, then? It shall have been worth the trouble to have arrested your attention at last. You have been in a maundering mood all morning.'

She held out a hand and Henry helped her down from the

monolithic stone. They had broken their walk in the grounds of the clifftop abbey whose ancient, crumbling walls offered the best prospect of Whitby and the North Sea. Henry sat his charge among the scattering of fossils his hammer had tapped from loose rock at the water's edge. While Agnes ran her fingers over ribs and furrows, Henry's talk was all of Cambrian trilobites and Palaeozoic brachiopods. Nevertheless, Agnes could feel that his mind itself dwelt still upon the ill-fortunes of his recent past.

A fortnight had passed since the limp and apparently lifeless body of Henry Hilditch had been scooped from the river by a wide-awake hand on a passing packet boat. He remembered nothing of the fall from the bridge and knew only by hearsay of how near he had come to destruction under the wheels of the paddle-steamer. Memories of the days that followed were like a shuffled pack of picture cards: a puzzled physician, who declared him recovered from his accident but could not account for the other symptoms of discomfort; the inn's small, cluttered room with its iron balustraded windows and views over the noisy Hungerford Market; the sporadic visits of George Devereaux, who locked the door behind him when he left. Most vividly, Hilditch recalled with repugnance the nights spent in glacial sweats and the voracious craving that clawed at his very being and dragged him to deepest Hell before it abated sufficiently for him to convince his new keeper that his dependence was a thing of the past.

When George had suggested he recuperate at Whitby, Henry seized on the idea with a fervour that had surprised even himself. A dose of Whitby air would be an antidote to London's noxious atmosphere and it was somewhere he might forget the worst of his recent pain. Over and above that, he felt himself drawn by some other attraction, though precisely what it was, he could not fathom. After only a few days at Sibthorpe Hall, high above his home town, Agnes had remarked on what a different person he presented against the poor specimen which her brother had let down from the coach late on Monday night. Only Henry himself knew how much of this metamorphosis was due to the

Scarborough apothecary who had carefully followed the receipt for Ratcliffe's vital tincture.

Though he had moderated his dosage to the extent that only another opium-eater might recognise him as a fellow traveller, to be denied these small amounts for more than a few hours was not tolerable. His continuing addiction impeded his perception and blighted his judgement. His thinking was often irrational and he spent long periods lost in dreamy contemplation. He meditated on an ideal future spent with Mary, but not upon the practicalities of finding her. Now, after a morning spent walking about Robin Hood's Bay, it seemed that no sooner had they settled upon the grass than Henry was itching to be away again. 'I had forgotten,' he said to Agnes, 'but there is something I really must be about doing.'

'What could be so urgent that we can't spend an hour up here enjoying the sun and the sea breeze, if not this awful cacophony of seagulls?' She stood up and directed useless eyes into the fresh westerly wind that was blowing briskly off the North Sea. 'I never tired of the view from up here. This was my Heaven. Tell me what you see. Tell me everything.'

'You must remember the limits of my descriptive powers,' Henry said. 'I let you down at Florence.'

'That was art but this is life,' Agnes teased. 'And now you have honed your skills as the mighty *Enquirer*, you have only to open your mouth and I shall see again, I am certain of it.'

Henry hesitated and began slowly. 'You see St Mary's Church directly before you. Hundreds of spray-weathered yellow head-stones toppling towards the cliff edge. The background, as you can see, is a wash of deep blue, speckled with sail and lightening to a cerulean sky.' He took her lightly about her waist and together they walked through the graveyard to the top of the steps that wound steeply down to the town below.

'Now you see it all,' Henry said. 'The clusters of roofs, the houses and fishermen's cottages, the lanes busy with people and the port thick with ships. Across the river-mouth some ware-houses . . .'

'I see your name on one. How famous you are, Henry!'

'And beyond,' he continued, as if he might overlook places he associated with past unhappiness, 'surmounting the straggle of houses and shops on the West Cliff and looking vastly more like a castle than a house, is your own Sibthorpe Hall.'

'Show me that, Henry.'

'I should need a telescope to do it justice,' Henry said. 'But it looks as grand as it ever did and at this remove the cracks in the east wall and the disturbances in the garden are quite invisible. Those ramparts and towers would deter any latter-day Viking or Corsican upstart.'

'And yet it was never intended as anything of the sort, but built to please the whim of a Derby cotton merchant little more than fifty years ago. Did you know his intention was to set a counter-balance to these ruins of St Hilda's, here on the East Cliff?'

'And he will have succeeded entirely if the place is under-mined any more.'

'The problem is as old as the house,' Agnes said. 'In his hurry he neglected proper building practice and now erosion and subsidence are tearing Sibthorpe apart. Only last week a great fissure appeared in the drawing-room.'

'But Mr Short will save the place, surely? There he is now, with an army of navvies, a forest of scaffolding, stout timber bulwarks, walls of shoring, mountains of earth going up and down the cliff in great buckets.'

'Is that how it appears? Then it must be graver than I under-stood. Father says that Sibthorpe cannot fall but I rather think that he cannot conceive of such a terrible thing.'

Henry, whose pernicious appetite had been nagging at him throughout their conversation, finally capitulated. 'Well, I must be about my business,' he said.

As Agnes made no enquiry, he added, 'It's time I looked in at Ryedale House. Risby the banker has been asking if I mean to sell.'

'Sell? I hope not. I pray you will live there again one day.

What is Whitby without a Hilditch at Ryedale?' She laughed. 'Well, you may go. And I'm glad of it – I had begun to think you were shunning the place.'

'I shall see you back to Sibthorpe first, of course,' Henry said, as he took the blind-woman's arm.

II

Such had been Henry's thirst for his elixir that he had no sooner reached the quayside than he had entered an inn and ordered a glass of brandy, discreetly pouring a large dose of laudanum into another of water, which he drank off in one long draft. He no longer felt equal to meeting the always bustling and needlessly officious Mr Risby, in whose keeping were the keys to Ryedale. Instead, he crossed the bridge and drifted towards the mole on which stood the stunted lighthouse. Fishermen mending nets and pots looked up as he passed – he cut a foreign figure in Whitby now and no one had yet marked him as the youngest Hilditch from Ryedale House. Here he spent the afternoon watching unclothed boys leaping in and out of the shining waters like salmon and later being mesmerised by the sparkles of sunlight upon the waves which slapped against the stone of the mole. When he was roused from his reveries by George himself, he found that it was evening.

At a table in a public house whose dusty window commanded a wide segment of sea below a grey crepuscular sky, they had talked of Mary Medworth and the event which had riven their friendship.

'If I had known that you loved her,' George was saying, as he extinguished his cigar, 'I should never have held her hand, let alone kissed her in public. And you know now that was done only in the heat of my triumph, do you not?'

'I do,' Henry said. The waiter dropped a great plate of pudding and gravy before him like a pig of lead.

'I had made a heavy bet with an uncle of Landini's, the biggest wager I ever made. I had expected to lose the entire thirty pounds. But then to see the horse win was beyond belief. No one who hasn't the passion for gambling can understand the life-giving thrill of it. I suspect that had you been there and not Mary, I should have kissed you, Henry.'

Still dopey with laudanum, Henry pushed away his plate and became lost in thought for such a long time that George was required to nudge him.

'When I awoke in hospital, after the race,' Henry said at last, 'I thought I must be dead. There were men in hoods about my bed.'

'The misericordia? The point of doing good deeds anonymously has always eluded me.'

'I hardly knew where I was or what had happened. It was days before I remembered a thing.'

'I should have stayed with you. But you were in good hands, a recovery was assured and I expected to see you back in England within a week anyway.'

'And so I should have been but for that awful mistake. I was convinced that you had stolen her from me.'

'We've been friends too long for that,' George said with a laugh. He patted the other man's arm. 'Really, Henry, I'm surprised you could think that of me.'

'I'm sorry for it, George. It was an error that changed the course of my life. But do please tell me what became of her? Agnes has refused to talk of it.'

'I'm not sure I can do better,' George said. 'You know Mary was anxious to avoid wasting away in Boulogne with her father. She would have done anything to avoid that.'

'Even take up with me, you mean?'

'No, I honestly believe she cared for you almost as much as you for her. When I took her back to Sibthorpe, where she had agreed to take a position as companion to Agnes, she spent those first weeks waiting for you. Time and again I found her on the widow's walk with eyes all at sea. She wrote to you care of Landini but I suppose you had already left Florence by the time the letter arrived there.'

180

'What happened, George? You wrote she left under a cloud. Surely you know more than that? And how did the butler come to lose his place the same day? I've met the man in London, but he won't tell me a thing. He seems to think that whatever he tells me will end up in the *Morning Messenger*.'

George paused for a moment while he cut the end off a new cigar. Once it was lit, and his face was obscured by thick blue smoke, he said, 'It was Touchfarthing who discovered her theft of Agnes's rings. That was his side of it. According to him, Mary had been helping herself to Agnes's jewellery. She denied it of course and blamed the butler himself, a far likelier candidate. My father wanted only to avoid scandal and sent them both away. I advise you not to mention the affair – it pains him.'

'Are you sure? I can't believe such a thing of her. I've met the butler – the man is an overweening ogre to be sure but I think he had too much respect for this family to steal from it. Where is she now?'

'As I wrote, the best information I have is that she may have gone to London.'

'Without a reference?'

'Without much at all, as I recollect.'

'And you have no idea where in London she might be?'

George considered the question. 'I suppose there are one or two places that a girl in such a position might find herself eventually. Enquiries might be made, but this sort of thing usually costs money.'

'I have money.'

'I know.' George's eyes brightened and he leant across the table, assuming a confidential attitude. 'And this brings me to the little business I wanted to talk to you about, Henry. I have not been fortunate lately but at last it seems that a chance has been put in my way. I have been offered an excellent opportunity to go into business with some men who are to invest in a South American railway. I've seen the plans and it's absolutely fire-proof. I did one of the consortium a favour one time and he's agreed to let me in. Of course, there is the matter of my own

181

stake to be raised, but any investment now will repay itself tenfold within twelve months. Lend me five thousand pounds Henry – I know you have it and more – and you'll see it doubled within the year, I promise you.'

'George, I should tell you that I spoke to your father today. He has asked me to restrain you from just such speculations. I can't let you have money I know you are going to throw away.'

'Throw away? Damn it all, Henry. Don't you see that an opportunity like this comes but once in a lifetime and must be seized at once? I know that if we miss this one we will both regret it for ever.'

'He said that you must prove some degree of personal responsibility if you are to inherit Sibthorpe.'

'There will be no Sibthorpe soon enough.'

'Short has saved it. All you have to do is to rein in your horses and wait.'

'And for how long must I live like a pauper, Henry? I tell you that this is money in the bank and food on the table. Don't make me beg, Henry. I'm asking you as my oldest friend to let me have that money.'

'And I'm telling you for your own good that I cannot, George.'

'You cannot deny me! Recall that I saved you from drowning in the river.'

'I was fished out by a sailor, I believe.'

'But I should have rescued you otherwise. And who was it saved you from those ruffians on the bridge?'

'You? But how could you know where I was?'

'I went to ask for you at the *Messenger*. Flynt said you were last seen with a soldier who was then drinking with a *Messenger* reporter. I followed him but the fellow lost me in the fog. It was a few days before I found his lair and lucky for you that I did.'

'Then I thank you for that and, believe me, it is in the same spirit of friendship that I must refuse your request.'

'Henry, I'm telling you that I must have that money!'

'Believe me, George, it's your own interest I have at heart.'

'You were always a tight-fisted fellow. And that's your final word?'

'It has to be, George.'

'Then damn you, Henry,' said George, knocking his glass from the table as he rose. At the door he turned. 'Let me tell you this,' he said. 'I hope you find her. You and Mary Medworth deserve each other!'

II

George likewise could go to hell, Henry thought as he climbed the steep path that led back to Sibthorpe Hall. He cared only for money. For George there was no problem which the application of a little cash could not solve. At a turn on the path, Henry stopped and gazed out at the moonlit ocean. His own case was not so easily remedied. He had been broken by his recent experience, had hit bottom; very nearly, he reflected, the bottom of the River Thames. His period of rest in Whitby had healed him in body only.

His mind remained fevered, agitated not only by his continuing use of laudanum, but by the obsessive idea that he had only to locate Mary Medworth and he would also find his salvation. He was certain of it. Who else had told him so much that he wanted to hear, had flattered his vanity and made him feel twice the man he was? Who else in the world would have his best interests at heart? He worried himself over George's parting comment, that he, Henry, deserved Mary. Of course he did, but he was sure George had not meant that. He believed that George had kissed Mary in the heat of the moment and yet he could not expunge from his mind the last, lingering doubts.

A week later, Henry having remained in Whitby, Agnes was assuring him that though she might be blind, she was still very much the mistress of Sibthorpe.

'And have been ever since the death of my mother when I was fifteen,' she said. 'I had my sight long enough to know the ways of the servants. It's easy enough to tell if windows have been opened and a room has been aired and I can distinguish a fresh-made fire from relit coals. My fingers know whether the piano top is dusted and I am satisfied that the hall is polished when I can smell beeswax and vinegar. I am not, you see, completely ineffective.'

'No, I only wondered how you managed, that was all,' Henry said, as he closed the glass case and turned the key in the lock once more. He pulled down the dustsheets over a thousand different beetles and took a last look around the room that had been his sanctuary at Ryedale House. He had opened drawers and looked upon hundreds of carefully categorised fossils, on boxes of unpolished pieces of jet found along the coast, at the great cases of pinned and neatly labelled insects but had failed to feel the welling enthusiasm he had known of old. He suggested they lock the house again and return the key to Risby, and there leave instructions for its sale. 'I hope you won't sell, Henry,' Agnes said. 'Whitby is your anchor.'

'Whatever makes you say that?' Henry asked.

'I know that you weren't happy here at Ryedale House,' Agnes said, 'but I remember you happy on the clifftops. And at Sibthorpe.'

'Is that what you remember?' Henry said. 'Perhaps I was.'

'And now, when you are in trouble, you have chosen Whitby as your refuge.'

'To come here seemed the natural thing to do,' Henry said. 'Perhaps you are right. But I may not be able to maintain my connection with the place much longer.'

'Oh, Henry, whyever not?'

'I have been talking with Risby,' Henry said. 'My affairs are not as healthy as I had thought. I may be obliged to sell to meet other claims on my father's estate.'

'I'm sorry to hear it,' Agnes said. 'If that is the case, could we not see the rest of the house? I should like to hear about every room. I never got beyond the drawing-room when your father was alive.'

'If that is what you wish,' he said.

They began on the third floor, where his elder brother's room was still full of rolled charts and sea-chests, fishing tackle and a rotting leather football. A guilty intruder, Henry peeked into his father's room: drab and smelling of damp, a dull brass telescope mounted by the window. They wound down the staircase and looked into the kitchen and back parlour and sat down upon the ancient chairs that Henry's mother had declared the glory of the drawing-room. The ships still sailed the walls, framed in mahogany and carrying a cargo of dust.

'And what will you do now, Henry, if you are not to return to Ryedale?'

'I am returning to London tomorrow. I must.'

'Because you are *Enquirer*?'

'No, Agnes,' Henry said and then, after a meditative pause, 'I didn't ask you out today only to show you Ryedale House.'

'Did you not, Mr Hilditch?' Agnes said.

'The fact is, I have received a letter from George.'

'George? Oh, how is he, Henry?'

'He has been in London these last days and is well enough, I think.' His voice was edged with excitement. 'The import was that George thinks that he can find Mary.'

'Why should he want to do that?' Her face betrayed the quickness of her thinking. 'Oh, I think I see.'

'I love her, Agnes. I have never in my life loved anyone as I did Mary. She discovered the best in me, showed me how to love life itself. And now I fear to think what might have befallen her in London.'

'Mary will have gone on well enough, I'm sure of that.'

'I do hope so,' Henry said, missing the bite in the blind-woman's tone. 'I know that above all things I must find her and discover her feelings towards me. If she can forgive me, perhaps I can win her again.'

Agnes, who had opened a window and was turned towards it as if she could see the harboured boats and warehouse roofs below her, said quietly, 'Don't run after her, Henry. She's not good for you.'

'What can you mean, not good? Didn't I just tell you she was the best thing that ever was in my life? How can she not be good for me? Sometimes, Agnes, you really presume too much!'

'I only say this as your friend. I would protect you as you would my brother, Henry. Can you not see what she is? Was her dalliance with George insufficient to open your eyes?'

Impulsively, he said: 'I know you are dreadfully situated, Agnes, and I feel for your limitations. But if this is the cause of your jealousy, I think you should try a little harder to make terms with it.' And even as he spoke, he would have swallowed those words though they choked him. His anger was blind.

'Henry,' Agnes replied, coolly. 'When Mary Medworth was my companion at Sibthorpe I got to know her better than you did then or perhaps ever could. I never wanted a companion – but George was insistent and wouldn't hear a word against the idea. For a little while it wasn't so bad, either. She was someone to talk to and take me on my walks. But then just when I needed her she would have disappeared, whether to the town or only another part of the house I never knew. Certainly she never came to my call. She was my companion only when it suited her. When she was found out, it was no great surprise to me. She was no more reliable than the weather.'

'I fully believe that she was innocent,' Henry said, shortly. 'I believe George thought so too.'

She turned, her face quizzing a commotion of noise from somewhere beyond the garden.

'George?' Agnes said, distractedly, 'George is the last person to believe that.'

'What do mean, Agnes? What did you know of all this?'

But Agnes's reply was stillborn as she answered the cry of a man, running up the road outside. 'Is that you, Tom Clarke?'

'Yes, m'm,' called the voice. 'I'm right glad we've found you safe. It's the house, Miss Devereaux, Sibthorpe has fallen into the sea, they say. Come wi' us, we'll take you there.'

I

Henry Hilditch stood back while the body was recovered from the rubble, glad that Agnes was unable to see the mutilations caused by crashing masonry. Gently, the workers lifted the man on to a rudimentary bier and, with as much care, carried him away, while their fellows stood by in mute shock and surveyed the extent of the cataclysm. Henry and the men had hurried to the place with as much speed as the care of Agnes allowed. She had said nothing, only held his hand tight. And then a child sent upon an urgent errand came skittering down the hill crying that someone had 'been hurt bad' and Agnes had implored the men to send a runner to enquire about her father's safety.

When they reached the rim of the gully, where the crowd had parted to allow through the bearers of the body, the first voice she heard was her father's, asking of no one particularly, 'What have I done?' Though the main part of Sibthorpe remained perched upon the cliff like a great yawning beast, the east wing had been torn away, leaving wallpapered rooms and leather chairs exposed to view and a colossal mountain of detritus and rubble filling the gully. On the beach below, washed over by the fast flowing tide, were newly-created islands of stones and lintels, earth and brick.

'I saw it all happen,' Edmund Devereaux said. 'Such a fearful thing. Whatever have we done to deserve this, Agnes?' She clung to his arm, understanding the extent of the devastation herself only as his words revealed it to her.

'I had come here to survey Short's workings.' He gazed upwards at the enormous empty socket in the cliff where once had been the terraces of shoring, the huge wooden posts and squeaking pulleys. 'The men had finished for the day and there was no one I could question about the earth I saw slipping from beneath the walls of timber. I had turned to go when I heard a great cracking and when I looked I saw the shoring give way like a broken dam, and an avalanche of earth crashed upon the rocks. There was more creaking, and then another part of the defences broke and the earth trembled. There was the most terrible noise, Aggie, as the land began to slide and slip and rocks started to smash into the sea. The house was still standing, though a chimney pot toppled and a great concavity had appeared beneath it. I was about to return to Sibthorpe and see what might yet be done for its preservation. I called to one of Short's men to summon his master – he was over the far side, came running and got caught under a sudden fall of clay, poor fellow. Before I could do anything for him I saw the house itself begin to shift, bricks falling and rents appearing in the walls. The front, the stones and windows of my library collapsed before my eyes. And then all was lost behind a thick cloud of dust.'

'I thank God you were not at home,' Agnes said. 'We will bear this, Father. I know that Henry will accommodate us at Ryedale. It is a terrible thing, but I am just thankful that you are safe.'

'I might as well have gone with it,' Devereaux said, as foam-flecked waves beat upon the shore, and bore away papers, a lampshade and a great fleet of books.

13

Calotypes

The display behind the shop window was regularly obscured by boys with hoops, curious old ladies and young girls playing with their tresses as they gazed at the dashing young hussar whose new-wedded image occupied centre-stage in the display. Families stood before it as they weighed the cost of dodging obscurity and preserving their likenesses for generations yet unborn. Mothers cooed over the pictures of babies and infants, both the blurred convulsives and those whose hidden restraints fixed them with fierce and indignant glares. People who wanted distraction without the attendant obligation of expense found it in the ever-changing shop window of Cornelius Touchfarthing, photographer.

This morning two men stood before the window in deep contemplation, each wearing a full beard and a pair of spectacles. One was tall and thin with flame-red hair, while the other had a pepper-and-salt greyness and the top of his hat was about level with the other's shoulder. The men had appeared to arrive at the window with some purpose in mind and they involved themselves in a lengthy conversation before, at last, they entered the shop.

Other street passengers who had noticed their animation now drifted towards the window to discern the cause. The picture of the actress, which had charmed passing boys the week before, had now been removed. The run-of-the-mill portraits, each one an authorised masking of familial cares and uncertainties, rarely excited anyone but the sitters themselves who had yet to pay and take away their pictures. The only photographs that attracted special notice were those whose subjects were unusual – a one-eyed sailor, a woman with a pronounced goitre and a picture of Siamese twins which might be seen in the windows of several other photographers in the metropolis. Otherwise the steely-faced, side-burned gents and bombazined widows were quite interchangeable. On more than one occasion a customer too pressed to sit for his portrait had happily accepted an off-the-peg photograph of a similar stranger.

But now there was movement behind the glass as the topmost parts of the shop's proprietor appeared behind the half-curtain and inclined over the lines of photographs. He pointed to some large, sturdily framed portraits of gentlemen of analogous appearance to his customers, but they shook their heads and indicated a group over in the corner, so hidden away that they had been unremarked by those looking in. The owner expressed surprise, perhaps even displeasure, and tried to redirect the focus of all to the sturdy portraits.

The three pictures that were the objects of the gents' fascination were unusual in that their subjects were eminently not of the kind to be able to pay for such large and probably expensive photographs. Hung one above the other on the side wall, they introduced to the world two female cress-sellers seated upon a kerb, neither aged above eight years, a group of shabbily dressed women standing outside a match factory and a family of gypsies, posed on the steps of their caravan. These photographs were removed from the window and shortly afterwards reappeared in the street, clutched beneath the arms of the interested gentlemen. Mr Touchfarthing stood at the glass pane of the door and glowered after their receding backs before disappearing behind the black curtain and calling for Mr Rankin.

'When did you last look in the window?' Touchfarthing

demanded of John Rankin, who was drying dishwater from his hands and regarding the other man with a mixture of forbearance and suppressed annoyance.

'Last night. I changed the display before I went to bed, like always.'

'And took it upon yourself to advertise your own pictures?'

'It ain't as if there wasn't room,' Rankin said.

'But I never gave you permission to discredit my window with pictures of vagrants and labourers! None of whom, I presume, gave you a penny for them.'

'Just a minute,' Rankin objected. 'How much did them gents give you?'

'They paid the price you had marked upon them,' Touchfarthing said. 'Although I was loath to accept so much. But that's hardly the point. That they were bought, I can only presume as freakish curiosities, does not vindicate you, Mr Rankin. This is not the way forward. And it won't support this business.'

'But that's just what it has been doing. Look at this.' And Rankin chinked out the contents of his purse upon the parlour table. 'That's five shilling for a study of lightermen at Wapping, two bob for an omnibus driver with his horse thrown in and another florin for a gang of crossing sweepers down by Charing Cross.'

'You've sold those from my window? It's my own fault for failing to inspect it every day, I suppose. Goodness knows what damage you must have done by now.'

'There was a few gone by the window, I own,' Rankin said, with a gleam of satisfaction. 'But mostly I've taken my photographs as and when the customers have asked me to.'

'You're not saying you've been commissioned? That's inconceivable. Intolerable. It is I who accept the commissions. Why wasn't I told?'

'It weren't your sort of thing, Mr T. It's some ladies and gents who are all for reform and likes what they see in my photographs. I show London as I know it and that's what they want.' He took a sheath of photographs from beneath a family Bible. 'Look at these. This is what they're paying for, not the sixpunny portraits.'

Touchfarthing handled the photographs as if they carried infection. He looked with obvious distaste at filthy scavengers upon a dust heap, a pair of mudlarks, knee-deep in river water, a toothless bird-seller, a band of midget street musicians, a beak-nosed nostrum vendor, a paper-thin flower girl. He looked at beggars of all descriptions and then stared at the last picture with disbelief. 'This is a public hanging!' he exclaimed. 'At Newgate! Can you have dragged us as low as that?'

'Hold your horses, Mr T.,' said Rankin. 'I ain't one o' them that sets up as souvenir-sellers and that. This was done for some respectable folks what thinks that some things are more properly done in private and that hanging's one of them.'

'And they paid you for this?'

''Ansomely. You've been eating the proceeds since Tuesday. And it's not only them what pays me. Word has got about. The Vice Society has assigned me to photograph the working gals on Haymarket and Regents Street.'

'Prostitutes? This is terrible, Mr Rankin, low gutter stuff!'

'It's proper business what turns a profit. And as respectable as you might like, Mr T. Just this morning I was asked by the Commissioners of the Great Exhibition to chronicle the dismantling of the Crystal Palace,' said Rankin, who repeated for the effect, 'By the Commissioners of the Great Exhibition.'

'I don't know,' Touchfarthing said. 'It seems you have been very close, very deceitful, John. I have to say that I am surprised at you. Disappointed, I should say.'

'How do you think we've kept our heads above water these last weeks? If you don't mind me saying, Mr T., you've made precious few contributions to the domestic economy of this household of late. You've not done one of your little portraits in weeks. All you've been doing is spending money. What are all these?' He waved a wad of thin papers under Touchfarthing's nose. 'Unpaid accounts is what. And they're not mine, neither. Look here – paint, burnt sienna. Brushes, medium and fine. Six yards of blue satin. And a bill of two pound ten for a seamstress. How do you account for that?'

'Might I remind you that you refused to do any further needlework? You've been much too busy with your own secret dealings of late to be of use to your mentor and saviour. Do you know that I had to dust the parlour myself last evening?'

'You are draining us of our capital, Mr T., and it has to stop,' Rankin said. He spread the accounts on the table and shook his head. 'What I've been earning, you've been spending. And all for what, I should like to know?'

The elder man drew himself up to his full and impressive height. 'I have been investing in our future. In the future of Art, Mr Rankin. I have been making preparations for the greatest photograph I have ever created. Perhaps the greatest photograph the world has ever seen. It will open eyes, it will prove once and for all that not only is photography the equal of painting, but that an expert photographist can sometimes improve upon it.'

'All this,' Rankin said as he totalled figures on the back of a bill, 'for the sake of a portrait?'

'Not a portrait, Mr Rankin. A painting made by a camera. This will be a masterwork of High Art.'

'And a very valuable one, I hope,' said Rankin, darkly.

The bell rang out and Touchfarthing tugged at his waistcoat, preparing to sweep aside the black curtains and make his theatrical entrance into the shop, when he appeared struck by a thought. 'No doubt you will see a little unusual activity tomorrow, but pay it no mind. I should prefer you did not see the mechanics of my art, only the finished work itself. I shall overlook your transgressions for the moment, John, but I ask you to admit the truth of our difference when you see what it is that I have done.'

'I will try not to get in the way of Art, then,' said John Rankin, dropping the rag on to the stack of dirty dishes in the sink and opening the back door. 'I 'ave some little friends to feed and then you'll 'ave to excuse me as I'm stepping hout. I'm takin' tea with a Commissioner.'

II

It was late in the morning when George Devereaux, collar raised against the lashing rain, shoes soaked in the filth of an over-flowing gutter, rapped at the low door that he had found only with dogged perseverance. The house was a slender, poorly-built interposition between a decaying Elizabethan manor house and the Grapes Hotel, which languished in the gloomy shadows of Christ Church, Spitalfields. So slim was the house that George had missed it on his first circuit of these alien streets. Henry Hilditch opened the door and, after apologising for taking him so far out of his way, hurried Devereaux to a damp-smelling, low-ceilinged apartment up two pairs of stairs, which was furnished with a threadbare rug, a tiny ash-choked fireplace, a three-legged bed heaped with Henry's clothes, and a cracked chamber pot. On a deal table stood two bottles of ink, and the nubs of a dozen spent candles. A flask and an empty glass weighted a sheet of paper that bore Hilditch's spidery hand.

Devereaux took it all in and frowned. 'Somers Town must have been better than this, surely?'

Henry, who sat at the table with the frame and dark lenses of the glasses he had been mending, regarded the place as if for the first time. 'The rent is very reasonable,' he said. 'And I'm where I need to be. Among the people of East London.'

'Where *Enquirer* can go about his work, eh?'

'No, George. Flynt and the *Messenger* can all go hang. I know now that a sneaking chap who feeds off the misery of others isn't the man for a girl like Mary. Here in East London I feel that any day she might pass by the window. A striking woman appearing in a neighbourhood cannot have gone unremarked. Someone must know where she is. I must be here, among these people.'

'You will become one of them if you are not careful.'

'I expected you yesterday,' said Henry, tetchily. 'Why could I not have come to you? It might have saved time.'

'You would not have found me, Henry. I regret that the

parlous state of my finances has denied me a proper roof of late. I have been sleeping at different lodging houses at thruppence a night.'

'I'm sorry it has come to that.'

'We have both taken a step or two down from Ryedale House and Sibthorpe,' Devereaux said. 'The difference is that you are here by choice.'

'Agnes will come around, George. Prove to her you won't throw it away and she will restore your inheritance.'

'She told you that?'

'She meant as much. Agnes wrote to me as soon as your father died.'

'That house was everything to my father. How has Agnes borne it all?'

'She has managed, as always,' Henry said. 'She took a small staff from Sibthorpe and set them to work at Ryedale. Your father would have died in comfort.'

'But without regaining the power of speech? Without, I must be plain, redrawing his will?'

'No,' Henry said, as he poured a small amount of liquid from the flask and brought it to his lips. 'But Agnes will not deny you what is yours, not without good reason, I'm sure of that.'

'Are you? She will say that I am thriftless and intemperate. You cannot imagine how I should have to change to satisfy my sister, Henry. I need the money now.'

'Write to her.'

'I have written. But I don't hope for mercy from that quarter. And as you are quite as harsh and refuse to make me a loan, I must rub along whatever way I can. But how would it be if I were to find Mary for you, Henry? How would it be then?'

'Your letter suggested you knew something,' Henry said.

'I do know something. Or rather someone else knows it. There's a fellow who makes it his business to search people out. For the police, among others. I gave him a photograph of Mary, one taken by the butler while she was at Sibthorpe. For a week or two I thought he had bolted with my money. But now he tells me she has been seen, Henry. South of the river.'

'Where, George?'

'He won't say more. Only tells me to trust him. He intimates that her position is not what I would call a happy one. And that it will take money to free her.'

'Good God, George! What has become of her?'

'For the moment we can only guess. I can follow this up, Henry, but he is asking fifty pounds to cover his fee and his expenditure, which he thinks may be high, given the circumstances.'

'What circumstances? What does he mean, George?'

'You must pay him to find out. I can get no further without this fellow's help.'

'I am not going to give you fifty pounds, George.'

'Not me. Samuel Wilkins. There is no one better at what he does. He knows it and he charges for it. But I tell you this, Henry, Mary's safety should not be jeopardised for the sake of money.'

'But fifty pounds, George,' said Henry, dazed. 'Fifty pounds that we don't even know will find her. It's too much, really, it is too much.'

'Henry, that fifty pounds could be the saving of you as well as Mary. Think what that girl meant to you. Remember how different you were. Not the cold clam you have become again, Henry, but warm, liberal, open-handed. You need to give things away, Henry. Not just your money, either.'

'I don't know what you mean,' Henry protested. He swallowed another tot of laudanum and slumped back in his chair.

'I don't think you do, old fellow,' George said, picking up a sheet of paper on which was recorded a conversation with one of *Enquirer*'s subjects. 'I must say, Henry, you've been a damned odd fellow ever since I first knew you as a child.'

'If you felt that, I'm surprised you spent your time with me,' Henry said, with a touch of petulance.

'I was not allowed to choose my playfellows,' George said, with equal heat. 'My father sent for you because your family had some standing in the town. I doubt that I should have befriended such a bloodless fellow otherwise.'

'Is that how you have seen me, then?'

'I tried everything I could to bring you out from the shell that your father chased you into. Sometimes I thought I nearly succeeded. But it wasn't until we were at Florence and you were with Mary that I finally saw what I always thought must be buried somewhere within you.'

'I was different with her, wasn't I?'

'Very. A new man, Henry.'

'And a better one? I felt that myself.'

'Much, much better. The love of a good woman, eh, Henry?'

Devereaux took Henry's flask, poured another small tot into the other man's glass.

'You are sure,' Henry murmured after he had drunk its contents, 'that the information is good, that your informant can be trusted?'

'I'm as sure as it is possible to be,' George said.

'I must see her, George. I will get you the money.'

'Trust me, Henry. I will walk with you to the bank. Now get your coat, the weather is foul.'

III

Mr Rawson of Cape Town was a stranger to London and to his inexpert eye, one photographer's shop looked very much like the next. If Mr Touchfarthing's new sign declared that it was to him and his partner alone that the British nobility went for their portraiture, then he might just as well believe it. However, Mr Rawson quickly discovered that the services offered by such top-class portraitists were at odds with those he particularly sought. Mr Rawson, a spectacularly mustachioed man with hair like gorse and skin the colour of tanned leather, had endured a troubled passage from the Cape, and his delayed arrival in England had thwarted his intended purpose of visiting the Great Exhibition before it ended. In compensation, he had requested that Mr Touchfarthing photograph him before the Crystal Palace. He also required further photography that might be labelled, Rawson at the Houses of Parliament, Rawson at the doors of Westminster Abbey and Rawson at 10, Downing Street. With considerable delicacy, Mr Touchfarthing suggested that while there were men in the parks who might happily accommodate him, the quality of this city always sat for their portraits in the privacy of a reputable studio, such as his own. Mr Rawson admitted that he would not like to do anything that might be improper, but the fact remained that he desired some photographic souvenir of his visit to London.

'I believe I have the solution,' Mr Touchfarthing said, and ushered his client through a small doorway that communicated directly from the shop to the studio itself. 'You will forgive the confusion,' the photographer said, indicating a great half-painted backcloth hanging from the ceiling and the many pots of paint, partly-built card walls, plaster columns with Corinthian capitals and other assorted stage properties, 'but you find me in preparation for my masterpiece. The photograph I will take here tomorrow will be the apotheosis of my calling, and, I might tell you, as much a bona fide work of great art as any oil painting hanging in the galleries.'

Rawson admired the enormous canvas on which were outlined some classical buildings and a crowd of agitated figures who might equally be warring or carousing with each other. 'Early Rome,' Touchfarthing explained. 'And after Rubens, of course.'

'Some distance after,' muttered Mr Rawson. 'Which of Rubens?'

'The Rape of the Sabine Women,' Touchfarthing said with pride. 'A sufficiently lofty subject for such a venture, I'm sure you'll agree.'

'The set is only half finished,' Rawson said, 'and you mean to take your photograph tomorrow?'

'The fellow who painted it isn't quite reliable, though he was a Royal Academician before he took to drink. Now he paints scenery at the Garrick. If he don't return this morning I think I'm up to finishing it myself. In fact, it is the backcloths I have already painted that I want to show you now.'

Touchfarthing took one of the three rolls of canvas that stood propped against a wall and spread it out upon the studio floor. 'Suppose I were to photograph you against that?'

Rawson walked about the canvas and eyed it from all angles. 'What is it?' he asked.

'St Paul's Cathedral, you must see that?' Touchfarthing said. 'Of course, it's not an exact representation, but quite sufficient to suggest Wren's majestic edifice rising out of the Great Wen.' Touchfarthing spread out two more cloths. 'This, of course, is the Pantheon and here's something gay,' he said. 'Vauxhall Gardens by night.'

'But it's full of women,' Rawson said. 'I shall look like I have spent my time debauching myself – this will never do.'

The bell in the shop rang but before Touchfarthing could excuse himself to answer it, they heard the clatter of pattened feet in the passage, and a small and breathless girl appeared in the studio doorway. Her dull and shabby attire was offset by the paint and powder on her face that might have been applied by the same unsteady hand which had coloured the garish backdrop before her.

'Mr Touchfarthing,' panted Jane Pipkin, bobbing a curtsey to Rawson and dropping heavily on to a throne borrowed of the Garrick Theatre. 'Mr Rutter says you can't have no more girls and that's flat.'

'Whyever not?' Touchfarthing said, with one uneasy eye upon his customer.

''E says you never paid them for what they already done for you,' Jane Pipkin said. 'And they won't do no more without you pays them their money.'

'Money?' said Touchfarthing. 'This is ripe! Didn't I buy them their clothes?'

Mr Rawson raised a bushy eyebrow. Touchfarthing said, 'You run along and tell Mr Rutter I must have twenty girls whatever the cost. I will settle with him after I have used them, but I must have those girls. Do you understand?' The girl nodded and ran out into the street. During this exchange, Mr Rawson had changed his mind. He admitted that the backgrounds were certainly unusual but realism was what he was after, and with that in mind perhaps he must after all try one of the men in parks.

Touchfarthing looked about in dismay, at his half-finished preparations and at another customer leaving the premises with his purse intact. The Royal Academician was no doubt still sleeping off his drinking bout in a gutter somewhere and Mr Rutter would most likely fail him on the morrow. Almost certainly, the execution of the great picture would have to be postponed. How disappointing that the world would have to wait still longer to discover the genius that slept in the heart of Cornelius Touchfarthing.

He sighed deeply, picked up a copy of the *Morning Messenger* and was about to start across the yard to the water closet where he hoped to move his troublesome bowels, but even this con-solation was denied him as John Rankin peered about the studio door. 'Apologies for intruding into the realms of art,' he said, 'but there's two fellows in the shop. One's got some armour as must be paid for today and t'other's got an 'orse and wants to know where to put it.'

IV

Hilditch awoke from a leaden, narcotic sleep with one word sounding within his skull. The word was 'different' and he was reflecting on George Devereaux's alluring assertion that he had been a different and much better man with Mary Medworth at his side. He let his drugged mind seize upon that thought and wander where it would. His face was turned against the damaged plaster of a wall and he watched complacently as the cracks diverged and conjoined until they had arranged themselves into the recognisable features of Mary Medworth. He groaned at the

200

abysmal emptiness he had known since he had returned to London.

He thought more on George's words. In Florence, he had indeed been a better man, happy for the first time since before his mother had died and before his father had been consumed by grief and failure. Henry had worn a confident aspect and had looked to the future without attendant fear. He would have shaken off the poor, solitary thing he had become and have been born anew. He was no longer alone, but had an ally with whom to march out into the world.

It was dawning upon him that there may be nothing he would not do, no price he would not pay, to know that happiness and that completion once more. Recent events had left him hollow. Stripped of self-respect during his imprisonment with Saggers, stripped almost of his life in the river, and his mind wildly disordered with tincture of opium, he felt close to destruction. He experienced frequent visions of Mary as she had appeared to him in the chapel at Florence, her face backgrounded by the brilliant fresco, and experienced a terrible, gnawing hunger worse even than his craving for the laudanum.

Early one morning of the following week, washed and shaved and wearing a second-hand frock-coat bought at the dollyshop next door, Henry Hilditch sat in a cab with George Devereaux as it crossed London Bridge, heading towards the Surrey side. The cause of this metamorphosis was the hope that had grown from a mere possibility into a thrilling certainty that he was about to see his Mary Medworth again. The night before, in response to a heated tirade from Henry that he was throwing good money after bad with never a sign of Mary herself, George had said that his man had finally located her in a part of Southwark. Now, though he had taken no laudanum that morning, he was able to look on the passing world with some complacency and feel tiny seeds of pleasure taking root within his soul.

He considered what he might say to her and what would be her condition. The droplets of information he had received were terrifyingly ambiguous. George had set on his agent to find

Mary Medworth as soon as Henry had paid him the fifty pounds. At first they heard nothing and Henry suspected that they or at least he had been duped. Then George reported that Wilkins had heard something and needed twenty pounds to follow up the information. Once again, Henry wondered whether he was being practised upon, but now the little details that Wilkins reported through George bore a convincing veracity – a garnet brooch she had worn at Florence; pretty little turns of phrase; the curling lock of hair that was for ever falling over her face. And yet Wilkins's information was never first-hand but reported to him from his network of informants. He could not say personally that Mary was well or that she was not in distress or even in trouble. London was a mortal, dangerous place for a young woman on her own, he said.

George had brought Mr Wilkins to Henry's door after another blazing argument in which George had asked for further funds and Henry had accused him of doing nothing but spending his money. Samuel Wilkins, a ruddy-faced fellow dressed in fustian, whose voluminous coat pockets appeared to carry his worldly possessions or the tools of some trade, had sat before Henry's dying fire smoking a long clay pipe. He had declared that finding a young person in the great city was not an easy job nor one that might be accomplished in a hurry. The places he had heard tell of her being at one time or another were not places in which he might reasonably suppose that she was well-housed and respectably employed. Mr Wilkins was firmly of the opinion that he must recruit additional informants, who must work quickly if they were to find this Mary Medworth safe and sound at the end of the day. It would cost money, of course it would cost money, but he could see that Mr Hilditch's regard for the woman far exceeded his regard for his purse.

And still Mary Medworth had not been found. Tantalising information reached Henry's ears. That she had been seen making bonnets in Poplar, that she had decamped from a lodgement in Shoreditch without paying the rent, that she had obtained a position as a governess in Richmond. He hoped that the worst report was mistaken. One of Wilkins's spies placed Mary at the Cremorne Gardens with an old and ugly woman following her every movement, leading him to deduce that the young woman was a dress-lodger, a young prostitute whose fashionable clothes were on loan and guarded by her companion. Any or all of these rumours might be true. Time went by and more and more money passed from him to George and presumably through him to Samuel Wilkins and yet still Henry had no certain knowledge of her whereabouts. Now, with George asserting that an informant of Wilkins's had certainly located her, he refused to let the chance slip by and was now arrived at the ancient rambling coaching inn at Southwark where Mary Medworth had been sighted only two days previously. With pounding heart and sweating palms, Henry followed George along the second-tier gallery that ran along the south side of the inn. 'We are early enough,' George was saying. 'I doubt she will have risen and gone at this time.' George rapped upon the door of the room at the end of the gallery and waited. He knocked again and when no answer was made to knocking so loud that ostlers in the yard looked up and whistled, he tried the door handle. The door swung open and, calling her name, George walked cautiously into an irregularly-shaped bedroom, one wall of which was formed by the eaves of the roof. They saw a rumpled, unmade bed, a wash-stand with a bowl of dirty water, a chair, a dresser and a chest of drawers, but no Mary, nor any sign that she had ever been there. Henry had the sensation of the ground opening up beneath his feet.

'You've tricked me,' he breathed.

'No,' George said. 'She was here.' He began to search the room. Henry watched without hope as George shook out the bedcovers, threw the bolster to the floor and peered under the bed. 'This is a charade,' Henry said.

'It's not, I tell you,' George said. He opened drawers and found them empty and then pulled back the curtain of a small alcove and momentarily disappeared from sight. 'There! What did I tell you?' he cried.

203

'What is it?'

'This,' George said. As he came out from behind the curtain, Henry saw that he was smiling triumphantly. What Henry saw then answered a question forming on his lips. Every nerve in his body felt as if suddenly shot through with a great bolt of electricity. In George's hand was a grubby and broken-spoked but quite recognisable pink parasol.

14

High Art

If John Rankin was surprised to see Henry Hilditch standing in his shop after so long, no sign of it coloured his thin and bony features. 'Well, Mr 'Ilditch,' he said. 'And 'ave you found her?'

'I haven't, John, but not for the want of trying. We know she is in London somewhere but I fear we are no nearer to finding her. I've come here to solicit your help.'

'Help you, Mr 'Ilditch? Thousands wouldn't, you know, not after a piece o' their private talk had found its way into the newspaper.'

'I don't think you were mentioned by name,' Hilditch said, and took a chair by the counter.

'As good as, it seemed to me,' Rankin said. 'And that wasn't right, Mr 'Ilditch, not by my book.'

'Yes, I know that now and I'm sorry for it,' Henry said, wearily. Prompted by a resolve to appear at his best before Mary, he had gone two days without his tincture and had not slept since. 'In fact, I asked the editor not to publish.'

'That's as may be, I suppose,' said Rankin. 'Well, what is it I can do for you?'

Henry pulled a photograph from his pocket. 'This is her picture,' he said.

'The one sitting down, I take it? She's a good-looking woman. With a headful of sense, I should say.'

'The person I seek stands at her side. The seated woman is the new mistress of Sibthorpe Hall.'

'Miss Agnes? Then Mr T. must have taken this hisself – he did a deal of portraits when he was butler at Sibthorpe. Mr Devereaux paid him to photograph the visiting nobs,' Rankin said. 'And so it's this one here is your Miss—'

'Medworth. I have people out scouring London for her but they need a likeness. Can you make me copies of this?'

'I'm not sure,' Rankin said. 'I'm precious busy now – but give me a couple of days and I'll do what I can.'

The dog-eared portrait Henry left with Rankin showed Agnes Devereaux seated on a drawing-room chair, attired in a simple, dark dress. Her hands were folded in her lap and her visage was plain and unadorned. Standing close at her side, Mary Medworth, dressed smartly and wearing necklace and brooch, gained everything from the comparison. 'I had almost forgotten what a fine-looking girl she is,' George smiled as he took the copied photographs from Henry's hand. 'But as for Agnes, Lord, what a bother she has become!'

'I never found her so,' Henry said, thoughtfully. 'Do you know, the more I think of your sister, the finer she strikes me.'

'I had a letter from her today,' George said. 'She comes to London shortly and is to stay until the repairs to Sibthorpe are effected. Repairs, forsooth! She will throw our fortune into that crumbling pile. There will be nothing for me. And now she is to be here in London, and will very likely watch my every move.'

'She can hardly do that,' Henry said.

'Oh, she has her eyes and her ears in Eliot, her maid. They are as thick as thieves, those two. I shall have not a moment's peace.'

'Where is she to stay?'

'Not with me. I have taken two rooms in Wapping, but they aren't up to that. I suppose they will put up at Milsom's. It's clean enough and the food ain't bad. Perhaps you will visit with them and make sure they are safely settled. I will be busy enough with these.'

George pocketed a stack of photographs and started for the door.

'Where are you going? If you are going after Mary then I must come with you.'

'No, we will do better by separating. You can begin by making enquiries north of Oxford Street. Here is a list of likely places at which it may be worth while presenting her photograph. I will take the south side. And after that I must meet with Wilkins.'

'Has he news of her yet?'

'I don't know. All I do know is that he has asked me to keep an appointment with him this evening. It may be nothing. However, he is up to something and needs more money.'

'I gave him another fifty pounds only last week, George. I can't bear so much.'

'But you have seen how this process eats up money, Henry. We are getting so close. Now is not the time to be illiberal.'

'It's not that, George. I have let you over-estimate the extent of my inheritance. It is not what I led you to believe, nor yet what I myself believed it to be. My father had debts. He had lost a fortune after the whaling ended in Whitby. I saw Risby the banker when I was there and he laid bare the full extent of my liabilities. By the time it was all settled I had mortgaged Ryedale and come away with only a few hundred pounds. So you see that I cannot continue to fund this Wilkins for ever. If he does not find her soon the game will be up.'

George bit his lip. 'You know he's closing with her, Henry. Lately there have been so many signs. Let Wilkins have his hundred pounds.'

Henry, worn down by his addiction and by the constant building up and wearing away of his hopes, opened his pocket-book without another murmur. George took the money and said that if he didn't return that evening with firm information about Mary Medworth, he'd repay the money himself.

Rankin had watched with bemused interest as Touchfarthing rushed in and out of the studio, ushering in noisy young girls and men carrying properties and fetching the horse from the livery stables, which he coaxed into the studio with compelling difficulty. Scarlet-faced and drenched in perspiration, he looked like a man attempting to organise and run the Great Exhibition on his own. So thought John Rankin, who wasn't about to lend a hand before the old fellow acknowledged that it was he who was earning their income these days and Touchfarthing whose ventures were like to bring calamity upon the newly-rechristened firm of Touchfarthing and Rankin.

The night before, there had been a fierce dispute between the men over Touchfarthing's alarming expenditure on his great picture. Touchfarthing himself had never totalled the figures on the accounts that lay crumpled and scattered on mantels and tables, and when Rankin showed him that stellar sum, even he had swallowed hard. 'Sometimes expense must be borne if Art is to take a great leap forwards,' he had blustered. 'There will never have been anything remotely like this before. Who knows what such uniqueness might be worth? I shall find somewhere to have it exhibited, John, somewhere it will be talked about. The patronage that results will likely set us up, let alone what the picture itself might raise.'

'I wery much hope that will be the case,' Rankin had said, 'because if it ain't, I think we will be ruined.'

With lingering reluctance, Touchfarthing agreed that the picture must be taken this day or not at all. He could not afford the further hire of horse and properties, nor another day's pay for Mr Rutter's congregation, who had agreed to pose as some of the Sabine women and auxiliary soldiers, so long as their dignity were not compromised and each person received a shilling a day, with sixpence to be paid in advance. Weeks of effort had been spent assembling the elements he needed for his masterpiece. He himself had completed the painting of the background and that of all of the properties, and the sewing of costumes had been done by the congregation, who had augmented their shillings by another ninepence for each costume they completed.

Mr Rutter's followers were a motley assemblage of penitents and saved souls, seekers after warmth and shelter and those who were infatuated by the perceived charisma of Mr Rutter himself. But not all of Mr Rutter's flock had seen their involvement in such a project as another milestone on the road to salvation, as the minister's lavish rhetoric had caused others to infer. Just that morning, Mr Rutter had been obliged to advise Mr Touchfarthing to reduce the scale of his ambitions.

'I can't do that,' he had argued. 'You can't shrink an epic, Mr Rutter. Are you to disappoint me again? I trusted you once before and I recall the unhappy result.'

'It would all have turned out properly had you only held your faith,' Mr Rutter said. 'And will do so yet. See here, Mr Touchfarthing, I can save the day for you, but I expect you to help me in return.'

'If you can get me twenty women in that studio by two o'clock this afternoon, I would consider myself deeply in your debt. What help do you want?'

'I want us to complete the *Accurate Scenes from the Bible*. The interest I had from the first pictures was quite extraordinary and I have dealers almost begging me for more. We stand to make a great deal of money, a very great deal, I assure you.'

'The pictures will be more tasteful?'

'And more instructive,' said the minister.

'Then I am in your hands, Mr Rutter.'

The acme of Mr Touchfarthing's photographic achievement might have been completed on a previous occasion but for the failure of several of his cast to attend and the fact that the horse, a mercurial colt, took it into its head to bolt the minute the livery door had been opened. Romulus, Touchfarthing had said, surely had less trouble abducting the Sabine women for the peopling of Rome than he, Touchfarthing, had organising his

209

heroic work. Once the scene-painter had absconded, he had worked alone to bring all to a state of readiness.

When it was understood that the picture would be widely exhibited, Mr Rutter had kindly offered his services as one of the picture's main compositional elements and would play the rapacious Roman soldier who, in the painting by Rubens, reaches down from his horse to snatch up a Sabine woman.

To this end Mr Rutter had wasted much of the morning arranging the folds of his robes and admiring the effect in a full-length mirror. He had at least proved useful in other ways, harrying and scolding his wayward congregation until all were properly attired and ready long before the appointed time. They sat on the steps of the Roman villa, knitting and gossiping and awaiting the influx of strangers who were to make up the numbers.

The women that Mr Rutter had located had begun arriving during the late morning, one bursting into the shop at the moment when Rankin was removing a facial wart from a customer with a rag and some nitric acid and causing a spillage that would probably scar the man for life. 'Go 'round the back,' Rankin had shouted, for this was not the first such interruption of the morning. Others, cheaply scented and painted and dressed in varying states of dishabille, had tramped through the shop full of saucy talk and suggestion, causing one family to flee in horror and another to remonstrate in the strongest terms. 'The back!' Rankin shouted at the latest troupe of bedizened girls. 'Use the tradesmen's!'

These girls had been loudly bothersome from the start. They complained about the costumes, which would be unfashionable even in Stepney, demanded advances of their money, caused a vicious dispute with the Berners Street congregation over their varying rates of pay and loudly scoffed as Harold Rutter made repeated attempts to mount the saddleless horse. Rarely were these girls all present and ready at the same time and, searching for a pair that had strayed from the studio, Touchfarthing discovered them in the shop, giggling over a photograph.

'I tell you it's 'er.'

210

'But don't she look all aristocratic done up like that?'

'Well, she ain't one o' us, is she? Running a night house ain't being an actual whore, is it?'

'Give me that,' said Touchfarthing as he snatched away the portrait of Agnes and Mary Medworth. 'Do you know this woman?'

'I should say,' said one and burst into a fit of laughter. 'But mayhaps you know 'er better! Come on, Bessy, let's go and get us own photos took.' The girls ran out the back of the shop. Touchfarthing followed in their wake, pondering whether they might have mistaken Mary Medworth for another woman. He doubted it, though: he thought he knew enough of Mary Medworth's character to assume the worst. But it was not a puzzle he would resolve then – there were more pressing problems assembled in the studio.

Now that Touchfarthing had decided to pose himself as Romulus, the founder of Rome, there remained the fundamental question of who was to expose the plate and for this service he would need to propitiate John Rankin. He found him in the yard, feeding his animals in their garden cages – the few he had felt quite unable to part with, despite Touchfarthing's protests. 'I have something to ask of you,' Touchfarthing said, and when Rankin only waited for him elaborate, said, 'The long and short of it is, John, that I need your help.'

Pausing only to slide shut the lock of the rabbit's cage, Rankin stood up. 'Well, seeing as how you have asked for it,' he said, and followed Touchfarthing through the doors of the studio, where he was confronted by such a scene of infernal pandemonium that he considered taking himself back out again. The studio more nearly resembled the Coliseum than an earlier Roman street. A vicious fight had broken out between one of the new girls and Mr Rutter's Moll Sargent and others were joining the affray as the combatants attacked each other with tooth and claw. On the right side of the setting, Mr Rutter was astride the nervous black horse, which was tethered to a high-standing dais. His high-pitched voice could be heard above all others as he appealed for peace, which did nothing to calm the agitated colt, which was depositing huge piles of dung upon the studio floor. Touchfarthing, resplendent in rich red robes which until very recently had served as his bedroom curtains, took up a Roman shield and beat it with a short-sword. 'Silence, please,' he called. 'Silence, if you want your money!' The fighting ceased and the noise all but abated. 'If we are all ready, Mr Rankin will make the exposure,' he announced. 'Take up your positions, please.'

While John Rankin scrutinised the inverted, grainy image on the ground-glass screen, Mr Touchfarthing swept away the dung and, with much trouble, arranged the girls on the steps of the villa in such a manner that they became a huddled and terrified mass of Sabine women under threat of abduction by the Roman soldiers, who were played by the small male contingent of Mr Rutter's congregation. Mr Touchfarthing now mounted a set of steps concealed behind the dais and set himself upon his throne, from where he looked down upon the scene with much regal complacency. 'I think we are ready,' he said. 'Mr Rutter, if you please.'

The minister leant down over the side of the horse and picked up Jane Pipkin. 'Mr Rutter!' she squealed, struggling in his grasp. 'Whatever are you about?'

'You must be ravished for the glory of Rome,' said Rutter, who had quite caught the spirit of the thing.

'No, you don't, you varmint!' Jane Pipkin cried and bit Mr Rutter's hand. But it was not his own piercing scream which rent the air loudest. At that very moment, a banshee shriek sounded and a hand pointed upwards. All eyes followed. There, swinging from window bar to window bar and pelting nut shells at whatever took its fancy, was a small monkey. It chattered and screeched as it depended from a beam, searching for John Rankin and his bag of nuts. Rankin called it by name and, spying its master, the monkey dropped suddenly upon the horse's neck, startling the beast and causing further alarm when it snatched at its mane. The terrified horse whinnied loudly and

212

reared up, immediately sending Mr Rutter slithering from its back to land squarely in a new pile of squalor and the girls to begin screaming and running in all directions. The horse tried to bolt for the open yard door but was momentarily prevented by the rope which tethered it to the wooden dais. Mr Touchfarthing, immediately perceiving his present danger, stood up and tried to lower himself upon the steps beside the pedestal, but the horse pulled sharply and the dais resisted for only a moment before toppling over, bringing Mr Touchfarthing, throne and all, crashing headlong upon the floor. A girl dropped her unfastened robe and flew from its path as the horse charged the door, knocking down and trampling the camera under hoof before it exited into the yard and cantered through the open back gate into the street.

In the studio Touchfarthing, who was experiencing considerable sharp pain in the region of his ribcage, propped himself up against the fallen dais, his red and bruised legs protruding from the disarranged bedroom curtains, and beheld a scene of considerable devastation. He picked up pieces of his smashed camera and regarded the tattered backcloth and broken properties. Mr Rutter was sponging excrement from his robes as several frightened and angry girls gathered about him and demanded their money. Others had pulled on their clothes and hurriedly exited by the shop door, where numerous women departing in varying states of dress and distress had no doubt caused interested speculation in the street. When the last of the women and a disconsolate Mr Rutter had left the studio, John Rankin, the monkey eating nuts on his shoulder, picked up the throne and sat down upon it. 'What a mess,' he commented.

'That monkey.' Touchfarthing pointed.

'It was that horse,' said Rankin. 'And your big ideas. Do you know there's folks experimenting with multiple negatives – they can do all of this without using half the Garrick theatre and a good many less Haymarket whores.'

'It would have been the making of me. My ticket back to society.'

'It's ruined us, it has. All those wasted hours when you might have been taking portraits. All those accounts still to be settled. Those girls to be paid. The props from the theatre all broken. A new camera. Do you know the total we're in debt for?'

'No, and I don't want to,' Touchfarthing said, with his head in his hands. 'I suppose it is the sponging-house and the debtors' gaol, then?'

'It should be and it would be under other circumstances,' said John Rankin. 'But it so happens that while you have been wasting your time and our capital on this, I have been making money. And I'm prepared to use it to set us straight. But mark me, Mr Touchfarthing, there will have to be some very large changes made at this here establishment. Very large indeed.'

John Rankin rose and began putting the studio to rights. Touchfarthing remained where he was, marvelling that he could ever have been brought so low. He mused upon the unhappy fact of his ruin for minutes and then his mind took refuge in happier thoughts, memories of the times he had been among the nobility at Sibthorpe. He had been only a butler, but he had prided himself that he was one who knew his business and had, he thought, gained the trust and respect of some very eminent people. Where had that all gone? How had this awful decline come about? Who was responsible for such a terrible fall from grace? The two girls he had discovered in the shop were preparing to leave the studio. 'One moment,' Touchfarthing said as he staggered to his feet and picked a photograph from the floor. 'I will not detain you long. It seems you know the lady in this photograph. I only want you to tell me all you know about her.'

15

The Final Frame

She held the rail and climbed the steps until her fingers met
with cold stone. Six steps in all; she would remember that. Eliot
caused a bell to ring deep within the house and small feet to run
towards the door.

'Miss Devereaux,' Eliot was saying, presumably with her
famous sideways glance.

'Ground-floor back?' replied a high and nasal voice that came
with the strong smell of pomade.

'Is that right, m'um?'

'Ask the young gentleman to see us through, Eliot.'

Eliot took her arm and led her across bare boards on which
her heels clicked and Eliot's shoes scraped. A key in a lock, an
unoiled hinge and then a musty smell, worn carpet underfoot,
an open window bringing the relief of a fresh draught. 'What
time is dinner?' she asked, so that she might better understand
the room from the sound of her voice.

'Eight for the travellers, miss,' the voice said. 'Nine for Mrs
Milsom's private guests.'

'Then we will join Mrs Milsom at nine,' Agnes said. 'Will you
take Eliot and show her the dining-room and anything else that
should be explained?'

When the door had clicked shut, Agnes moved a few steps in

each direction, returning to somewhere near where she had started after encountering and comprehending each new obstacle. Soon she had a picture of the room. An over-stuffed sofa, three chairs, a sideboard on which was a tall unlit oil lamp and a bowl of wrinkled apples, a mirror suspended by chains above the mantel, a table and chairs, and a piano whose top was thick with dust. Two doors led from a rear wall, presumably to the bedrooms, which she would explore later. No sooner had she congratulated herself on mastering the lie of the land than she tripped over a valise left on the floor by Eliot. She fell against the table, which she was unable to grasp before landing heavily on the floor close to the fireplace. Stifling tears of frustration, she sat up and went through the process of orientation once more, and then sat down upon the sofa.

'It reeks of boiled cabbage and laundry,' she told Henry Hilditch when he visited her the next day. 'There are doors slamming at all hours of the night and there's dust everywhere. But George used to stay here and says it's all right, so I suppose it must be.'

'It looks comfortable enough,' Hilditch said, thinking of his own lodgings. 'But will it be sufficient for you until Sibthorpe is ready?'

'I don't need much, Henry,' Agnes said. 'Certainly not a pretty view. Mrs Milsom is rather a dragon, but I can breathe a little fire myself so I expect we shall make our accommodations.'

'You could have stayed at Ryedale, you know.'

'I know, Henry. Only I particularly wanted to come to London.'

'To look out for George, I can see that,' Henry said. 'Well, then: now I have seen you are settled, I shall be about my business. If you find there is anything you need, send to me at Spitalfields at once.'

'I hope we shall see you often here, Henry,' Agnes said. 'But I suppose *Enquirer* will be busy reporting London's misfortunates?'

'I am finished with all that, Agnes. I have been doing a deal of thinking lately and it seems to me it was not such a very noble thing to be doing.'

'But I hear that *Enquirer* fascinated London, Henry,' she said. 'George tells me that you opened eyes.'

'Perhaps, sometimes. But what insufferable vanity to think I had the right to treat human beings as a species to be categorised, labelled and displayed in a newspaper. A certain Mr Treby is the new *Enquirer*. I will continue to observe and to write, but my subjects will not be my neighbours. And I won't be writing only to satisfy my own curiosity. It seems I will have to earn a crust in future whether I would or no.'

Agnes took his hand and squeezed it. 'I'm sure you are right, Henry. Goodness, how cold are your hands. You are still not well.'

'I am better than I have been in some weeks,' Henry said. 'There was a time not so long ago when I was brought so low that I thought myself in Hell.'

'But you are getting better now?'

'Now I am only in limbo. I have overcome my dependence, I think, but I shall not find my Heaven until I find Mary. I'm getting close now, I know it.'

'Oh, Henry, don't say that.'

'Whyever not? I don't follow you.'

'Don't go after that woman. She will pitch you back into the blackest pit, nothing is more certain.'

Henry dropped her hand. 'What is the matter with you, Agnes? Sometimes I am at a loss to understand you.'

'I knew her better than you, Henry,' Agnes said gently.

'You most certainly did not!' Henry exclaimed. 'No one could say that. Did you not sense how good she was for me, what a difference she made in me?'

'I think it was love that made the difference, not Miss Medworth alone. She deceived you, Henry. She is not what you took her to be.'

'I don't know what you are saying,' Henry said. 'Indeed, I don't wish to hear it. I am sorry to see you behave like this, Agnes. You know that I care for you very much but I have to say I am disappointed in you, severely disappointed.'

'Let me tell you everything about her,' Agnes said. 'Then you may decide for yourself.'

'I should not believe you,' Henry said. 'I don't know why you do this. Unless it is jealousy for a pretty woman who has her sight.'

He took up his hat but at the door he stopped and turned to her. 'I'm sorry,' he said. 'That was unforgivable. I must go. But, remember, if there is anything that you need.' And left Agnes alone in her darkness.

II

Eliot handed Agnes down from the cab and paid off the driver. He opened his glove and looked at the small coins within, said something that provoked a sharp northern response from Eliot and cracked his whip. Eliot stood in front of the photographer's window with her arm through Agnes's. She looked with some alarm at the pictures of urchins playing in fountains, ragged beggars in shop doorways, newspaper sellers bundled up against the cold, a couple of grimy girls with trays of ribbons no older than Eliot's six-year-old niece, two warders by their prison van and a grinning clerk with protruding cheekbones and the elbows out of his coat.

'Are you certain this is the place, m'um?'

'Does not his name appear upon the sign?'

'Yes, m'um,' Eliot said. 'But I wonder if it's the right one. There's pictures in this window our Mr Touchfarthing would never have took. Not never.'

'Show me in, Eliot,' Agnes said.

Eliot found a thin man in the shop, busy fitting a backing to a large photograph. 'Where's Mr Touchfarthing?' Eliot demanded of him.

'Miss Devereaux?' Rankin easily recognised Agnes from the photograph. 'Half a moment, miss. He'll be considerable pleased to see you, I'm certain of it.' He popped his head behind the curtain and called. They waited a few minutes in an

218

uncomfortable silence until Touchfarthing's own large and bald head appeared and his eyes bulged with astonishment.

'I never thought to see you here, Miss Agnes,' he said. 'Whatever can have brought you to London? But it's a pleasure, miss, really it is.'

'Touchfarthing,' Agnes said warmly. 'You have your own business, then.'

'Yes,' he said, and then, 'With John Rankin here, I do.'

'And it thrives, I hope?'

'Oh, I think I may say that,' said Touchfarthing, with a glance at Rankin.

'I'm glad you have succeeded,' Agnes said, causing Rankin to smile thinly and to choke back a cough as Touchfarthing said, 'Is it about a portrait? Because if it is, we would be honoured to do you the best we can, at no charge at all.'

'It's another matter,' Agnes said, and turned towards Rankin, who took the hint and disappeared into the house. 'I think you know a man called Henry Hilditch?'

'I know him as well as a man might hope to,' Touchfarthing said. 'Though he's a close and strange cove, that one.'

'He has become so, I know,' Agnes said. 'Mr Hilditch is searching for Mary Medworth.'

'I know that, m'um. He was for ever asking me about her. But I never said anything. Your father might have let me go, but he paid me off properly and I wasn't about to see the family's name spread all over the *Messenger*, not I.'

'Mr Hilditch mistakes Mary Medworth for some sort of a saint.'

At this, Touchfarthing ignited. 'A saint? That one? I should be more than happy to undeceive him. And if I were ever to see that woman in the flesh again, I should know what to do. I hardly like to tell you what I have heard about her doings here in London.'

'I wish you to meet with Henry in my presence and tell him everything about her.'

'Everything? Sibthorpe too?'

'That as well, Mr Touchfarthing.'

Mr Rankin then returned to the shop and picked something from a shelf. 'Don't go, Mr Rankin,' Touchfarthing said. 'I think we see Mr Hilditch tomorrow?'

'We do,' Rankin said. 'If you remembers right, sir, you 'ave been commissioned to photograph the dismantling of the Great Exhibition and in your turn, have commissioned Mr 'Ilditch to record its passing.' Mr Touchfarthing glanced again at Mr Rankin.

'Then I shall meet you there at a time of your choosing,' Agnes said. 'There will be another party present: my brother George. I will send a message to him by you today, Eliot.'

'You'll not persuade him to go anywhere he's not a mind to, miss,' Eliot said.

'Tell him I must speak to him about his father's estate and that he will hear something to his advantage,' Agnes said. 'He will come.'

III

Hyde Park Corner on a morning in November, 1851, is thick with traffic. Growlers and cabs and wagons of bricks and wheat and slaughtered pigs threaten the lives of pedestrians and road sweepers as they weave across from one pavement to the other. The far side of the road is busier, indeed at this moment is jammed. A great pantechnicon, pulled by eight horses, is presently describing a huge arc as it exits from the gates of Hyde Park, loaded to the gunnels with huge girders of iron. Other such vehicles have been choking Piccadilly: the Crystal Palace is on the move. When the pantechnicon is clear of the gates and the waiting traffic has moved on, Touchfarthing flicks his whip and their own small wagon turns sharply across the road and, with a great clinking from the chemicals in the box, enters the verdant space of Hyde Park.

The scene here is a very different one from that of a few months ago, when the Great Exhibition had recently been opened by the Queen. The great crowds have gone, as have the enormous block of coal, the giant anchor and the heaps of raw materials that were on display before the fabulous glass building. A line of wagons belonging to the men charged with the dismantling of the palace are queued up on the wheel-rutted grass and great pieces of ironwork are being swung aboard them by means of ropes and pulleys. The flags of all nations that fluttered from the roof line have disappeared, as indeed has a good portion of the roof itself. The Exhibition is now open to the late-autumn elements.

Henry Hilditch has engaged the overseer in conversation and is scribbling his findings in a notebook. The photographers have gone inside and have been amazed at the enormous space within, which seems so much vaster now that the treasures of the world have been carried off. All that remains are the brown-leafed trees that will continue to grow long after all Paxton's remarkable building is gone, the lines upon lines of stacked glass panels, great trunks of bundled guttering, pyramids of window bars and boxes of fixings. Weak sunlight illuminates clouds of dust and falling leaves, causing Rankin to look up. The mezzanine floor has been taken away and much of the gallery has been removed. Ladders are everywhere propped against walls or secured to high gantry walkways, along which men are carrying stacks of glass, heedless of the dizzying void beneath their boots.

The photographers, among whose equipment is a new rosewood camera of advanced specification, set up by the trees. It is Touchfarthing who does all the work, Touchfarthing who makes repeated trips to the wagon outside for the various items of equipment needed in the production of a high-quality photograph and who is sent to fill up a pail with water from the Serpentine.

A photograph is taken of a gang of demolition men, crowbars in hand, and then the overseer, in top hat and side-burns, is posed and exposed against a sign that advertises cheap shilling entrances to the Great Exhibition. But the photograph that best pleases Rankin is a carefully composed picture of the vast empty space itself in which is not a single person. Shortly after this photograph has been processed in the portable dark-tent, Rankin hears the men remarking something unusual and, turning about, sees Agnes and Eliot making their way carefully around various stacked obstacles until they are within speaking distance of the two photographers.

IV

'We waited until Eliot had seen that you were finished,' Agnes said to Mr Touchfarthing. 'We did not like to disturb an artist at his work.'

Touchfarthing takes some comfort from the knowledge that Agnes could not have witnessed what all these workmen have: that John Rankin is the photographer and he the assistant. 'Mr Hilditch is here,' he says to cover his awkwardness. Henry Hilditch smiles as he sees Agnes and pockets his notebook.

'What an agreeable surprise,' Hilditch says. 'I had hoped to see you soon. We parted so badly. Are you here to see the fall of the Palace of Vanities?'

'I'm here to see you, Henry,' Agnes said. 'But I should be obliged to hear all about it. You may find it easier describing a temple to science than a church full of art.'

Henry laughed. 'What you would see,' he said, 'is only a vast skeleton. The beast itself has begun to hibernate, to be reawoken at some other location, I understand. Only the ribs remain, great iron peers supporting a vast tracery of iron window bars. The noise from above is the workmen walking along the gantries, taking apart and sending down thousands of panes of glass.'

'How I wish I could see it all,' Agnes said.

Henry offered further description and then enquired about the progress of the repairs to Sibthorpe. He expressed his sorrow that he had not been well enough to attend the funeral of Edmund Devereaux, who had collapsed and died only days after catastrophe had struck his house.

'You had to return to London,' Agnes said. 'For whatever reason. And now you are here, what do you propose?'

'Surely you know that I have only one purpose now and that is to find Mary,' he said.

Agnes was silent for a moment and then she put out a hand and touched his shoulder. 'Oh, I hope I can open your eyes, Henry,' she said softly.

Tracing the contours of his face, she removed his coloured spectacles and he allowed her fingertips to brush lightly over his eyelids. 'These will heal,' she said. She did not move and Henry's nose was filled with the smell of her washed hair and a delicate scent.

'You know that I care for you, Agnes, deeply,' Henry began, but before he could say any more, a deep and resonant voice boomed across the empty space.

'Have a care, Henry, that's my sister you're toying with!'

Smiling broadly, George Devereaux shook hands with Henry and introduced himself to the photographers.

'Now then, Aggie,' he said, when he thought that sufficient pleasantries had been exchanged. 'What's all this you have to tell me about the estate? Or should we excuse ourselves and go somewhere private?'

'This will do, George,' Agnes said. She steadied herself, resting her back against a propped ladder. 'I asked you to come here, George, because it is time that Henry knew the truth.'

'Truth, Aggie? The truth of what?'

'Henry must know what occurred at Sibthorpe, George, if he is to be saved from making a dreadful mistake. Touchfarthing, *Mister* Touchfarthing I must say now, is here because he knows what happened there as well as you do, George.'

'Oh, no, Agnes,' George said, his composure evaporating. 'Leave things as they stand.'

'I can't do that, George,' Agnes said. 'Matters must be set right.'

'Agnes, I beg you to reconsider,' George said. 'What good can it do now?'

'If Henry wishes to remain deaf to the truth then I will indulge him,' Agnes said. She paused, but on hearing no reply from

Henry, she asked him to recall the time that George had returned from Florence and had persuaded their father to employ Mary as her companion.

'I did not want a companion,' Agnes said. 'But I took her to please you, George. Foolishly, I thought I was only gratifying your generous desire. I love you best when you are warm and generous.'

'I meant you to have someone to talk to, someone to take you out. I could not always be there and Henry was still abroad. I intended to help you, Agnes.'

'If that is true, then I thank you for it. But afterwards, George, when she was spending more time in your company than my own, I would hear you whispering together. I knew something was wrong then.'

'If you please, ma'am,' Touchfarthing said. 'This isn't fit for a lady to tell. I was there.'

'But it's not for you to shame them, Touchfarthing,' Agnes said. 'Even though, of course, it was you who discovered them together in the blue room.'

'No, no, not that!' Henry Hilditch said, quietly. He took off his dark glasses, as if he could not see George and Mary clearly enough. George looked quickly about him and said in a low voice, 'It was not my fault, Henry. She was ambitious and snared me like a rabbit. I expect she had planned it all while we were still at Florence. She set her cap at you, Henry, but as soon as she discovered we were the better family she switched horses. I never suspected her designs. I offered her a position at Sibthorpe because I knew she would be company for Aggie and, yes, a diversion for me. It was never supposed to go any further than that. There was not a chance in the world that I would marry her. I wasn't such a flat as to marry a companion or a governess. But I reckoned without her cunning, Henry. She led me a dance, gave me her favours until one day she made such a noise as to have us discovered.

'My father expelled us all – Mary, me and, because he was a witness, old Touchfarthing as well. I thought to leave her and win my father round, but by that time Mary knew all about my losses at the races and threatened to tell him of that too. There was no returning to Sibthorpe then. She said we must bide our time, wait until we might both be accepted back within the fold. In the meantime I have been without any resources but what Mary can provide by this means and that. I tell you, Henry, I wish it had fallen out any other way but this.'

A shrill and derisive laugh resounded in the cavernous space. Though they looked about them, the source could not immediately be perceived. 'We should have married at Sibthorpe and had it all, but for your carelessness, George.' A figure emerged from the shadows of the trees and walked quickly over to the group. Henry looked hard at the approaching form and then his heart missed a beat. She was changed: she wore her hair in a different style and her dress was less appealing and more showy than those she had worn before but, unmistakeably, the newcomer was Mary Medworth. He was startled beyond measure and yet, as she came nearer, he saw clearly that this was not the paragon who had fettered his mind since Florence. This, somehow, was someone else. In his confusion, he looked closer, as if he might discover the flaw he had missed, while a thousand questions crowded his mind.

'Well, George?' she said. 'What have you heard of the Devereaux estate? Are we to have it or not?'

'We?' Agnes whispered. 'What does she mean, Henry?'

But Henry was too overwhelmed by hideous revelation. He tried to impose his angel of Florence upon the countenance before him and could not make it fit. She was pretty, no doubt; everything was in the right place, yet something essential was missing. The lodestone of his attraction to her was gone.

George said, 'There is nothing to be had here.' He looked at his sister's unsmiling face. 'Not after this.'

'You deceived me,' Henry said at last. 'Both of you. I was horribly duped.'

'You deceived yourself,' Mary said. 'I never said I loved you, Henry.'

'And you were my friend,' Henry said to George, 'yet you drained me of money and kindled false hope. How could you?'

'I'm sorry, Henry,' George said. 'But you brought it on yourself. I needed cash, you know that I did. At last I had a chance in life, a once in a lifetime investment opportunity. It would have been the making of me. And I counted on you as my friend to loan me the stake I needed. I would have repaid you every penny.'

'You would have lost it as you do everything else in life,' Henry said.

'You said you refused me for my own good,' George said. 'What rot. You were always too mean and self-absorbed to be much good to those around you.'

'Let's go, George,' Mary was saying. 'I at least have business this evening.'

Agnes was touching Henry's sleeve as she told him to come away.

'Wait,' Henry said. He might have been addressing anyone. 'What am I to do now?'

Mary said, 'I'm not your saviour, Henry.'

'Then I have nothing.' As hope drained from his face, he did not notice when Agnes let go his sleeve. For moments, no one spoke. All attention was upon the stricken individual whose wound was too new and too raw to be plastered over with conversation. Mary Medworth was turning to leave, her hand tugging at George's coat, when a voice shrill with alarm cried, 'Up there! Look up there!'

Workmen were pointing at a woman, high on a ladder and groping for the rails of an adjoining gantry. 'Good God, it's Agnes,' Henry breathed.

'Do something!' Eliot cried.

Agnes had turned about, pressed herself against the ladder and begun to climb, unnoticed by all until she caught her breath as she stepped off the ladder and on to the gantry which her hands had found in the blackness. She held tightly to a rail and appeared to look directly at those below.

226

'Do you see me, Henry?' she called out, the quiver in her voice betraying her fear.

Henry swallowed. His heart was beating so furiously he thought for a moment he could not speak. 'Yes,' he said at last. 'I see you.'

Indeed, he could do nothing else but see, transfixed as he was not only by the sense of imminent danger but by something else that was quite as galvanising. Looking, he saw clearly for the first time. The meretricious distractions of Mary Medworth dissipated in the dusty air; he saw with perfect clarity that what he desired above all else was teetering on the brink of destruction. His head swimming with the turbulence of this discovery, he tried to move but consternation and his own stark terror rooted him to the spot.

Now upon the gantry, Agnes grasped the rail and the precarious construction began to sway. Henry watched with horror as she moved slowly along it. It was as clear to Agnes as it was to the onlookers below that she had placed herself in great and immediate danger. The gantry moved at her every tread. She stopped and steadied herself to speak. 'Oh, Henry,' she said. 'What have you driven me to?'

'Come down,' Henry called.

A workman, at the same elevation, but an unknown distance away, was urgently shouting to Agnes, 'Go back! It ain't fixed this end. Go back before it gives way!'

She swallowed her panic and gripped hard. Her mind began to spin. 'I can't!' she cried out. 'I can't move!'

'Do someone help her!' Eliot was crying.

Agnes had turned about and could not recall the direction she had come and so, dizzy with fear, she remained where she was, clutching the rail and feeling the walkway moving wildly beneath her feet. There was a moment of silence while all below watched the gantry swaying above them. There was no question but that the unsecured structure must fall and she with it. A scream died in her throat. Then she heard, far below, a London voice saying he'd fetch the lady down. And then that was Henry

227

who was saying, look out, he would do that. She waited, as metal creaked and strained and Henry's feet sounded upon the ladder.

Agnes gripped the rail and prayed as Henry stepped upon the iron platform, which complained of its additional burden and swung still more crazily.

'Quickly but carefully there,' John Rankin was calling softly. 'She ain't likely to take much more.'

His quick, short breathing was coming closer. 'I'm coming, Agnes,' he was whispering. 'Only hold on a little while more and I shall have you safe.' He edged closer still and then caught his shoe upon a loose fitting and stumbled. Agnes let out a sudden cry as the walkway shook and the unsecured end began to tip. They held fast to the rails until the shaking was stopped. 'Only a little longer, Agnes,' Henry breathed, pulling himself towards her, step by step.

'Where are you, Henry?' Agnes was asking and a moment later she felt Henry's arms around her and his breath in her ear whispering, 'I'm here.'

With infinite care, he guided her slowly and safely back to the ladder. When at last she reached the ground she discovered that Henry was shaking more than she. He held her in his arms and rested his chin upon her head. 'Aggie,' he said, 'I was so terribly frightened.'

Some men who had been watching the drama cheered loudly and then went about their work. Cornelius Touchfarthing, wiping his cherry-red face with a handkerchief, thanked God and Henry for her delivery.

Agnes said nothing. Her face was hidden in the folds of Henry's coat. There was a moment of quiet, when perhaps all there were giving thanks. But then John Rankin's strident Cockney voice broke the peace. 'Oh, you're goin', are you?' he was calling. 'Well, good riddance to the pair of you.'

Henry looked up and saw Mary Medworth walking briskly towards the shilling entrance, her shoes clicking on the ground as George Devereaux followed meekly behind. Nothing in her gait or demeanour reminded him of the girl he had worshipped

228

at Florence. Without thinking, he began to polish his spectacles. He wondered if he could have been seeing clearly. How could he ever have been so short-sighted? Without thinking, he dropped the coloured glasses into his deepest pocket and watched Mary leave with cold indifference.

V

That evening he had yet to register the force of the shocks he had received and he stood by the window at Milsom's and only looked out in the street at the swollen tide of Londoners returning from their places of work. Men of business in tailored coats, boys with slates and strap-hanging books, artisans with bags of tools, street traders with depleted trays of food and haberdashery, young soldiers in scarlet, costermongers wheeling barrows, cabbies cursing the traffic, skinny clerks and courting couples and a man lounging against a lamp-stand, watching the world pass by. Agnes stood behind him, a hand resting upon his shoulder. 'I would never have hurt you had there been another way,' Agnes said.

'Perhaps I am not hurt,' Henry said. 'Perhaps you have saved me from further humiliation.'

'I imagined I was saving you from a dreadful marriage, but I see my brother will have that.'

Henry thought of George and Mary living shabby lives and gaining nothing by their improbity. 'Poor George,' he said. 'Do you know, I think she would have accepted me at Florence. She took George for the richer man.'

'Of course she would,' Agnes said. 'But now that the scales have fallen, Henry, what do you intend?'

'I intend to become something more than an observer,' he said as the crowds passed by. 'To come off the sidelines.'

'And how will you do that?'

He continued to follow the multitude without. A coffee-seller was pushing his creaking vehicle towards the corner where he would set up for the evening. By a stationary cart on which was mounted an enormous placard advertising a grand and unmiss-able entertainment at a nearby theatre, a boy was performing cartwheels on the pavement, for the benefit of a girl in a beribboned bonnet who laughed and applauded.

'I shall find happiness, Agnes. That's what I shall do,' he said. 'Though where I must begin to search I hardly know.'

They watched the scene in the street a moment longer in silence.

'Of course, I couldn't say,' Agnes said, as Eliot clicked open the door. 'But Yorkshire might be as good a place to look as another.'

When he turned from the window, he wore a half smile, though she, of course, could not know that. Eliot said, 'Mrs Milsom's respects, but if you like your dinner 'ot, you should go now.'

'Are you hungry, Henry?' Agnes asked.

He thought for a moment. 'Hungrier than I have been in an age,' he said and turned away from the commonplace spectacle without.

VI

John Rankin sits in the long damp grass by the camera, where the tripod legs have been set firmly into the ground, and uses his pocket-knife to cut a slice of the pie. He takes a bite and offers the remaining portion to Mr Touchfarthing, who looks as if he needs some sustenance after the long walk up the hill loaded with camera, tripod and a bag of necessities. 'Tasty,' says Mr Touchfarthing, gratefully, as he wipes crumbs from his lips with a parti-stained handkerchief. 'Very tasty indeed.'

'So it would be,' Rankin said. 'It's from Simpson's, and their pies is full of meat, with no rubbish.'

The pie is soon finished and Touchfarthing refreshes himself from a bottle of ginger beer.

'Must we wait here any longer?' he asks. 'There's not been a break in the clouds since we arrived. I shall catch my death of cold if I continue to sit here, I know I shall.'

'Just you catch some patience, old fellow,' Rankin says, and returns to watching the clouds. At this time in the afternoon, with the sun low in the sky, he had hoped to utilise the contrast created by strong and oblique light. The shop had been bathed in sharp winter brightness when they set off but now, two hours later, the sky is leaden and soon the obscured sun will be too low in the sky.

'We could come back another time,' Touchfarthing suggests. 'In the spring, when it's a little warmer.'

'I expect to be too busy then for little things of my own,' John Rankin says. 'We may even have to take an apprentice.'

'I must confess I am surprised we have time for this,' Touch-farthing grumbles. 'It's not as if you are even going to offer it for sale.'

'It's an extravagance,' John Rankin admits. 'Ah, but what a stunning centre-piece it will make for the shop winder!'

'Not today, I think,' mutters Touchfarthing, who had advised against this afternoon's enterprise from the start. Rankin ignores him as he has become accustomed to doing, and studies a lightening in the western sky. 'We might be lucky yet,' he says. Time passes as he watches and follows the clouds. Just when Touchfarthing has begun to complain again about damp and cold and wasted money, Rankin suddenly leaps to his feet and ducks his head under the cloth. Touchfarthing looks up from his pie crust in time to see brilliant rays of sunlight streaming down and gilding the scene below.

Beyond the trees and the backs of a dilapidated terrace of houses and stretching away until the last shadowy shapes dissolve into the haze on the horizon, is a remarkable panorama of London. From his vantage atop Primrose Hill, Rankin can make out famous landmarks and public buildings, can see the roof lines of squares and crescents, the treetops of parks and commons and can even estimate the approximate location of his shop. Even at this remove, the city is too vast to be contained upon the ground-glass screen and Rankin has selected a section that will represent and hint at the enormity of the whole. As if for his convenience, the sun continues to illuminate his chosen scene. Rankin reaches out and removes the lens cover and takes his photograph of London. 'There,' he says, to no one in particular. 'Now I've got it all.'

Acknowledgements

The greatest debt I have is to Henry Mayhew's four-volume work *London Labour and the London Poor* (F. Cass, 1967). Also invaluable has been Donald Thomas's *The Victorian Underground* (John Murray, 1998). My thanks to Roger Pickles of Whitby Museum, Stuart Gibbins, Kay Mitchell, Lesley Shaw at Gillon Aitken Associates and to my very excellent editor at Fourth Estate, Leo Hollis.